Wealde

Also available from Grey House in the Woods

the Voice within the Wind
of Becoming and the Druid Way
Greywind

the Path through the Forest
a Druid Guidebook
Julie White & Graeme K Talboys

Arianrhod's Dance
a Druid Ritual Handbook
Julie White & Graeme K Talboys

Wealden Hill

Graeme K Talboys

Grey House in the Woods

Copyright © Graeme K Talboys, 2005

First published at Samhain 2005 by
Grey House in the Woods
PO Box 8211
Girvan
Ayrshire
KA26 0WA
Scotland
www.greyhouseinthewoods.org

Graeme K Talboys has asserted his right under the Copyright, Designs
and Patents Act 1988 to be identified as the author of this work.

ISBN 0-9540531-3-3

Set in 11 point Times New Roman by Redwind
Cover by Greywind

for
Barbara
with all my love

ONE
(7 July 1883 - 16 July 1883)

(Friday 7 July)
Rowland Henty woke from the dream. Floundering in the cool, pre-dawn light, stranded in that brief infinite moment between sleep and wakefulness, he struggled instinctively to retain the vision. But the charm of the dream was weak and the light of the sun is a strong and rough magic, no matter that it was then still pale and new to the day. It was enough to dissolve the spell that had been cast about his sleeping soul.

The young woman, a gentle beauty, an ephemeral image of the mist, was gone. The words of her song, which had beguiled him in the uncertain and deep regions of his sleep, were scattered wholly from his memory like the fallen petals of an exotic flower caught in a summer breeze.

Only the music lingered - a fragrance clinging where the gentle wind of the waking day had yet to reach. For that sweet, fleeting moment, he was able to savour its special delight, heartstruck with an inexplicable and painful joy.

It, too, faded. He was left once more grasping for something that had never been real and was no longer there. All that was left was the memory of a memory.

With nothing but that to cling to, he finally reached the solid shore of the day. Washed up and stranded, he sat with his knees under his chin, arms tight about his legs. Droplets of sweat stood out along the frown lines in his brow. The rough cotton top sheet was gripped tightly in his fists.

A dull and viscous confusion washed languidly through his mind. An equally dull and slow throbbing began at his temples as the hard, stinging fire of tension began to burn deeply in the muscles along his shoulders.

Outside his room, in the eaves by the open window, a bird gave startled voice to a short burst of song in protest at some disturbance. The bright notes cut sharply into the still air and dispelled the confused greyness in Rowland's mind. He began to relax, a faint gasp of despair slipping between his lips as he looked down at his tightly clenched hands.

With a conscious effort he released the crumpled sheet and forced his shoulders back. Tension eased and the dull ache began to fade.

Slowly, having foregone the struggle yet again, he lay back on his bed. He heard a collared dove in the distance and was soothed by its call. Elsewhere, by the schoolhouse and across the valley, other birds gave song. There was the sudden squabbling of sparrows in the garden below; the piping of martins and swifts on the wing; a thrush close by on the schoolroom roof; and the gentle click-twitter of a starling. Much muted by distance, the raucous bellow of rooks from the wooded slopes on the far side of the river was a base line to the chorus.

The outburst of song lasted several minutes. It rolled gently northwards as if the birds in the valley had been woken from their sleep by a passing presence. Then, once the first chorus had swept away, there followed the quieter pattern of song as the creatures began their day in earnest.

His body still heavy with sleep, Rowland turned his head and glanced across to where his watch hung by its chain from a hook on the side of the dresser. He lay still, staring at the second hand as it swept around the face.

It was a plain, simple, knowable part of the universe. About as much as he could cope with when the pattern of his sleep was disturbed. But by what, he wondered? What could have woken him so early in the day and pulled him from the now familiar dream? And such a dream.

He closed his eyes and sighed. As with every time before, he tried to recall it, but the brightness of waking had drowned the fragile vision. There had been flowers of ineffable fragrance. That he knew. A song of overwhelming sadness. That he also knew. The indefinable presence of a woman, young and beautiful...

Try as he might, he could never remember more. Nothing else lingered save a deep and incurable pain, as of something dearly and passionately loved and now irrevocably lost.

Yet this morning there was a difference. He opened his eyes again to see the second hand circle in its steady sixty-step dance. Turning away, he lay there, drifting back to the edge of sleep, convinced that something new had entered the familiar pattern. Rather, that something new had entered his understanding of it.

This morning there was in his mind an element of uncertainty. He frowned briefly as he recognized it for what it was. But of what was he uncertain? It took him a long time to pin it down

4

for it was as elusive as the dream itself and so obsessed was he with the content that the act of dreaming did not enter his thoughts. That is, until he wondered again just what it was that had woken him.

Then he knew where the uncertainty lay, saw at last the haze that obscured his way forward. And that allowed him to ask the first useful question of his puzzling experience. Had it, after all, simply been a dream? Or had he, perhaps, heard someone singing as he slept? A song that gave birth to his dream - evoking, for some reason, the heartbreaking emotions that always lingered when he woke.

He considered the idea for a while in the dispassionate and detached way that half sleep sometimes allows, but it became entangled in his imagination and he felt himself become attached to the idea. It gave rise to hopes of unravelling the deeper feeling of mystery that surrounded the recurring vision.

Yet who could it be? Sarah Elam, perhaps? She had the sweetest voice of all those he had heard hereabouts. And of one thing he was certain; the voice was that of a young woman. Yet if it was Sarah Elam, then why was she so close to the schoolhouse on so many mornings and at such an early hour?

Sweeping aside the single sheet that covered him and shaking loose the remnants of sleep that fogged his mind, he rose naked from his bed and stepped lightly across the bare boards to the main window of his room. There he felt the sweet freshness of the night-cleansed air against his flesh.

Leaning on the high sill, he pushed the casement wide open and looked out northward onto the valley. Even in this early light he was forced to squint to protect his eyes. For once, however, he did not reach for his tinted spectacles. There were times when he felt the need to see the world in its own colours - no matter what the pain.

A thick sheet of faintly iridescent mist obscured the valley floor. It moved in a slow and soft swell, stirred in places by the light dawn breeze into dancing ephemerae with haloes of prismatic colour - dilatory dream waves that stirred again the nameless sorrow within him and afflicted him with crawling shivers along the flesh of his bare back.

He stepped back from the window a pace, finding some security in his room whilst still being able to see beyond it. In the far distance, where his gaze now fell, the mist washed up against the smooth curves of the northern downland. It was an unfocussed shoreline in this first light of day, yet solid and unmoving before the sea of mist. And dominating the massive silhouette was the high, symmetrical swelling of Wealden Hill.

Wealden Hill. Rowland gazed at it intently. Beyond it, and to the east, the stars had been bleached from a sky already bright with the light of the unrisen sun. The ancient ditch and ridge that sat like a crown upon the hilltop was sharply marked.

Yet the strength and solidity of the hill owed more to some inner quality it offered to those who beheld it than to its shape, or its size, or the way in which it was silhouetted against the early morning sunlight. It was not even the highest of the hills hereabouts. But still, somehow, it dominated.

Rowland shivered again. It was difficult for the intellect to assert itself in such primordial moments. The self was, for no matter how short a time, alone in the world - defenceless against its elemental magic.

Eventually, he managed to draw his eyes away from the ancient and spellbinding upswell of the earth. To the left, where he looked, lay Rushy Edge. The river cliff at its western end was still in deep shadow, as was the market town of Hamm which lay below it astride the river. It was a safer view, mundane.

Rowland moved back to the window and leant out. He cast his gaze quickly back across Wealden Hill to its eastern slopes and thence to the gap beyond. It was from there that the waters of the Cobb flowed to join the River Rushy. Beyond Cobb Reach he could see the end of the high ridge of the downs directly across the river from the schoolhouse. There stood the twin peaks of Cobb Hill and Beacon Hill.

Carved into the thick turf on the slope beneath those hills sat the giant chalk figure of the Newelm Man, seated and with head in hands. Rowland could not see it from his room, but he was only too aware of the implacable presence, was touched by its mystery in the pre-dawn stillness. It had been sitting there through unnumbered centuries, a grieving guardian of the quiet valley, staring endlessly out across the Cobb to the slopes of Wealden Hill.

Wealden Hill. A centre of dormant power that drew the unwary eye always to its slope. As now it drew Rowland's gaze once more. Innocuous and strange, a bare hill of smooth, sheep cropped turf, with the mist now rolling back from its lower slopes as if it were slowly rising upwards. All was still. All was quiet. All was alive with a tense potential.

Unable to shake off the unsettled feeling evoked by the dream, Rowland stepped back from the window once more. Tears now ran from his light-plagued eyes. He moved to the dressing table beside his bed, anxious to anchor himself to the familiar, scared momentarily by the feeling that something was stirring, something was rising.

Drawing a deep and deliberate breath, he opened the top left-hand drawer of the dresser and removed a clean kerchief. With great care he wiped away his tears using different sides of the heavy cotton square for each of his eyes.

Satisfied, he picked up his spectacles and put them on. The dark-green lenses brought relief to his eyes. There was no such easy relief for his puzzled soul. No relief from the inexplicable sadness of a lost and nameless joy.

With his eyes protected from the growing light, he moved to the southern end of the room where there was a smaller window at the head of the stairs. This, too, was open. He looked out from there to his right, towards the village.

The small, irregular cluster of cottages and houses seemed to him, after the view to the north, to be a cold and dead place, wrapped in the vestiges of the night as it faded in the western sky beyond the gentle slopes of Brook Down. Nothing stirred between the buildings that he could see, nothing but tenebrous tendrils of summer mist.

He sighed. There was nothing there that would answer his question. Turning away, he moved slowly back to the larger north-facing window. The night's shroud of mist finally dissolved as he watched the dawn caress wary life into the valley.

He shook his head slowly. The singing must, then, have been a dream, lost now to the growing day. He sighed again, letting his gaze wander slowly up the wooded slope of Cobb Spur to the summit of Cobb Hill and across to where the rays of the rising sun were burning dry summer colours into the surface of

Wealden Hill. Somewhere behind him, in a distant part of the village, a door closed, loud in the early morning.

*

Wearing his shirt without its collar and with the braces of his trousers hanging loose down the sides of his legs, Rowland left the shade of the kitchen and walked barefoot across the yard towards the small cast-iron pump. As he walked, he yawned.

Some time would pass before the sun cleared the heights of Cobb Hill. The air was fresh and invigorating, but already warm. It still carried faint traces of the scents of the night - like dreams. Rowland stopped for a moment and looked up. The sky above was clear and there was no wind, the early breezes having chased after the tail end of the night. It would be another very hot day.

Cool water, drawn pure from the chalk deep beneath his feet, sparkled as it filled the large ewer. No time, he thought, for being indoors. With the world to himself, this was a chance to be savoured, a time to be enjoyed.

Walking back to the kitchen door, he pulled his braces up onto his shoulders one at a time, changing the ewer from one hand to the other as he did so. The water shifted in the overfilled vessel and some of it slopped over the lip. A brightly spangled, amorphous mass of liquid turned in the air as it fell toward the solid earth of the yard. Rowland watched it fall with a feeling of dread.

The water hit the ground with a dull splatch, breaking into smaller masses that shot outward in shallow arcs from the point of impact. Dark stains spread as the liquid soaked into the packed soil.

Old scenes of terror that he had tried so hard to subdue over the months flickered through his mind. Blood splashing, like water, from the bullet wound in his leg, soaking into the hard packed snow. That is how it began. That was the first he knew of it.

He left the door wide open as he washed so that he could feel the warmth, see the green hills and the English summer sunlight - even though it pained his eyes.

When he had finished washing, he put his round, wire-framed spectacles back on. Even in the shade of the kitchen the green tinted glass gave him considerable relief. Without them he

8

would have been reduced to tearful and swollen-eyed helplessness by mid-morning.

His eyes had always been sensitive to bright light, even as a child. The condition had become slowly worse as he had grown older. A bout of snow blindness when he had first been posted to the Afghan had done nothing to help.

With his ablutions finished and his mind somewhat settled after the succession of unnerving events, Rowland gathered some bread and cheese from his larder, and wrapped them in a cloth. As he left, he carefully closed the kitchen door, then crossed the schoolyard to the road. There, he stepped over the low perimeter wall and turned away from the village.

He walked slowly along the hard-packed cart road to the bridge that crossed the River Rushy. It was a favourite spot of his at such rare and precious times when there were few people about. A simple sanctuary above the flowing water, free of the weight of contact with the earth beneath his feet.

It was not a large bridge, but it was solid and well made of dressed stone with a broad parapet where he sat cross-legged. He unwrapped the food he had brought and there, in the calm and silence of the early morning at the centre of the valley, broke his fast.

From this vantage point he was able to gaze downstream to the south. He sat quite still when he had finished eating, his body like some decorative carving placed as a guardian of the bridge. The dawn mist that had filled the valley floor had already been replaced by the first intimations of a heat haze that teased his vision of the more distant hills.

Beyond the interlocking feet of those southern heights was the coast. There, the water of the Rushy ran out to sea, shallow and dispersed, across an ancient and wave-built bank of shingle. There, the fishermen of Meeching would be hauling their boats up the steep beach to secure them beyond the tide line. Having spent the night at sea they would now be looking forward to another day of restless sleep in the heat.

Rowland paid no heed to this as he sat on the bridge. The cares of the world were not his concern because the inner peace that the valley had begun to offer him was now disturbed by the recurrent dream of the singer and her song. If dream it was.

9

Strangely enough, it was the identity of the song that most disturbed his equanimity. The strangeness of the dream he could accept as simply that, the strangeness of the dream. But the song itself was a different matter. Although it was strange, he felt he knew it. Yet, try as he might, he could recall neither the tune nor the words to help him in his attempt to remember just what it was. And that voice. Sweet. Penetrating his spirit. Stirring up the sadness. Always just beyond the grasp of his memory.

The same feeling of loss that he had experienced earlier returned to him now. It was a gently aching emptiness that he could not define and did not know how to assuage. He sat alone and felt his loneliness, surrounding him in its vastness. And now, with that splashing of the water on the ground in the yard, the terror of the nightmare was also back.

The vision that had flashed out from his memory had been so vivid it had swamped reality and left him shivering with fear while he had washed in the kitchen. It had taken a real effort of will to subdue the panic. Panic that came not so much from the actual event but at the thought that his memories of it were still so strong within him. It had taken a long time to shed those visions from the surface of his mind. But they had not gone completely. They never would.

For a long time he stared unseeing at the waters below until a movement distracted him. One by one and preceded by the ripples that had caught his eye, a family of swans emerged from the tall reeds at the river's eastern edge and began to swim upstream towards him.

The cob, a regal bird, eyed him warily with bright, black eyes and recognized there was no threat. It nodded its head gently, in greeting, as they passed beneath Rowland into the shadow of the bridge. Rowland nodded back before he realized what he had done. Overhead, a grey heron flew in great and lazy circles looking for a fishing spot for the day.

Once the swans had disappeared from view, Rowland turned his head and looked across to the village. Bobby Hall, one of his pupils, was walking along the road towards the schoolhouse, a milk can swinging gently from his hand. When he got to the schoolyard he slowed his pace and crept, almost on tiptoe, to the kitchen door. There, he left the can on the doorstep and crept quietly away from the house.

Smiling at the boy's efforts to avoid disturbing him, Rowland swung himself round and lowered his feet on to the road. It was time, he thought, to prepare for the day ahead. No time there for the unsettling thoughts and emotions that had assailed him since waking.

He shrugged them off and bundled them away with some difficulty as he stretched his legs. A vixen, late home from her night hunting and resting now in some shade among the tall grasses by the river bank, watched him carefully as he returned to the schoolhouse. She was panting already from the heat.

*

Sunlight blazed at the small windows high in the wall and poured into the room, illuminating the dust he had stirred in passing. He watched the motes for an instant as they reflected the indirect but still fierce daylight and then added to the slow and silent fury of movement by clearing the blackboard of the previous day's copy.

He worked methodically until the board was quite clean. When he was satisfied, he shook the duster and then clapped his hands to free them of the chalk dust. With chalky fingers he eased his stiff, formal collar. Already the room was uncomfortably warm.

As he was about to write the day's date in the top right hand corner of the board, a sudden shout from one of the boys in the schoolyard, wordless and loud, made him stop. He turned to the schoolroom door and listened. Beyond it, in the yard, the boys continued more quietly with their game.

In his mind, Rowland could hear the echo of a shouted warning in the mountains followed by the volley of rifle fire. In his mind he could see his own blood splash across the snow as the bullet passed through his leg. The man who had shouted the warning fell an instant later, spilling more blood. Much more. Too much.

A bead of sweat, rolling from his forehead, eventually found its way beneath his spectacles and into the corner of his eye. He blinked as the salty liquid began to sting and the oaken desks and chairs in front of him came suddenly and sharply back into focus. Slowly and with deliberate care he drew the familiar surroundings of the schoolroom to him as a shield to block out the cold terror of his waking nightmare.

In his hand the stick of chalk he had been about to use was broken to small fragments. He placed the fragments on the easel and slowly wiped his hands on the duster. They were too unsteady to attempt writing on the board. Instead, he picked up a pile of text books from his desk.

Slowly, he walked up and down the room, laying one book at each place. He took long, deep breaths as he did so, concentrating on the task in hand.

The methodical, measured activity helped to calm his body. His mind, however, was not so easily soothed - agitated still by the nightmare's return as much as it was by its content. He really had thought it was all behind him. He really had thought that he had seen the last of those grim months when his dreams and his guilt kept forcing him back to that distant mountain side.

Dreams. Suddenly he wanted very much to cry, to let go, to run. But he did not. He knew there was nowhere to go, no sense in giving in. For he knew it was not what the dreams were about that disturbed him. That had passed. The shooting was done and long gone. He was alive and safe. The song... that was just a dream and no more. That could not harm him.

What dismayed him was the thought of enduring yet more of the torture of the long sleepless nights, of slipping back to where he had been two years before when there had seemed to be no end and no prospect of any end to the dark loneliness of the small corner in the shadowed caverns of his mind where he had cowered for so long.

In growing desperation, and for want of a better or more permanent distraction, he picked up the brass hand bell. With a key taken from his waistcoat pocket he unlocked the schoolroom door. It was not yet nine o'clock, but he slipped quietly out and stood on the wide stone step.

Directly above him, the roof of the schoolhouse extended some six feet beyond the wall that supported it, forming a shelter along the length of the southern side of the schoolroom. Designed to shelter boys from rain, it offered little protection from the relentless glare of the sunlight and Rowland squinted behind the dark lenses of his spectacles. However, it was there he stood and watched the boys at play, drawing some comfort from their bright life.

"Eaver Weaver, chimney sweeper,
Had a wife and could not keep her,
Had another, did not love her,
Up the chimney he did shove her."

With a victim chosen there was laughter and an explosion of boys running in every direction away from the small circle in which they had just been standing. They were being chased by the smallest.

"Bobby Hall's Tig!" shouted one boy in his excitement as he hurtled away.

The schoolyard had already gathered a fine haze of dust, like mist, lifted by the heavy boots of chasing demons. Bobby Hall, small but with great strength and quite some athletic ability, quickly succeeded in trapping another boy in the far corner of the yard. "Tig. Tag. Never Tig back. Touch cold iron."

Rowland heard the familiar formula as the 'Tig' was handed on. Bobby Hall sped away and the new 'Tig' raced off in search of a new victim.

Several of the boys stood aloof in the sparse shade of the shelter, close to Rowland, their running days not so very long passed. They were caught in that uncomfortable age when childhood and adulthood pulled at them with equal attraction. They followed the game eagerly.

Rowland watched them unheeded. It was not an easy time for them, but it would be gone all too soon in this community. In but a very few weeks time, the responsibilities of their fathers would begin to weigh on their shoulders and the pull of the schoolyard would quickly weaken.

With the older boys stood a tall, thin lad with a pale, hollow, and infinitely patient face in which were set the darkest of eyes. Rowland turned his gaze to him. This was a boy who had never had running days. He had never had the strength. In many ways childhood had escaped him. His had always been the burden of pain and of worry - yet some things would be spared him. Some things not. As the haze of dust reached his throat he began to cough.

Rowland spoke to him above the clamour of the game. "Get yourself some water, John," he said.

The boy turned and shyly smiled his thanks. As he crossed the yard to the pump, a handkerchief held across his mouth and nose, Rowland looked at his pocket watch. It was nearly nine o'clock so he raised the heavy bell and rang it five times.

The noisy hoard of boys came quickly to order and formed a line, smallest at the front and tallest at the rear where John Elam joined the rank after finishing his drink. Rowland surveyed them briefly and then ordered them in.

In a way that simultaneously managed to convey military precision and the casual swagger of carefree youth, the line marched through the door carrying summer dust inside with it. Once inside, each child sought his seat and stood waiting with a barely suppressed energy that seemed to sparkle throughout the room.

Rowland followed them in, leaving the door open. He placed the bell carefully on the corner of the table in front of his desk and then stood silently and still until his outward show of calm infected them all.

"Sit."

They obeyed quietly and, as they did so, Rowland took the School Register from his high desk and laid it on the sloping lid. Without hurry, he settled himself comfortably on his chair and proceeded to call the names, each boy answering until all were correctly marked as present with a careful stroke of the pen that could be heard throughout the room. There were rarely absences from Rowland's school and then only with good cause, something that pleased the School Board. Rowland blotted the Register and replaced it in his desk.

"Open your books, please, at page thirty-seven," he said, doing the same with his own copy. He surveyed the class, deciding which of them should start. "Trickett," he said, choosing one of the older boys who had stood in the shelter, "read to us please, from the top of the page."

So the school day began. Each boy in his turn read a few sentences of the history text and when the passage came to an end, they listened carefully while Rowland read it again. If their teacher seemed somewhat distant, his air that of a man who saw more than was immediately apparent, they did not notice. They were remembering what they could of the life and times of the Venerable Bede for the test that would surely follow.

(Saturday 8 July)

The fresh, clean scent of rain kissed earth was still strong in the air as Rowland walked at a gentle pace along the road from Swann and through the outskirts of Hamm. He felt at peace. A deep sleep had been soothed by the sound of the rain in the night. The steady patter had filtered into his subconscious and washed away the dreams that threatened his rest, had calmed the worries of the previous day. Now he was back to his routine and much content.

As he walked through the outskirts of the town, the freshness of the air became increasingly spoiled by the flat, dry, staleness of the dust of long buried chalk. The dull smell of sweat and alcohol also hung in the air as he approached the remains of the Norman Cluniac Priory.

Despite the smell and the dust, both of which found their way into everything and were difficult to shift, a sizable crowd had congregated on the nearby pavement. They were looking over and through iron railings into a deep, steep-sided cutting where a large gang of navvies and labourers was hard at work on the last stretch of the new section of the railway.

On the far side of the cutting a smaller gang of better dressed men also dug into the earth, supervised by several local notables. The new branch line of the railway had already cut through the centre of the Priory cemetery and was now heading for the remains of the cloisters.

Henry VIII had started the work of destruction. The railway company was finishing it. Some wit, who had wisely elected to remain anonymous, had written to the local newspaper to suggest that the Archaeological Society, newly formed and now busily supervising their own dig to salvage and protect what they could of the Priory, would make a better job of it than either Henry or the navvies.

Rowland slowed his pace, but skirted the crowd without stopping. He did not much relish the presence of large numbers of people. Crowds were unpredictable and unpleasant forms of humanity as far as he was concerned. And crowds gathered to watch their repressed brethren slaving to maintain the status quo were very nearly the worst form of humanity, only a step or two above the louts who chased, terrified, and slaughtered animals

15

for their pleasure. Besides, he had seen more than enough destruction in his life.

At the railway station itself, several hundred yards further along the road, another crowd was forming as passengers alighted from a train recently arrived from London. There was excitement and an air of purposeful confusion. The whistle of a porter summoning a hansom cab from the distant rank cut through the busy hubbub. Rowland paused awhile rather than mix with a bustle that he could not otherwise avoid. Taking his straw hat from his head, he wiped his forehead with a handkerchief. He replaced his hat and stowed the handkerchief in the canvas satchel that was slung from his shoulder.

While he waited for the crowd to disperse, he looked at the collection of station buildings. He did not altogether approve of the railways. It was partly association. Most of his journeys had been with the army either to or from destruction and death. But they seemed to him also to represent the new age that excited many and impoverished so many more.

The station itself was much larger now than when he had arrived a year ago. A new ticket hall of brash yellow and red brick had been built with a pretentious and ill-proportioned canopy of cast-iron and glass over the main entrance. A new footbridge, balanced on ornate pillars, also of cast-iron, was being erected to service the new platforms.

Hamm had grown in importance as a market town and the new lines of steel that would link it with the major coastal towns to east and west would accelerate that growth even further. Men were making their fortunes. And their gain was had at the loss of so much. A man cannot grow rich as these men were growing rich without making others poor in direct proportion and ravaging the natural world. Rowland sighed quietly. The speed of all these developments astounded him. All this expansion had happened in a year and showed no signs of slowing. And much more than fortunes were being gained and lost.

Musing on the past seemed inescapable these recent days. Hamm had been an unfamiliar town when he had first stepped off the train, but he had felt instantly at home. He had always supposed, whenever he had bothered to think about it at all, that it was because he had family connections with the area. His guardian, a great-uncle now dead, had been born here. And that had been the major factor influencing him when he had applied for the teaching post in Swann. It was a reason when reason had been lacking. Just who his other relatives had been, or even if they still existed, he did not know and had never felt inclined to discover.

An amiable, if somewhat tenuous, relationship had grown between himself and the Reverend Lemuel Beckett, incumbent of the parish of Swann. The age difference of forty years between the two men kept the relationship at a pleasingly distant level. Rowland had quite successfully convinced himself that it was all he needed. That and his books, of course. But this little paradise had its flaw for there was also the Reverend Beckett's granddaughter, Ruth. Rowland sighed again as he thought of her. Dear Ruth Beckett. She was gentle, kind, and of independent mind; and altogether too fond of Rowland for his comfort.

When the arrivals from London had finally dispersed, Rowland resumed his journey. He passed the station on his right and, afterwards, the flint and brick bulk of the Ragged School on his left. Then came the steep climb up to the High Street. As he plodded slowly upwards, he smiled to himself a little confusedly at his dalliance with his memories. He made some vague excuse to himself about the heat and finally came out from his inner self to touch the day.

People moved all about him in the hot sunshine, weaving their lives together into a slow and rich tapestry that to them was everything, but which would one day be forgotten and visible only in its broad design to those who cared to take the time to look.

A police constable, visibly sweltering in his uniform, saluted Rowland as he passed the Law Courts. He hailed from Swann and Rowland stopped as they exchanged pleasantries for a few moments in the shade of the imposing portico.

Beyond the Judges' Lodgings, which stood next to the Law Courts, the commercial section of the High Street began. Rowland went into a large and well kept grocery shop that he favoured. The proprietor was a florid little man who moved cheerfully from behind his counter, smoothing his apron as he came. "Good morning, Mr Henty," he said, contriving to give the impression of bowing servitude without actually bending at the waist.

"It is, indeed," replied Rowland conventionally and handed the grocer a list of his requirements.

"Thank you, sir. George will be delivering to Swann as the per usual day. If you would care to settle your bill?" He raised his hand slightly as he caught the eye of his cashier.

Rowland bade the man a cheery farewell and went across to the cash desk. Behind the grille sat a pale and painfully shy young girl. She took his cash and, with a mumbled "Thank you, sir," counted it carefully. With equal care, she entered the amount in a vast ledger, wrote out his receipt, and blotted it before handing it through to him.

Rowland returned to the street. He had, in that single visit to the grocer, satisfied the needs of his larder that could not be met in Swann itself and had thus satisfied the needs of his body. The rest of the morning in the town he could devote to satisfying his intellect. For this singular pleasure, he sauntered further along the crowded High Street to Mr Parslows book shop. There he spent a pleasant hour in the dim, cool interior, away from the crowds and the bustle and free of the need to wear his spectacles. After much deliberation, he finally selected a copy of John Ruskin's *Elements of English Prosody* and a new book, *Treasure Island*, for the library shelf in the schoolroom - a luxury for the boys that was subsidized by the legacy that Rowland's guardian had bequeathed him.

"Ah, Mr Henty." Mr Parslow, who had spoken, appeared from a back room that was even darker than the shop. "How are they faring with that wretched railway?"

"Too well, I fear. It will not be long before the lines are laid up to the platform."

Mr Parslow shook his head sadly. "It is a dilemma. Progress can bring such delights." He waved his hand at the books in his shop.

"Is it progress if so many suffer?"

"Now that is a good question, Mr Henty. But you know my answer."

Rowland smiled. "What will we talk about when the railway is finished?"

"There is plenty left for the likes of you and I to complain of."

"True, Mr Parslow. Very true." Rowland placed the books he had chosen on the small writing table that served as a counter. "I will take these volumes if I may."

"Ah. Yes. Now wait just a moment." With that Mr Parslow disappeared into the deeper gloom at the rear of his shop and returned with a two volume set of books. "I have something just in which may interest you. It has been published these several years. Edited by Mr Wedderburn."

Rowland picked up the top volume. "Ah, excellent." With pleasure he scanned the first page and then closed the book to look at the title. "*The Arrows of the Chace*," he read.

"Yes, something of a treasure, to have collected Mr Ruskin's letters to the press."

"I will take them as well, Mr Parslow. If you would be so kind as to add it to my account. Is there news of any new publication?"

"I fear we shall have to be patient. He is, by all accounts, giving some fine lectures on art this year which will doubtless be printed in due time. But he is no longer a healthy man."

They shook their heads together in silence. John Ruskin was not the hero he had once been to many. The Age, they said, was passing him by. The Age, some said, did so at its peril. Rowland was one of those some. But, by and large, it was those with money to lose whose voices were being heard, and they were adamant that the Age was passing Ruskin by and a good thing too.

After further small talk, Rowland left the shop. Emerging from the pleasant haven of the cool, dim interior was a shock. The heat pressed in about him and light beat at his eyes. All about him, the town continued to move in its business but it seemed now to be a lethargic randomness. Certainly it was much to be avoided, so he crossed the High Street and walked down a steep, cobbled lane called Priory Twitten that ran between the backs of houses. Large oaken gates punctuated the flint and brick walls that surrounded the large gardens. The last one on the right was open and Rowland caught a glimpse of piles of brick stacked neatly on the large corner plot. Several bricklayers were at work. As he passed, his eye was caught by a sheet of paper pinned to the open gate. On it, in a laborious and awkward hand was written the name of the new property, 'Newelm House'.

At the bottom of the lane he turned to his right and walked down a stepped slope with a high buttressed wall to his right, part of the old town wall and now garden wall to the new house being constructed above. Crossing a road at the bottom, he passed the front of The Grange, a fine brick built Jacobean house with extensive private gardens that straddled a small stream that flowed only in the winter. Beyond the gardens was the small suburb of Southover, once a small village in its own right. There, he made his way up a small slope onto his road home.

The crowd that had gathered to watch the new dissolution of monastic buildings had grown larger, spilling from the pavement onto part of the dusty roadway. And now they had two entertainments. In addition to the railway work, which proceeded with little variation, a matronly woman had alighted from a grand carriage and was loudly scolding her daughter for her wanton behaviour in being in the street so close to the workmen without an escort. The reputation of the navvies had come before them and doubtless grew with local retelling.

Rowland shook his head sadly. The tough working men were probably too drunk to notice the crowd, let alone any daughters of the town who might be there without an escort. Alcohol was the only anaesthetic sufficient to dull the pain and monotony of the gruelling labour they undertook day after day. And any reputation they may have had, other than as hard men, was largely false. They had neither the time nor the inclination to go chasing local women. It would have cost them their job and put them on a blacklist. Most, in any case, had wives and women of their own at their nearby shanty town.

As Rowland left the town behind, he felt muscles relaxing in his neck and shoulders that he had not realized were tense. It was always the same. Being close to so many people and their 'civilization' bore down on him. The streets of London had been a constant nightmare. But that was passed. And so too was the town for he had soon left the last of the houses behind him. The atmosphere seemed less stagnant and breathing came more easily. Were it not for the visits he made to Mr Parslows book shop, he would not bother to make the journey each Saturday.

Vegetables, after all, could be had from many sources. Meat he had no use for at all.

As he walked, his books in the satchel slung across his left shoulder and resting on his opposite hip, he looked across the head of the valley that lay to his left. The chalk face of the river cliff, clumps of greenery growing from ledges and cracks in its surface, was bright in the sunshine. Beyond it showed the sun-parched crown of Wealden Hill. He looked away from it, strangely discomfited, and his eyes found the carved outline of the Newelm Man. The melancholic figure, seen obliquely from this road, filled him with a peculiar sense of longing that brought him slowly to a standstill.

He stood there for a long time that felt like no time at all, gazing quietly from beneath the shadow of his hat across the valley, lost to the many and varied emotions that filled him. Strange feelings of loss and desire that had no apparent focus and no apparent cause. Strange feelings that held him in thrall and cast him adrift at the boundary of some other place and some other time. It was a boundary he could not cross, merely one along which he could wander, back and forth, confused and uncertain about which way to turn.

It was the hard rolling sound of an approaching wagon that finally broke the spell that had charmed him. He turned, automatically at first but suddenly emerging into the world with a sudden inrush to his senses. It was as if it had all been dammed up beyond him by a circle of silence and now it entered in on him like a sudden flood. As he turned, he stepped up onto to the parched grass of the verge to allow the wagon to pass. The driver nodded to him and pulled the vehicle to a halt.

It was Farmer Hall. "Warm day for any folk to be walking," he said and shifted his bulk to one side of the seat. Rowland accepted the invitation, glad to be distracted from the peculiar trance into which he had fallen. He threw his satchel up onto the foot board and climbed up after it, settling himself onto the hard plank seat. "Walk on," said the farmer, quietly. The great horses strained against their harnesses and began walking. As the wagon moved, Rowland cast a quick, stealthy glance across to Wealden Hill. The enchantment was broken.

The heavy shires pulled the wagon on along the road at a slow, steady pace, heading for Swann. Their ears twitched and tails flicked at the flies. One or the other would occasionally lift its head and shake it. Farmer Hall paid them little heed. They knew the route well enough. The large wagon, filled with sacks and a new plough, rumbled behind them over the hard, baked earth of the road and both men swayed and rocked in unison as it lurched and bumped.

They travelled in silence for some while. Neither one of them was given to talking for the sake of making noise. Rowland sensed, though, a growing desire in the farmer to say something. It would be of import to his being for the large, weathered man had never been one to speak of trivialities. Rowland waited patiently. It was one lesson he had learned very early in his army life and which he found to be of inestimable value in dealing with these great, solid men who worked their annual miracle with the soil of the valley. If you let them speak in their own good time you will hear exactly what it is they want to say. If you tried to force the process with questions or other such fripperies of speech you would get nothing worth having and it would be no man's fault but your own.

When Farmer Hall did eventually speak, it was a question framed as a statement. "Robert."

Rowland sighed inwardly and pursed his lips. Young Bobby Hall, just turned fourteen, was the smallest and brightest of his pupils. A compact and muscular lad, he excelled at and enjoyed academic work. And not only was he quick in the classroom. He knew the soil as well, better than some grown men in the valley. It was a dilemma that confused the boy's father for he was not used to the idea of schooling. Rowland was also aware of the problem and, though apprehensive, was glad it had been raised. Here was a father's obvious pride for a clever son and a farmer's ever desperate need for another pair of hands.

Rowland spoke quietly. "I will, of course, urge that you allow him to stay on and try for his scholarship."

"Yes. You will. And rightly so. 'Tis your job. As mine is the land. But I have need of his hands."

It came slowly from the man and not without some difficulty, each short sentence carefully weighed before being offered. Rowland listened and accepted what the man said, but he felt he must try to persuade Farmer Hall otherwise. Bobby had a real chance of scholarly success. And not just some schoolmaster's post at the end of it, though that was far from a disgrace. There was a spark in the boy that might ignite a flame of real brilliance. If given the chance.

"How many hundreds of years have farmers faced this problem?" asked Rowland, and knew at once that it had been the wrong thing to say – idle and abstract.

"None hereabouts to my knowing, Mr Henty. And I know nothing, nor yet care, for other farmers now dead. Their problems are passed. It is my problems that I look to. I understand your concern. Understand mine. And the boy's. What he has never sown, he will never need to harvest."

The wagon moved slowly on. Both men still swayed in unison but that was their only communion. The farmer had spoken his mind and that was all there was to the matter. Rowland, however, brooded. He damned his insensitivity in dealing with adults. Children he knew and understood instinctively. Their ways and wants were usually straightforward and honestly voiced. What is more, their ways and wants were usually concordant with a peaceful and gentle existence. So too were these farmers, but they were adults and the adult mind in all its rigidity remained largely beyond Rowland's understanding. There were exceptions. Kingsley. Ruskin. Morris. MacDonald. The rest of the world... why were they all so fixed on such destructive ways?

Rowland turned to the farmer. "In the end, Mr Hall, I must of course give way to you, but at least allow the length of the summer before making a final decision."

The farmer turned to Rowland and looked at him for a moment, considering the request. He turned back to look out over the broad backs of his horses. "This I will do, Mr Henty, but be not surprised if I do not change my mind."

Rowland looked out over the horses as well and saw the rooftops of Swann through the trees ahead of them as the wagon breasted a small rise in the road. Rowland watched them and wondered why the sight did not feel so much like home as he was sure it had done just a week ago.

*

"Good day to you, Rowland. You are returned from your excursion to Hamm much earlier than usual."

Rapt of his recent conversation with Farmer Hall and of more general ideas about the direction a life might take, the Reverend Beckett's voice startled him. He stopped and turned to face the vicarage, slightly startled that he had passed this far through the village without realizing it. The Reverend Lemuel Beckett had paused in his tending of the sadly parched rose that grew over the front door. Both men stepped to the garden gate from opposite sides and stood in the sparse shade of a small lime tree that grew there.

There was a gloss of perspiration on the old man's face and he produced a large, red handkerchief from the pocket of his white linen jacket. Removing his wide-brimmed straw hat with a tremulous hand, he carefully wiped the kerchief across his brow and around his neck. When he had finished he replaced his hat carefully on his head and smiled.

"I rode back with Farmer Hall," explained Rowland during this.

The Reverend Beckett looked mildly surprised. He replaced the crumpled handkerchief in his jacket pocket. "I did not hear him come along the lane."

Rowland looked at the old man blankly for a moment. "No," he said, finally breaking out of his reverie. "He stopped outside Mrs Reeve's house and let me down there. He was driving up to Brigg Farm with Mr Brigg's new plough."

"Ah, yes. Of course. Good. Then I need not worry for my ears."

Rowland again stared at the old man for a moment before he understood. The Reverend Beckett peered back at Rowland as though over the top of spectacles that he wasn't at that moment wearing.

"Is something the matter, Rowland?" he asked.

Rowland sighed. "I tried to persuade Mr Hall to allow Robert to stay on at school and try for his scholarship."

"Ah. Yes, Rowland. It is a problem."

"I am afraid that I was not very convincing. But," he added, more in an attempt to convince himself than anyone else, "Mr Hall did promise to delay his decision until the end of the summer."

The Reverend Beckett smiled sadly in response and scratched the back of his head. "He will not change his mind, Rowland.

He is not a dogmatic soul. He will have given this a great deal of thought - with young Robert in mind as much as himself. And I have not the slightest doubt that he will now think it all through again. A very fair minded man. Very fair. But in the end it is he alone who knows the realities of his situation."

Rowland looked questioningly at the old man. He knew it was not meant as a criticism, but he could not help feeling put down and it showed in his face.

"I am sorry, Rowland," said the vicar. "I could, perhaps, have phrased that a little more tactfully than I managed." He thought carefully for a moment before continuing. "Mr Hall is a farmer. You are not. He has worked hard all his life on the soil, has adapted to the changes of our age where others have failed. He knows that if his son is to survive, he must start his education on the land now."

"Yes." Rowland knew it was right. More than most other folk he knew and appreciated that education consists in a great deal more than just schooling.

"Do not let it worry you. You must not think of it as a failure. Young Robert will do as well as, if not better than, his father. And that is due, in part, to you."

Rowland smiled, although it needed a little forcing. "It seems such a shame, though."

"Let it pass. There will be other scholars. And as this little community grows more used to the idea of education they will be more inclined to give it a chance. Bobby Hall will be a parent one day. You mark my words and see if he does not give his children the chance he is to be denied. Yours, Rowland, is a work that will have its effect for many generations."

"I had not looked on it in that light." It was a heavy responsibility yet one that he felt could easily be borne.

"Of a more cheerful note, I have promises from both Mr Hall and Mr Elam that we might have their wagons for the picnic on Thursday. I hope you will join us, Rowland. You will enjoy it, I am sure."

Rowland knew he had no choice.

*

Pausing a moment at the track's edge to catch his breath, Rowland turned to look back across the dry but still verdant landscape of the Rushy Valley. Below him, at the foot of the hill, his own village of Swann lay woven amongst the trees. Just beyond its far boundary was the schoolhouse with its pale, dusty yard and his own lush garden. Further beyond, much further, clear in the bright afternoon sunshine, was Wealden Hill. All else that was within the scope of his vision seemed to have been pushed away to the edge as if the places most in his thoughts and deepest in his spirit were in some way magnified and strung out along an invisible line.

Apart from the slow drifting motion of sheep in the distance and the occasional glint of sunlight bursting like diamonds of fire from fish ripples on the river's surface, the whole scene was still. A masterpiece caught by a hand and eye infinitely more skilled and knowing than any mortal artist. A canvas touched by the breath of life for, despite the stillness, the spirit of being was also there, imperceptible but unmistakable.

The land breathed, just as Rowland himself breathed. It was a vast living thing, benign at this moment, warm, nurturing the creatures that lived within its protective and enclosing arms. It was a prospect pleasing both to the senses and to the spirit and he felt within himself that same sense of comfort that had come to him when he had first arrived in the valley and discovered its ways. It was his home. And it was his home in some sense that went deeper within his being than he yet fully knew or understood.

Somewhere out there in a reality beyond the shield of the summer haze and his sparse knowledge, his forbears had lived. From there they had set out into other worlds - journeys that would continue for centuries yet to come. So much had his great-uncle told him. So much and no more.

It was precious little to know of one's history, but it was sufficient for Rowland to realize that something of his past had been hidden. Talk of his parents, for example, had always been vague. It took little enough of intelligence to realize that he was most probably born out of wedlock. A bastard. Yet he did not much bother himself with that. What was past was beyond anyone's ability to change. It could not hurt him. And his great-uncle had given him security, if not love. It had been enough.

He looked again, scanning the world before him. His home, this valley, was green and welcoming - even in this increasingly fierce summer. It was an ancient place, solid and well founded, its roots running deep into a fertile past, deep into a mysterious otherness.

About him, the hilltops were scattered with the tombs of kings and heroes long dead and as long forgotten. The whole landscape was shaped by the countless generations of farmers who had felled the forests, had grazed their sheep, and had worked its soil. A people who had gentled nature, altered her and learned her secrets in order to work with her to their own advantage, created new and verdant landscapes teeming with life. A people who had developed a way and a knowledge that was now almost lost. A people who had a communion with the land.

It was a gentle place filled with the presence of the spirit of those people and touched with something else even more tenuous and indefinable - a deep and green magic that caressed the soul. After the high Himalay mountains with their cold and alien past and their justly hostile peoples...

He shivered, recalling the jagged fragments of memory that had shot through him the day before, released, as it seemed, by the strange recurring dream. He looked down to the ground at his feet, shadows crossing his mind. "No," he said quietly. "I will not succumb. It has gone. I am safe here."

With that spoken, like a spell strong with the magic of his homeland and held defiantly in his mind, he turned his back to the valley and continued along the narrow upward road.

The way was hot and dusty, but partly shaded from the afternoon sun by tall, thick hedgerows and the occasional wind-sculpted tree. Quietly, treading gently on the earth, he made his way westwards and southwards. Insects filled the air about him with their soporific song.

After breasting a low curving ridge of the downs, the road descended into a hollow where the village of Cross lay. A pair of russet butterflies danced together across the road and about his legs before disappearing into the long grass at his side. He encountered no other living creature as he walked through the small sun baked huddle of cottages and was thankful. Although his mood was lighter, he knew he would not have brooked interruption without ingratitude.

Leaving the small village, he followed the road back up out of the hollow. It gradually diminished as it began to climb away from the cottages until it became no more than a narrow path that led to and then beyond the church. Rowland looked at the flint building with its squat spire of red tile as he passed but did not feel compelled to stop and explore. Instead he carried along the path as it trailed up onto the western shoulder of Cross Down. There he did stop; surveying a scene of complete contrast to the one he had left behind. Before him lay two small hills, covered in scrub and divided by a narrow dip. Beyond and below that lay the sea.

It was silent from this distance and it was seemingly still, shrouded by the faintest of heat hazes. The steely surface was a desert to the soul, a clean place. Each time he came to this spot he felt fiercely alive, yet he was also filled with a great calm. All the worries and confusions of his life were, for a while, put to one side. And it made no difference what the mood of the scene might be. It could be such as he saw now, magnificent serenity, or some other scene altogether; sultry anger, wild frenzy, bleak solemnity. There was always, for him, an escape in this view of the sea.

Breathing deeply of the fresh, salt air as it blew gently past him, he strode down to the cliff top and stood with the very edge of the world at his feet. Dry crumbs of earth broke away from under the soles of his boots and fell unheeded down the chalk face to the beach below. Across the face of the bleached blue sky myriad gulls soared and cried, riding the upward winds.

In the far distance, close to the horizon, a white sail, flapping impotently, caught the sun. Lazy sparks of sunlight moved across the distant surface, speaking of a gentle swell. Looking directly below, Rowland could see the waters push gently against the pebble shoreline. He watched the sea breathing thus, taking its rhythm for his own and stood, free and clean as the world turned.

Unnerved by his presence so close to their young, great gulls began to climb away from their nests below his feet. They circled his head, screaming abuse. He stepped back finally, conscious of the disturbance he was causing, and left the birds to their offspring.

Back on the path, he hesitated for a moment and then decided to head eastward, passing a row of deserted, roofless cottages and skirting the heights of Rushy Head with its view of the broad maze of shallow water at the mouth of the river. Walking at a near marching pace he strode along the path through the scrub and down into the valley towards the village of Meeching.

Later, in the darkening evening, he settled himself on a bench in his garden beneath the large climbing rose that surrounded the kitchen window. Bathed in its rich scent, he watched the stars appear, their light flickering as the shadow of the planet darkened sufficiently for their faint fires to be seen. It was the time of day he treasured the most. A brief time, soon lost to the night, when the light was dim enough for him to be able to dispense with his tinted spectacles yet still see the true colours of the sunlit world. A brief time when a quiet magic, derived of that deep and green enchantment but somehow stronger in the stillness, filled the air with an indefinable sense of something other.

As he scanned the sky, picking out the familiar star mosaics as they appeared, his eyes ready to follow the quick trail of a meteor, he massaged his left thigh. He had walked too far and too fast and the muscles ached with a dull pain. Gently back and forth he ran his fingertips, feeling, even through the thick material of his trousers, the ragged wound where the bullet had made its exit. It sickened him, an ugly thing in image of the war that made it. War, made in the image of man.

The exhilaration he had felt after his walk was gone. So, too, was the discomfiting restlessness that had sent him on his way in the first place. He had settled now into a sadness both nameless and gentle beneath the summer night sky.

From the village, the faint sound of ale inspired laughter drifted through the dark. Some part of him, albeit briefly, yearned then for company, for the ability to cast off all worries and fears. Yet, who could? Only in sleep was that possible, and his sleep now was haunted by strange dreams and songs.

(Sunday 9 July)

The hymn came to an end. A last echo of voices was swallowed by the rustle, scuffle, clatter, and cough of the congregation as they sat and settled themselves on the pews of ancient oak. Silence filled the space.

Rowland, as always, was sitting where the shadows were deepest. He had always felt out of place in churches - an observer in an alien world. And always with the same thoughts. Turning his head slightly, looking at the faces of those others that he could see, he wondered, if they were any more comfortable than himself within those walls. Did they feel the mystery of their god, or did they just fear him? Perhaps they feared their neighbours more. Just as he did himself. It was his position in the village as schoolmaster and the patronage of the Reverend Beckett, after all, that made his presence an obligation.

As his eyes wandered idly about the cool spaces of the interior, they were caught by those of Ruth Beckett. She smiled at him in greeting and his eyes slid quickly away, firstly to a window where the bright sun was painting many colours that hurt his eyes, and thence to the cold stone floor. Her smile had become a brief frown as he looked away, betraying her lack of understanding at the way in which he so resolutely cut himself off from human company - especially her own.

No matter how often he had expressed content with his self-imposed solitude, she failed to comprehend that there does not need to be a reason beyond the natural dislike by some of the company of others. No mater how he tried, she would not be convinced and, not for the first time, he wondered how she might be persuaded. Further speculation, however, was cut short as her grandfather began to speak in a soft voice that, with the practice of many years, filled the church.

"Isaiah, chapter fifty-three, verses four to six. 'Surely he hath borne our griefs, and carried our sorrows: yet we did esteem him stricken, smitten of God, and afflicted. But he was wounded for our transgressions, he was bruised for our iniquities: the chastisement of our peace was upon him; and with his stripes we are healed. All we like sheep have gone astray; we have turned every one to his own way; and the Lord hath laid on him the iniquity of us all.'" A quick shadow moved through the church, the passing breath of some distant object. "A prophecy in its own time of the coming of Our Lord. But it is no less relevant to our good selves It was the Infinite mercy of God that gave us the Saviour, his only Son, to bear all our sins and die for us that we might see the way. We must not assume from this, however, that we may sin and expect others to take that burden. We cannot blame others for our own faults as many in this world are prone to do."

The Reverend Beckett continued in like vein for some time, but Rowland soon stopped listening. His mind was elsewhere, lost in a vague and uncharted realm of disquiet in which some very real and very frightening but equally anonymous emotion had started breaking the threads of the protections he had woven for himself.

The lunch that followed was a strained affair. Rowland, a regular guest at the Beckett table, despite the problems and embarrassments his vegetarian diet had first caused, did not feel disposed to conversation. Attempts to draw him out had all but ceased. Ruth and her grandfather continued to make small talk, to which Rowland responded monosyllabically, but the effort was increasingly onerous. His gloom settled upon the other two until the room eventually grew silent apart from the sound of cutlery on the best china-ware. Outside, beyond the latticed windows, the sunshine was bright, hot, and solid.

Ruth and her grandfather exchanged looks but seemed unable to break the silence that had filled the room. They had tried many subjects but Rowland was obviously not in a receptive mood. Indeed, the gloomy spell was eventually broken from without when Mrs Black, a widow of the parish who kept house for the Becketts, came through the door. She cleared away the plates and when she had gone Lemuel Beckett rose from his chair.

"Perhaps we should adjourn to the garden," he said. "Smiles might more easily be found there."

Rowland rose. "I am sorry to you both," he said quietly. And he was because, apart from his reservations about Ruth's feelings toward him, he normally enjoyed his Sunday lunches with the Becketts. "I have allowed my preoccupations to cloud the day," he added, feeling the need to offer some explanation.

"Preoccupations?" asked Ruth. "Do you mean Robert Hall?"

"No," he said automatically and then regretted it. It would have been a convenient half truth with which to forestall further enquiry. He thought quickly. "I strained my leg yesterday. The pain has evoked memories." It was only part of the truth, but it would serve. "Perhaps," he added, "the warmth of the sunshine will do me good." He knew, despite his ignorance of the problem, that it would take more than sunshine.

Arranging a smile on his face, he opened the door for the others.

*

The airless heat of late evening enclosed him, as did the gathering darkness. He lay upon his bed staring at the ceiling, haunted by the events of the last few days, fighting a battle with the feeling that somewhere beneath the surface of his calm, ordered little world all was not well. It was a battle he was slowly losing.

It was not the sensation of dancing on a volcano, desperately trying to ignore the coming catastrophe with a wildly enthusiastic and unnatural devotion to the false world through which one whirled. It was more like journeying on ice over unknown depths. Thin ice. Ice that whines and crazes beneath each careful step long after the shoreline has faded beneath the horizon. There would be no explosion, he would simply slip through the surface and be no more.

He was haunted, too, by the attentions of Ruth Beckett. For all that she was his age; she seemed to him but a girl - intelligent, well read, kindly, but somehow a surface entity, a creature of convention. He liked her, but that was all and he had no desire to encourage her beyond their present relationship. Her life had not been easy, he knew, left in the care of a grandparent whilst her mother and father had sought out South American heathen with an anachronistic zeal that had, quite possibly, put them beyond the pale. They had not been heard from, or of, since well before Rowland had arrived in Swann.

Rowland felt that he was losing control over what little there was in his life to regulate. He knew that circumstances were pushing Ruth and himself together. Yet she was not what he wished for. He was too familiar with her ways. She was open and known, not possessed of the mysterious he so suddenly desired. A desire that startled him as it was so strong, so suddenly and newly articulated in his own thoughts, one that he could not understand.

Silently he rose and moved to the window in the north wall. His spirit was restless and he did not understand. That was not the worst of it, however. The worst of it was that the disquiet he

32

felt was not some imagination wrought of tiredness. It was real. It had a real source. But that source, as yet, was deep in the heart of an unknown darkness. Across the valley a hill blotted out the stars. He looked, unseeing, into that darkness and tried to recall the words of the song, tried to recall the tune.

(Monday 10 July)

An air of wellbeing filled the almost silent room. Outside, the sun once more shone relentlessly, flooding the windows and open doorway with a painful liquid glare. Inside, within the thick walls of flint and brick, the brightness was just bearable and the air was still comparatively cool from the night. It would not, however, remain cool for too much longer. Leaden breaths of sun baked air were already venturing through the open door and touching Rowland's face where he sat.

With their heads bowed as they worked hard at their copy, the boys seemed oblivious to the warm breezes. A face lifted occasionally to look at the blackboard where Rowland had written the text they were to transfer to their books, and then dropped once more to concentrate on the labour of letters. Rowland watched them with drowsy but watchful interest, feeling some peace within himself. He was too occupied by the smooth running of the day's lessons to worry about anything that might lie beyond his immediate field of vision.

Sitting at his desk in the schoolroom, in confident control of his domain, he felt a degree of freedom from the troubled thoughts of recent days and he was able to push them into some dark recess of his being. The gentle order he had imposed within these walls during his tenure now helped to impose a sense of order within himself. Whenever there was a specific purpose in life that made personal sense there was little room for doubt.

A shadow filled the open doorway, followed a moment later by the slight frame of the Reverend Beckett. Rowland smiled and got down from his tall chair quietly so as not to disturb the boys. He joined the vicar in the doorway, surveying the class before they went out into the yard. The heat clamped itself about Rowland's flesh and the pervasive brilliance of the sunlight made him squint, even through the heavy tint of his lenses. He stepped back into the scant shade provided by the overhang of the roof.

The Reverend Beckett decided to join him there, mopping his face with his red handkerchief. "I expect you are used to such heat as this," he said.

"Not really," replied Rowland, looking out into the glare and into some great distance beyond it. "The heat of India and the Afghan is... different."

Lemuel Beckett silently berated himself for once more dragging the schoolmaster's past into the present. He was not one to mollycoddle, but he knew the young man had suffered more than most, and wounds in the mind take longer to heal than those in the flesh. He really should, he told himself, take more care when talking to the schoolmaster.

Rowland shifted uneasily and drew his eyes away from the brightness, sensing unease in the old man. Perhaps his reply had been somewhat abrupt, but he knew that there was a tendency to tiptoe round his sensibilities and he really wished that people would not. He removed his glasses and, with a large handkerchief, he wiped away the tears that had formed in the corners of his eyes. "It does not worry me now."

The vicar frowned, seemingly uncertain, after the pause, just what Rowland meant.

"Talk of India. The Afghan. The fighting," added Rowland, clarifying his remark as he replaced his glasses and put his handkerchief back in his pocket. "I have learned to... accept that I shall carry the horror with me. But it is passed. I was, after all, one of the lucky ones. I can live with the memories of what happened there. Others have to live with much much more. Many simply did not live."

Living with the memories was a problem he had no choice but to try and cope with. If he could not come to terms with that, then his life would be nothing more than one long nightmare. But the body could not remember physical pain. And the mind was good at tidying the pictures up into neat little packets of memory, making subtle alterations in the process, and then tidying them all away into dark recesses of the mind. Eventually it would be no worse than taking out an album of photographic prints, looking at a series of strangers who are your past selves. Eventually.

Understanding the way he had been treated afterwards was an altogether different matter. That still turned and churned in his mind, increasing his frustration, for he knew that as time passed he would be further and further from any sort of solution. And knowing that he would never know merely compounded the problem. Not knowing was what had started it all.

It had been as if they had blamed him for what had happened. It was, after all, the Intelligence Officer's job to know. He had not known. And he had been the only survivor. Yet how could he have known? They hadn't been part of the opposing forces. Just a group of bandits, on the run from both sides and hungry, brutalized by the war, dehumanized by dogmatic tradition, and as fond of committing atrocities as the regular Afghan, his woman, or common British soldier. He took off his spectacles once more and pinched the bridge of his nose, rubbing at his closed eyes before running the palm of his hand slowly over his cropped hair. He replaced the spectacles. The peace of the day was gone.

For a while the two men stood still and stared silently into their respective thoughts, brooding on life and coming no nearer to answers this time than they had at any time before. Quiet sounds of restlessness from within the schoolroom restored them to the present. Rowland walked to the doorway and stood there for a moment looking in at the boys. Silence returned. He went back to where the Reverend Beckett waited.

"Ah, yes, Rowland," he said, as if they had just at that moment met. "The Reverend Turner came to see me earlier."

"Reverend Turner?"

"From St John's at Stone."

Rowland nodded as he recalled a small, rather curt man in his late forties who, popular gossip had it, beat his wife with a cane. Having met the man, Rowland could well believe it to be true.

The Reverend Beckett continued. "He told me of a small band of gypsies, five caravans it would seem, that had come along the coast from Hastings. They had been moved on from there. Apparently, the men have heard that the railway company are in need of labourers to help with the new line."

Rowland was surprised. "Does the company not have enough workmen?"

"I believe they have a full complement of navigators, but are still in need of common labourers, especially when they begin work on the eastern stretch. They prefer to hire them as they move along. It is likely that these men will be taken on. If that is the case, they will probably camp up at Brigg Farm for a while. Mr Brigg often allows the field behind his orchard to be used by travellers. He does not share the prejudices of many hereabouts." He paused for a moment, perhaps trying to decide whether he himself shared those prejudices, perhaps thinking of some other thing altogether. Rowland waited and was suddenly discomfited by the piercing gaze that was turned on him. "Be that as it may, there are several children with these people and they may have provision of this school."

"I see. And you would like me to extend this... invitation to them?"

The Reverend Beckett smiled. "If you would, please, Rowland. My legs are getting a little too old for the climb up that hill."

It was Rowland's turn to smile. At seventy, the Reverend Lemuel Beckett could outwalk most men, including some of the local shepherds.

"Besides," added the old man, placing a hand lightly on Rowland's arm and lowering his voice unnecessarily, "some of these travellers have a deep mistrust of the Church. Not that it is not always unwarranted, I am ashamed to say. I think the only thing they fear more than the Christian Church are the fraeries and the Old Religion. But that was ever the way. Hereabouts was the last place in mainland Britain to forego pagan worship." He smiled defensively, as if it were a subject not suitable to be heard from the lips of a priest. "Now, Rowland, if I may, I will go in and take my scripture lesson."

(Monday 10 July - Tuesday 11 July)
School was over for the day. The boys had rushed off into the sunshine leaving the schoolroom empty - an emptiness that was more than just an absence of people. Some spirit, which was the group both present and past, and which normally lingered in faintest form, had this time gone with them into the heat of the afternoon to escape the sombre confines of the room. Shadows of deep silence had settled quickly over the oaken desks and

hung like dust sheets from the shelves, covering the books and oddities that were on them.

As soon as the boys had gone and the strange quiet had settled, Rowland had taken a small book of folk ballads from the shelf by his own desk. He had paid it scant attention since he had bought it some months before as part of a boxful that Mr Parslow wanted rid of. Now it held the promise, if but faintly, of an answer.

Rowland sat quietly at his desk with the book open before him. Some faint feeling of recognition had come as he had flicked through the pages earlier in search of something to read to the boys. It had been no more than the merest whisper of déjà vu, flirting with the very edge of his reasoning mind. Yet the occasional phrase seemed to echo the voice he had been hearing in his dreams.

It was only that - the slightest of echoes, a rhythm that seemed almost to match, words that seemed almost to say something. But how could he know? There was nothing about what he read that matched sufficiently for him to latch on to anything. Even the language was wrong.

And suddenly he had something - a breathtaking certainty catching him unawares as he sat in the deserted room. Whatever the song, whoever the songstress, it was not in any language he knew. This realization sent shivers crawling across his flesh. The song was coherent. He knew it had meaning. In his dream it was quite clear. Yet it was not in any form familiar. And he was certain it was not that sort of dream in which some great truth is revealed that cannot be remembered on waking. It was not that at all.

The timeless space that Rowland had entered into in the exploration of his dreams was not inviolate. Bobby Hall, who had left with the others and raced home, had now returned. He hovered in the doorway to the schoolroom, a book in his hand, caught between his desire to be out and away with the other boys for the few precious spare hours that were his and the imposed need to speak with his teacher. He watched the pale, thin figure for a while and then, drawn by respect and a kind of love, yet hesitant because of a slight fear, he approached the tall desk where Rowland sat, head down, reading.

"Mr Henty, sir?"

The boy's timid voice drifted into Rowland's consciousness. It was a strange and harsh arrhythmia cutting into the formless world where his soul was increasingly more easily drawn along a path that was at last, if only slightly, beginning to show itself in a dense undergrowth of uncertainty. He raised his eyes from the book before him. Slowly the thoughts he was exploring dispersed and the room came into focus. He turned to the boy, pulling his gaze from some great and secret distance. Bobby Hall watched cautiously.

"Ah," Rowland said, as if trying to remember the boy's name. His hand went to his mouth and he took a deep breath through his nose. He took his hand away and breathed out in a great sigh as his eyes finally focused. "Robert. Bobby. Hob."

The boy hesitated, his face showing the bewilderment normally reserved for the more onerous tasks set by his teacher. Rowland saw the look of disquiet in the boy's face and quickly pulled himself back into the old and well trodden world of his daily life. His voice and bearing returned to something close to that of his normal mien. "What is it that you want, Bobby?" asked Rowland.

Reassured, the boy spoke. "The book, sir."

Rowland, momentarily confused, frowned and cast a quick glance at the book which lay open on his desk. "The book I just lent-"

"Borrowed."

"Borrowed, sir."

"*At The Back Of The North Wind.*"

"Yes, sir."

There was a pause. It was clear that the boy did not know how to continue. He looked at his teacher as if mesmerized. Rowland sensed his discomfiture and filled the gap for him. "Well, Bobby, and what of Mr MacDonald's extravaganza?"

"My father found it at home, sir. Today, sir. He said..." His nerve failed and he looked down at his feet as he continued, "He said 'it was nonsense to be filling a boy's head with' and that I'd to bring it back." The speech came out in a rush, almost one continuous word, and the boy proffered the book, his face a beacon of the embarrassment he felt.

A sudden flash of anger flared within Rowland and tried to burst free; anger at the narrow, interfering farmer who saw no further than the hedgerows of his miserable farm and would not allow his son even a brief chance to fly, as Diamond flew, even if only in his mind. And as quickly as the anger flared, it died. There was no real kindling for it to burn upon, no real target for his anger. Farmers, he thought, looking at the boy standing before him. They had, most of them, unremittingly hard lives, even here where the working was good. Confrontation would solve nothing.

Gently Rowland took the book from the boy's hand. "Well..." he hesitated for a moment until a solution presented itself. "I'll put it back on the shelf. The schoolroom door is not usually locked until late. Do you understand?"

The boy frowned momentarily and then smiled as he realized that the book would be available without his father being disobeyed. The smile surprised Rowland. For the briefest of moments it was a smile of knowing and wisdom as much as it was a smile of joy. Bobby Hall, who loved books as much as he loved the land, had seen something of his own future and knew that it was a good thing. It was always a shock to see such an expression on the face of a child. And yet, Rowland had seen such a thing many times before. On the faces of babies at rest in the cradle, on the faces of children in the last throes of starvation. They have seen in their own way and calmly accepted a reality that no mere adult can even begin to comprehend.

"Go on," said Rowland, breaking his mood and smiling. "Off you go."

Grinning his thanks, the boy ran from the room, stirring the dust in the air as he passed, kicking up clouds in the yard as his heavy boots pounded the dry soil. Rowland watched through the open door as the boy went off towards the village and continued to stare at the outside world for a long time after the boy had disappeared from sight.

His smile faded slowly. And just as slowly, his gaze returned to the open book on the table. With an involuntary shudder, he focused his eyes and mind on the words, dropping once more into the unmixed vision that danced the misty stretches of his unnamed longing. And there he sat until long after the sun, eclipsed by the shoulder of Brook Down, cast the last of its light across the valley.

Only when it became too dark to read comfortably did he rouse himself from his search. He held his head haught, blinking, stretching the pain from his neck. Carefully, he closed the book and replaced it on the shelf. The night was coming. He locked the schoolroom and retreated to the downstairs room of the house via the connecting door. In that, too, he turned the key.

The song had not been in the book, but that had not really surprised him - it was, after all, only a dream. Nothing more than a dream, obsessed with it as he was. That is what he kept telling himself. Just a dream. But somehow he could not really convince himself of it any longer. The words and phrases, despite being in a language he did not know, had dislodged ghosts from obscure parts of his memory and sent them spinning briefly across the wasteland of his mind. Far too briefly for him to recognize, let alone grasp.

*

The quiet, scented evening drew steadily on to night, peaceful and calm. It was a deep sea on which he felt he was floating, above which the air lay still and allowed the ineffable vastness of the universe to reach down and touch the very mantle of the earth, disturbing the minds of mortal beings.

From his bedroom he looked out on the eastern sky at the bright stars blazing at the beginning of their dance. Some there were that formed a crooked crown about the head of Wealden Hill. It was a wild sight that brought up the gooseflesh in a thrill of wonder.

Turning away, disturbed and overwhelmed, Rowland walked to the dresser and blew out the candle that stood there. In the sudden dark he stepped across to his bed and lay down. As he pulled the thin sheet over himself, the after-image of the flame flickered purple inside his eyes. Enclosed by the comfortable warmth he lay, outwardly still, his mind wreathing in and out of the strange and tangled melancholy that had been laid upon him.

At the centre of the labyrinth, the song. Shimmering and brightly formless as if fashioned of fire, the words were unfolding petals, emerging flowers. They danced in the hot air, blown by the wind, quick, elusive, and free. Sometimes one would be trapped between his reaching fingers, only to become insubstantial, slipping away with the rest. If he could only just hold on to one. It was all he had to do. Nothing more. Just that. Chase after them. Follow them through the silent wind. Yet, hard as he tried, his legs would not move and a heavy, inevitable sadness gripped him.

Trying to mark where they went, that he might follow later, he found his sight blurring. Only when he looked down at his motionless feet and beyond into the deep snow-filled ravine did his vision clear. There came a silence, absolute and terrifying. A suspended silence. A silence of anticipation. A silence that lasted forever, frozen like the snows across the peaks of the high mountains. A silence during which a horrifying clarity filled him with dread. He could see each crystal of frozen snow as they lay bluish-white on the slope, each flake like an elusive flower.

And what was it that someone was shouting? He wanted to look, to see who it was, but his vision was blurring again, fogged this time by an expanding cloud of red mist. Gunfire and hard echoes cut sharply into the silence, rolling like thunder in the chill, clear air. Someone screaming. A long, wild, desperate scream tearing razor thin layers of pain from the cold and still air, wrapping them around the echoes as they faded across the distant snow fields. The words were completely lost. He never did know. Never would.

There came a second cloud of red mist, steaming across the frigid air. A falling body, collapsing as though life were strings that had just been cut. Suddenly he panicked. He wanted to get away because he knew what was coming next. He was desperate to move and panicking because he knew he would not - knew he had not. And he was still staring down past his feet when, half way down his left thigh, the leg of his trousers bulged and blossomed in an explosion of shreds of coarse woven wool and flesh as the rough-cast lead ball passed through him. The ruin of his limb was turning slowly in the red mist of the mountain air as he was lifted from his feet in a painful twisting motion and dumped on his back with a jerk and was awake, the sheet clutched painfully in his closed fists, his mouth open for a scream that would not come.

Only when the sweat had dried from his body and he had relaxed sufficiently to move properly did he rise and go to the window. He leaned on the sill and drew in deep draughts of the warm night air trying to cleanse the nightmare from his system. He shivered. It had been a long time since he had endured that.

A tear born of frustration rolled from the corner of his eye and he wiped it away. Yet the dream had been different this time. The replay of reality had been intermixed with more recent visions. Flowers and words. The aching sweetness of the song. Perhaps it had woken him again? Any speculation that would lead his thoughts away from the bloody horror of the shooting was worth entertaining. So he listened to the night with exaggerated care. And he knew with sickening certainty that the nightmare alone had kicked him out of his sleep.

In a movement more of tenderness than savagery, he buried his face in his hands and pummelled the flesh, pushing his hands up over his head to the back of his neck. He stood silent and still. A semblance of peace settled over him if not, at first, within him. In the passing minutes, as he stood alone with the disinterested universe, something finally worked to restore the complex and settled patterns within him as well.

The night air was warm on his flesh. It did not stir and drew no sound from the nearby trees. He sighed and looked down across the back garden of the schoolhouse and beyond to the water meadows that ran to the river's bank. Moonlight picked out rough detail and painted a clear, still picture. Doubtless there was movement and life there, but he could see none. In the far distance, a tawny owl called. Its sudden screech echoed in the dark. Nothing more. Just stars and the darkness of the hills.

He turned away to return to his bed and then, with a slow, cold tingling in his stomach, went back to the window. It was, he reckoned, close to half past two. No one would be about at that time of the morning. At least, no one who would want their presence known. So why, he asked himself, were there stars on the side of Cobb Hill? Not the steady, yellowish glow of a lantern as one might expect in such a place, or the fitful capering, orange glow of a fire, but points of light, flickering with many subtle hues, moving northward and upward along the hillside, continually eclipsed by the trees as they moved. Stars. There was no other word he could think of to describe them for that is what they most closely resembled. And not those hard points of light scattered like living frost across a winter sky, but the great, lazy, pulses that jewelled the summer darkness above him.

He watched them in awe, willing himself to see them more clearly, touched by their light as he had been touched by the song in his dream. Heartstruck and empty. Yearning for some unknown thing. Alive to all the confusions of that which is new to the heart.

Slowly they went on their way. He tried to count them but could not be sure of their number, nor yet their purpose. And then, all too soon, they were gone.

For some time he waited in case they should return, but he was disappointed. Had they been real? Were they dream lights? Both fear and excitement, nameless and fierce, filled him in equal measure, turning slowly to wonder and longing. Eventually, he returned to his bed feeling as a child might that anticipated some unspecified treat. In the darkness he lay, all prospect of sleep gone, and waited for the sun.

(Tuesday 11 July)

"I know that I should not dwell so upon such pleasures, but that was an excellent meal. Do you not think?"

Ruth and Rowland voiced their agreement as Mrs Black cleared away the plates. Her expression did not change, but her pleasure was quite evident in the brisk way in which she moved about the table.

"Now, Ruth, would you be so kind as to fetch my shawl? Rowland and I will take a turn about the garden."

Ruth smiled in acquiescence and left the room ahead of the men who made their way across the hall and into the study. They crossed the quiet, book-lined room and stood in silence by the french windows that stood fully open. A cooling breeze stirred through the stale air of the day. Rowland breathed deeply, grateful for the freshness. The long and over-hot summer days were beginning to induce in him a feeling of claustrophobia.

When Ruth re-joined them she placed the shawl she had brought around her grandfather's shoulders. It was done without fuss, a commonplace ritual, but the action nonetheless betrayed a deep tenderness. Rowland saw in it only one of many small threats to his over-precious sense of freedom. While she settled the shawl in place, she looked at Rowland. Speaking directly to him, but informing both, she said, "I shall sit beneath the oak and read."

So saying, she picked up a book from a side table, Catherine Macaulay's *Letters on Education* Rowland noticed. Walking between the two men, she led the way outside. When she was happily settled on the tree seat, in a reciprocal ritual performed by her grandfather, the two men left her and strolled along the gravelled path between the lawn and the flower beds. When they reached the end of the garden, they passed through a gate in the low hedge and sat themselves upon a bench at the top of a low bank. From there they looked out across the valley.

"A fine prospect, Rowland."

The crown of Wealden Hill was just visible away to the left between the church and some cottages.

"Yes."

"Now, what is it that prompted such worries that need my attention this evening? Is it your... leg?"

The oblique reference to his troubled memories of the war amused Rowland in a distant kind of way. He allowed himself what he considered the luxury of a slight smile. "No. No. In fact, it is nothing that should... and yet..." He searched for the words. "There is something that I cannot explain."

It was the old man's turn to be amused. He smiled. "You are not alone in this, Rowland."

Rowland turned to look at the old man. He had been trying to work out how to explain his dilemma and, although he knew that his companion had spoken, he had not consciously heard what had been said. He frowned. "I beg your pardon?" he asked, just as the words pierced his conscious mind.

Before Rowland could continue, however, the Reverend Beckett spoke again. He had decided not to attempt to be light-hearted. It often seemed to miss its mark in conversations with Rowland Henty. "Something puzzles you?" he asked.

"Yes."

"Is it serious?"

"I really do not know. That is why I wished to speak with you about it."

"Then, by all means, do so."

Rowland paused to take breath. "Yesterday, you recall, you told me that a small group of gypsies would be camping in Mr Brigg's field."

"Are you worried about going to their camp?"

"No," said Rowland, surprised at such a suggestion. "It is not that. In fact, there is no need for me to go. The children, two of them at least, came to the school this morning."

"Did they?" asked the vicar, somewhat puzzled. "I wonder how they knew? Perhaps Elias Brigg... Still, it matters not. Unless," he added, hurriedly, "it is this which worries you?"

"No. Not at all. I was surprised, I must admit to that. But it was not their unexpected arrival that gives me concern." Rowland thought back to the events of the morning. "It was the children themselves. Their behaviour."

"Behaviour?"

"It was most strange."

They paused to watch a group of yearling swans as they flew northwards along the valley. In the distance they turned eastwards along Cobb Reach where the unpaired juveniles gathered each year. The silence between the two men remained after the swans had settled out of sight.

"Strange behaviour, Rowland?" said the old man eventually. "I am a little apprehensive."

"There is no need to be worried. They were not badly behaved. Far from it. The strangeness was in the change that came over them during the course of the morning." Rowland paused once more in order to recollect the events he was about to relate, gently rubbing at his chin. He pushed his glasses tight to the bridge of his nose with his forefinger. When he continued, his voice sounded as if it were coming from a great distance. "When they first arrived they were, quite naturally, objects of curiosity for the other boys and, I must admit, for myself. I watched them from the doorway of the schoolroom, unseen as I now think it. They were better dressed and fed than I had expected, but I have no doubt my expectations were fuelled by prejudice. The village boys obviously had fewer prejudices than myself, or at least kept them better hidden. It was not too long before the travellers' children had been accepted and were playing with the others, for all the world as if they were village children."

45

"Most commendable."

"Indeed, it was. At nine o'clock I called the school in. And then it was that some barely perceptible change occurred. It was from the very moment that I introduced myself and asked of their names. They seemed to... I really do not know how to describe it. They began, slowly, to withdraw. They became tense. That is, perhaps, the best word. They were like... cats, strolling and playing, who suddenly see a dog at some distance from themselves. They do not run or hide, but everything that they do thereafter is subtly altered to take into account the fact that there is some potential threat nearby."

"Surely, Rowland, that is a natural reaction on meeting a strange adult, and a teacher at that. With all respect due to your good self, the children of travellers do not normally fare well in schools."

"And thus was my interpretation. At first. But as the morning progressed, I could see they were afraid of me."

"Afraid?"

"Yes. They did not shiver or cower. There is too much strength in them for that. However, by the end of the morning, the younger of the two was very close to tears. When I dismissed the school, they left as if I were the devil and snapping at their heels."

"Did they return?"

"No. Some of the boys asked me about it during the afternoon for they too had noticed. I was at a loss as to how to explain it. And the more I thought about it, the stranger it seemed. Those two children were genuinely and deeply afraid of me. And it was not the fear you associate with an unpleasant past experience. It seemed to me, at least, to be that sort of fear that you feel when belief or superstition or..." and Rowland was once more struggling for words.

The Reverend Beckett watched him, waiting quietly. He was a great respecter of words and knew their importance to Rowland. But Rowland was struggling because he suddenly knew what sort of fear it was. It was the fear that discovery brought. Discovery that there are things greater than yourself. Discovery that the world holds secrets that are not possible but just the same are all about you. Discovery that there are things one can only dream about. Discovery that sometimes dreams can be the truth.

"Most disquieting," said the Reverend Beckett finally, seeing that Rowland had become lost in a train of thought. "I suspect that someone has filled their heads with nonsense and they were waiting for the worst."

Rowland felt very frightened, but dared not show it. It was not the kind of fear one experiences when one is in danger. It was the thrilling fear of the great unexplored spaces that come into view when a person discovers their mortality - not in the sense that they realize they will die, but when they suddenly realizes that they are alive. "Should anything be done?" he asked finally.

"I leave that to you, Rowland. Wait until tomorrow. If they do not attend school, then perhaps you could walk up to where they are camped and talk with their parents."

"Yes." Rowland gazed across the valley to Cobb Spur. "Yes."

"And now, if you will excuse me, Rowland, I must go and start preparing my sermon."

The Reverend Beckett rose stiffly and left Rowland sitting on the bench, staring across the valley and back across the hours at the woods on Cobb Spur. He contemplated the hard fact that the stars on the hillside represented something in his life that he knew nothing about - a complete and perhaps vast unknown.

What they might be, he was not even able to begin to imagine. Guiding lights, perhaps, or just the first signs of dementia, although he very much doubted that. But then, he told himself, he would think that anyway. Whatever they did represent, however, their very existence electrified his soul.

For Rowland, the unknown had always been a challenge. It had made him a good scholar and it had made him a good Intelligence Officer. So, as he sat, he tried to trace the route that the lights had followed. It was as good a starting point as any other, and a thread that could be followed to some use.

There seemed no path across the hillside, but it was not really possible to tell with the trees in leaf. He was not familiar with that side of the valley for he rarely crossed the river. Even if there was a path, he reasoned, it would lead nowhere but the hilltop.

He shook his head. This puzzling over the reason behind the lights was an attempt, he knew, to avoid speculating on the effect they had on him. Yet simply calling them to mind, bright and attractive, threw him into confusion. And there was also the fear they inspired. A thrill of fear and confusion that he found to be strangely and in itself confusingly pleasant. But, it was only a fear of the unknown and the unknown, he kept telling himself, was not necessarily harmful.

Having wandered deeply into the deep green forests of his thoughts, Rowland did not notice that Ruth had seated herself beside him on the bench. When she spoke, he was startled. He turned to face her. "Yes?" he asked sharply, annoyed by the interruption.

A frown crossed Ruth's face, leaving behind it a shadow of disappointment and hurt which Rowland saw but chose not to notice.

"What is wrong?" she asked with quiet restraint.

"Just a school problem. I have sorted it out with your grandfather."

A fire ignited behind Ruth's eyes and the twitch of her arm betrayed a restraint from swinging at his face with her book. "What slight veneer of social civility you have managed in my regard has worn somewhat thin of late," she said, her voice tight with anger. "I am not talking of your precious school. I know what the problems of teaching are. I have taught the young ones of the village their letters for the last ten years. There is no mystique to what we do." She had calmed slightly. "Can you think of nothing beyond the school? Nothing beyond yourself?"

"Beyond?" He was too taken aback by her tone to consider the content of what she had said.

Ruth took a deep, slow breath. "I cannot believe," she said, "that you are being deliberately obtuse. Do you think of me?"

He looked at her closely for a moment, by now fully aware of the intent of her question. He was tempted, for just a moment, to play the innocent. Whatever else he might be, however, he was not a liar, by deed or word, and the temptation was resisted. He shook his head and said, "No."

He searched her face for some sign of a reaction. He saw nothing. "I do not think of you in the way you imply, Ruth."

"But why?" she asked.

"There are many reasons."

"And do any of your reasons consider my feelings?"

"Your feelings?"

"Yes. My feelings." She sounded uncertain. "You have... toyed with them ever since you arrived."

"No." He looked at her in astonishment, alarmed by what she was saying. "There is no truth in what you say. It is melodramatic, self-flattery and it ill becomes you. I have done nothing to suggest anything to you other than my true feelings."

"But-"

"But nothing. If you choose to imagine things, or put false interpretations upon them, then you must be prepared to face the truth. I am surprised that a woman of your good sense should be prey to such shallow, penny novelette emotions."

She gripped the book tightly in her hands. "I fear," she said in a voice so measured that it signally failed in masking the welter of emotions Rowland saw in her expression, "it is your deliberate misinterpretation of what I say that betrays your own enrapture with things melodramatic. And to impute such false emotions to me is nothing but cruelty."

He stood and took several steps away from the bench before he turned to face her. The low sunlight sparked from the green lenses of his spectacles and hid his eyes. His voice, when he spoke, was controlled, but tight with anger. Its expression was most pronounced in his face.

"Cruelty. What do you know of cruelty? Your upset, caused by believing your own fantasy, is nothing." Shifting his weight from his bad leg, he was about to tell her something of real cruelty, but he stopped himself. Slowly, he let the anger drain from him for it was a poison that fed on what he dimly perceived was some misunderstanding of intention. This whole conversation, he was beginning to see, was a kind of baroque fantasy of words and emotions for both of them.

"No," he said gently. "I am not cruel, Ruth. Telling you lies would be cruel and I have told you no lies."

A silence grew between them and he turned away, walking across the rough turf to the edge of the low bank where he stood and stared, once more, across the valley.

"Then what is wrong with me?" Her voice was small and she sounded lost.

Rowland turned back to her. "There is nothing wrong with you."

"So why do you ignore me?"

He sighed. "I do not ignore you. Neither do I have any desire to know you better than I do already."

There were tears shining in the corner of her eyes. "I am sorry," she said. "I have been forward. If you will excuse me."

She rose and hurried through the garden, disappearing into the vicarage through the open door of the kitchen. Rowland watched her go. Now more confused and fearful than ever, he turned away and crossed to the churchyard and thence on to the road to the school.

(Wednesday 12 July)

Beneath the cool, quiet shade of the trees, the cart lane of packed earth climbed steeply up to Brigg Farm. Rowland took the long slope at a gentle pace. Bursts of hard sunlight peppered his sight. Bird song, gentle and sweet, was in the air. The green tranquillity of the shade eased the faint claustrophobia that had begun to cling to him in the valley below. He breathed more freely. It was a place of peace and Rowland felt in no hurry to be moving on. It calmed his scattered and confused thoughts and, for a few moments, he was able to assess them in the perspective of this daylight world.

There was, he finally decided in a burst of groundless optimism, no problem. Things had happened, it was true. Unusual things that had disturbed his ordered existence. But they were not catastrophes. Not the singing or the dreams or the nightmares; not the nocturnal lights; not even Ruth's outburst. They were all, perhaps, just a slight summer madness induced by the excessive heat. All things that had a simple explanation, all problems that could be resolved with a little calm and patient thought. He smiled smugly. His decision was made with all the certainty of a drunken man and with all the authority of a fool.

Heedless of his own fallibility, he came at length to where the eastern wall of Mr Brigg's orchard turned a corner and became the north wall that ran alongside the lane. In that corner there was an old wooden door in an arched stone frame. Rowland stopped. By the farmhouse further up the slope, he saw Mrs Brigg and waved, pointing then at the gate and thus in the general direction of the field where the travellers were camped. She squinted in the sunlight before shading her eyes and then smiled when she realized who it was. Rowland opened the door, one of several, went through, and closed it carefully behind him.

Brigg Orchard was large. The wizened trees, many with branches held aloft with props, were clustered haphazardly within the confines of the ancient, moss covered walls of flint. So old were the walls that they resembled natural outcrops of rock as much as they did the artificial constructs of some long dead labourer. Mr Brigg was fond of claiming that it had been an orchard since Roman times, but no one took him seriously - which was a shame because he was substantially correct, the site having first been planted by a deserter from one of the recalled Legions.

It was a peaceful place, even more so than the lane. The still spirit of the tended trees filled the garth. The ancient walls seemed to provide an extra layer of insulation from the rest of the world. Rowland stopped for several minutes inside the door. He allowed himself to become infected by its green and living calm before moving on between the gnarled trunks to a small door in the southern wall. Reluctantly, he passed through.

There were apple trees and pear trees beyond the wall as well. They were scattered across the field, less dense the further they were from the orchard wall. Several horses grazed in their shade, legs hobbled to prevent them wandering too far. Way down the hill, to his left, Rowland could see the road that ran dustily between its thick hedges from Swann to Lower Cross on its way to Meeching and the coast.

The travellers' camp was well beyond the last of the stray fruit trees beside a stand of oaks at the top of the slope. He approached the camp from behind as the five, travel-stained caravans were arranged in a semi-circle that opened southward. A thin plume of pale blue smoke rose straight and unbroken from a cooking fire. It was the only sign of life he could see as he drew near and he thought at first that the camp must be deserted.

A movement caught his eye then and he saw, standing on the edge of the driver's seat of the nearest caravan, two ravens. Rowland had never been so close to a raven before. The sunlight on the black feathers of their plumage produced a sheen of the darkest gun-metal blue. From the underside of the forward thrusting head of each hung a small ruff. Their dark eyes gleamed coldly as they watched him intently, one with its head held low so that the other could look over it. Rowland shivered. Still and other-worldly the ravens stood. Rowland took several, faltering paces further forward and then stopped.

One of the ravens, the furthest from him, stretched its wings full width, quivering, and then settled them back again. The other bird, having watched the wing stretching with one eye and Rowland with the other, suddenly turned and pecked at its companion's head with its long, heavy, down-curving bill. The other dodged with a practised motion and then pecked back. A strange, totally silent, almost comical, dance-like movement ensued, with each bird pecking and dodging in turn, the actions slowing until they were still once again. They eyed each other and then, satisfied that all was as it should be between them, returned their attention to Rowland - motionless, watching, waiting.

Of a sudden a hand was thrust between the birds and they rose in awkward fluttering disorder, their anger voiced by a deep croaking 'pruk pruk' that faded as they flew away. Rowland stood, too startled to move, with his heart heaving painfully in his chest and blood banging in his ears. High above, the ravens wheeled and croaked and tried some reckless tumbling aerobatics for good measure.

With deep breaths, Rowland restored some calm to his body and looked at the hand. It was old and claw like. Tanned flesh, loose and wrinkled across long, slender bones. Hard, yellowing nails. The thumb was tucked under, holding the two middle fingers against the palm, leaving the two outer fingers extended to form the horns that ward off spirits.

Still trembling slightly from the surge of adrenalin, Rowland walked carefully around to the front of the caravan. The person to whom the arm belonged sat on the driver's seat, propped against the door. Wrapped in a dirty cloak, a broad brimmed hat cast a deep shadow across their face. The hat and cloak, such strange clothes to be wearing in such heat, together contrived to cover much of their wearer's body but could not conceal that person's deformity. They contrived, also, purposely no doubt, to create an effect of mystery and menace.

Rowland stood silently before the obscured figure and allowed himself to be scrutinized. Despite the shadow beneath the brim of the hat he fancied he could see that one eye was missing. It made the flesh on his spine crawl, though he could not think why for he had seen plenty of such deformity and much worse during his time in India and the Afghan. The contrived effect of the clothing was obviously working on Rowland.

Aware, suddenly, of the aura of mystery he was starting to spin about this so far silent figure, Rowland spoke in an attempt to re-establish some air of normality. "My name is Henty," he said with a clear, strong voice. He paused and then added, "Rowland Henty."

He waited but there was no reply. The outstretched arm, however, was slowly withdrawn into the folds of the cloak. Almost immediately afterwards, with barely a disturbance of the air and taking Rowland by surprise, one of the ravens returned to its perch, wrapping itself in the cloak of its wings. It watched Rowland carefully with one eye.

"I am the schoolmaster in Swann," he continued, half convinced now that the person he addressed was deaf. "I have come to ask about the two boys who came down to the school. They are quite welcome to return. There is nothing for them to fear."

"No!"

Rowland span round at the force with which the word was spoken and found himself faced by the person who had spoken it. He was now thoroughly confused. None of it made any sense to him. The whole encounter had wrong footed him and kept on wrong footing him. The peace he had experienced in the lane and in the orchard seemed to him to be alien, long past, and, with a terrible sense of dread, irretrievable. At some time and at some place in the very recent past, he now felt, he had crossed a threshold, moving into some realm from which there was no permanent return. And for a moment, before she hardened her face against him once more, the woman before him showed him with her eyes that she knew he was lost.

Unseen and unheard, a group had gathered behind him. The woman, who was at their fore, looked old but there was an air of youthfulness about her. She looked beyond Rowland to the figure seated on the caravan as if looking for some signal. Rowland looked at the others who had gathered. They were close, but not too close. Several small family groups, the men worried, the women half hiding, children peering from behind their skirts. The two boys were there as well, watching him with wary eyes. They all stared at Rowland in silence, unmoving, a mixture of reverence and fear discernible in their faces. It made Rowland feel most uncomfortable to be the centre of such incomprehensible attention. Just for a second he felt like a man on a high mountain path who had stumbled. A man who knew there was no way back and who knew that the path forward could only get worse.

The old woman spoke again, softly this time, almost gently. Her tone was almost apologetic as if determination had overcome fear. "The children will not be returning to your school."

"Why?" he asked, genuinely puzzled.

At his question there was a sudden change in the group that stood before him. He sensed that a great deal of hard gathered bravado had been swept away by that one word and that they were all suddenly floundering in a sea of bewilderment, even fear. He knew the feeling all too well of late.

"Why will your children not be returning to the school?" He asked it mildly, saw glances quickly exchanged.

"It is… We cannot allow them to be…" The woman faltered. She looked down for a second, gathering her own courage. "It is forbidden," she finally said, in a tone that strongly suggested that Rowland should know better than anyone else why that should be so.

But Rowland did not know why. "Forbidden? By whom?"

"Please."

He frowned. The fear had become more palpable. The old woman was pleading. She was desperate for him to be gone. Desperate for him to stop tormenting them. The whole situation had become absurd.

"Enough, woman. Go." The voice, deep and soft, old and tired, came from the cloaked figure on the caravan. The raven nodded.

"Tell him, if he really does not know," the woman demanded.

"Go!" he replied testily.

The woman went, suddenly and without argument. Perhaps she was glad to have the responsibility taken from her. The others went with her. They shuffled away, dazed, casting occasional glances back at him. Rowland watched until they had passed beyond the caravans and faded into the deep shadows beneath the oak trees. Then, slowly, he turned back to face the shrouded figure.

The other raven had returned. It was on the ground and walking majestically towards the caravan. It stopped close to Rowland and looked at him with its head cocked on one side. Something in the way it looked at him reminded him of the swan he had seen a few days earlier when he was sitting on the bridge. Some assessment was being made by an intelligence that Rowland had always believed in but only now saw for himself. Whatever the criteria the bird had applied it seemed suddenly satisfied and leapt with a single beat of its wings to its perch. Once it had settled its feathers both birds sat silently and still once more, their eyes blank but always watching him.

"They are scared. They are fools."

Rowland turned his gaze from the birds to the man, for man he now supposed the figure to be, and stared hard with seeing eyes. He saw now the effect that the clothing contrived. In conjunction with the ravens, the man's clothes offered a visual affinity which was probably enough to impress the unthinking or superstitious. Closer inspection dispelled the aura for they were just dirty old clothes wrapped about some shrivelled old body to keep it warm.

Angry at having been taken in by the impression, Rowland was further angered by the old man's words. "Fools?" he asked, doing nothing to hide the hard edge in his voice. "Fools to fear? I knew some who would be alive today had they been so foolish."

The old man, shrivelled as he was, seemed visibly to shrink into his cloak. He, too, was afraid. But, wondered Rowland, what is it that they all fear? Is it me? He knew it to be true as soon as he asked it of himself. But the realization was painful and hard to accept. What is it about me that is causing this, he wanted to know. And why with these people? To what are they sensitive? He stepped up to the caravan and leaned forward, placing his hands on the edge of the driver's seat for support. "And what, old man, do you fear?" he asked very quietly.

The ravens looked at Rowland enquiringly as if the word or even the concept of fear was new to them. They turned their attention suddenly to the old man as if waiting for him to reply. Something important to them hung upon the answer. The old man shifted, trying to push himself away from Rowland and from the gaze of the ravens.

"The only thing I fear," he said in a dry-mouthed whisper, "is that which is hidden."

Rowland stared at the old man, somewhere close to the edge of anger. One of the ravens gave a soft 'pruk' of disappointment and took to the air, beating its great wings in slow strokes as it flew off down the hill barely clearing the hedge at the bottom before it climbed to settle finally in a distant tree. The second bird looked at the old man for a while as if giving him a second chance. When no further explanation was offered it lifted its head and then hopped down from its perch. Without looking back it walked away from the caravan and finally took to the air to join its companion.

Suddenly all the anger and confusion ebbed away. Rowland stepped back wearily and turned to face down the hill. The ravens were just visible in the tree they had adopted. They had set an example that Rowland felt should be followed. All this cryptic talk was leading nowhere. So many questions. No answers. All of it disturbing the quiet certainty of his life. It was time to leave.

Drained, empty, confused, and suddenly feeling very lonely, he walked away from the caravans, crossing the field toward the orchard. When he reached the road on the other side, he stopped in the shade of a tree and removed his glasses. Gently he massaged his eyes, cleaned the tinted glass with a kerchief and put them back on. Fear. What is there to fear? He listened to the flutter of wings and looked up to see one of the ravens looking down at him with blatant curiosity. Whatever it was that frightened those people it had no effect on the bird. He smiled sadly at the creature, drawing some comfort from that, and made his way down the hill.

(Thursday 13 July)
Enveloped by a silence that seemed total and which was dismaying, Rowland lay in the empty darkness of the first hours of morning. He had no idea of how long he had lain there after waking from the unconscious darkness of sleep. He was completely adrift in the night, cut off from all that made sense, straining to hear some sound of life beyond his own. But there was nothing. Eventually he lost all sense of passing time and lay paralysed by his feelings of helplessness.

In whichever direction his mind explored, the roads and pathways were blocked or severed. There was nowhere to go. There seemed to be no way he could see of overcoming the problems that faced him. He could think of no reason to try, what there was beyond to achieve, what normality he wanted. He did not even have any understanding of why they were problems at all. So it was that he lay staring into the void, adrift and wracked with anguish.

Faintly, through the enveloping silence, came the screech of a distant tawny owl. It unlocked the paralysis of his soul and released his thoughts from their slow inward collapse. And he wondered, suddenly, about dreams and songs. Just as suddenly, he swept aside the sheet that covered him, rose from his bed, and went to the north facing window which was open to the summer night.

There was a vision set out before him. The still, silent world in seeming miniature, painted in starlight on darkness and devoid of all perspective. It was a subtle picture drawn with the minimum detail necessary to make it comprehensible. He looked at it for a few seconds and then withdrew. Hurriedly he dressed himself in the dark, filled with the desperate need to be outside and a part of what he had just seen.

Quietly closing the door of the schoolhouse, he crossed the schoolyard and stepped over the low wall onto the road. The warm night air caressed him and drew him to the river. The valley was a whole new world at this hour. Vibrant with a life that had its own metaphysic, one that was, root and branch, different from that which was driven by the sun. The stars provided a gentler, if more dangerous, logic for life. Exhilarated by this discovery, glad to be free of the need to wear his glasses, he walked slowly but with purpose to the bridge.

Gentle sounds came to him now that he had learnt how to hear them. The water ran so quietly that it was almost silent. Solid and black, it threw back the starlight so that it filled the air, imperceptible, until he was breathing it in, feeling its glow run brightly in his blood. Throwing back his head, he felt himself spin, slowly dancing the star dance with joy, his arms stretched out as though he would embrace the sky and its philosophy. Soft, gentle laughter filled his head, kindly and joyful.

Across the glory of the sun-dusted night sky a meteor ran silent and bright, its incandescent trail a pale green in the high space above the valley walls. He held his breath as it passed and held it still as a second and then a third seared the brilliant darkness with thin, sharp light. They passed over his head with speed and simplest majesty to be eclipsed by the eastern hills - dark presences in the dark emptiness.

After the first savage fire of joy had burned to a warm and gentle ember, he sat cross-legged upon the parapet of the bridge, free of the earth, breathing the night air, staring into the darkness that was the slope of Cobb Spur. He had been released, was intoxicated, no longer in control of the thoughts that had welled up from within. They drifted unchecked across the years, alighting briefly on bright scenes from his childhood, his youth, university, days abroad, the war. Each was like a wound cut into him, each causing pain when explored. They all seemed such alien intrusions into his being yet they were everything that had formed him. Was there any escape from their pain, he wondered, any way to break from the past? Any way to forget the loneliness? Even here, in this valley, where he had until recently felt most at home, he now felt a misfit, lonely and haunted.

As his thoughts ran their all too familiar course, his eyes followed the stars moving across the hillside. He snapped out of his reverie and watched carefully now with all of his being that which only his eyes had seen before. Ahead of him, on the slope of the spur, a dozen or so bright points of light, starlike in their intensity, but warmer in their appearance, moved northward, just as they had two nights before. As they went, they were constantly obscured by the foliage and the trunks of trees, giving a flickering impression to the vision.

Drawing breath, feeling apprehensive, he slowly unfolded his legs, placed his feet gently on the road, took several hesitant steps in the direction of the lights and then stopped. He was confused. Whoever it was, they were not on any path, but were moving slowly upwards through the trees. Nor were they travelling as others travelled for there was a peculiar motion to the lights as they cut in and out of sight. And such lights. Like exotic and fabulous jewels in candle light, rich, precious, subtle, and rare in the night.

Feeling again as he had when he had first woken, he knew there was no menace in the strangeness. They drew level with the bridge and then passed on. And upward. A fire in the night, a candle in the window of home, burning for him. A beacon that called. Familiar. Friendly. Strange. On and on they moved, weaving their sinuous way in a visual spell that bound him to them.

As they approached the summit of Cobb Hill he wanted to be there with them. His first step off the bridge came as they vanished. In his head was an echo of the song. For a moment - just for one short moment - he had felt hope.

(Thursday 13 July - Friday 14 July)
Although it was early, the whole village was awake and alive with movement. Laughter and the distant sound of voices filled the air, weaving brightly about a rich tapestry of other sounds less easily identified. Rowland had seen children move in darts and flashes between the cottages. One small group, composed mostly of his pupils, trailing curious sisters and toddlers and dogs, had come in a great and bright fizzing ball of life to make sure he was up and about, chattering excitedly about the day to come before rushing off again.

He resisted the drawing power of the festive spirit as long as he could, needing a moment of calm on which to ground the coming day. In the brief moments of solitude the day would afford, he went to the garden at the side of the schoolhouse to tend the great climbing rose that covered much of the lower wall. As he twisted back the suckers that were growing across the kitchen window, he explored carefully about the perimeter of the hope that had entered his heart. A brief hope, nameless and uncertain, which, he believed, was likely to fade. But you cannot once feel hope and then forever be free of that feeling. It was a strange thing and he backed away from it, letting his mind wander over the events of the past weeks instead, glancing ever over his shoulder to the hillside across the far side of the valley.

It was his first summer in Swann and each day thus held some unlooked for surprise. But these last few weeks burned brightly with strangeness. Even from the safe retrospective of summer morning sunlight, they refused to conform to the sensible belief that he, in some way, was mistaken. It was all too real, and the ravens sitting side by side on the edge of the water trough in the yard were potent reminders.

Vivid, also, was the haunting sadness that had been conjured by the recurring dream-song. There had been the return of the nightmare. There had been the lights across the valley, dancing in the trees. There had been the peculiar confrontation with the travelling people who had shunned and feared him. And just what had the old man meant? I fear what is hidden. It annoyed Rowland, gnawed at the shadowy edges of his mind. And then, in the early hours of the morning, there had been the lights across the valley once again. Dancing.

*

Two great haywains, freshly whitewashed for the day, had been brought into the village. They stood outside the vicarage, one behind the other, bedecked with ribbons. The great draw horses that stood patiently between the shafts were all shires. They too were decorated in their finery, manes and tales all neatly plaited, short ribbons gently a-flutter, brasses gleaming in the early morning sun.

In a small group by the vicarage gate, the horsemen stood talking quietly, relaxing with a rare, early morning pipe. They wore their Sunday clothes and occasionally a finger would ease a collar. A writhing, ever changing knot of children had gathered about the wains and now and then one of the men would quietly warn them away from the horses when they came too close. Gentle beasts as they were, accidents were not unknown and could well be serious.

With breakfast out of the way, with kitchens cleared and set straight, with baskets prepared, the womenfolk began to appear, trailing their menfolk. Most of the men of the village looked highly uncomfortable at the prospect of a day's idleness. It was not in the nature of these dour faced men to waste daylight hours.

As they all gathered, the noise increased, merry and free. A short ladder was brought and people climbed up onto the wains, to sit on the benches that had been roped in place the evening before. As the villagers began to settle themselves, after much mirthful re-arranging and careful stowing of baskets of food, the Reverend Beckett appeared at the doorway of the vicarage, Ruth close behind him. They walked to the gate, returning greetings, and there paused, Ruth to check that she had all they needed, her grandfather to talk with the horsemen about the route they were to take - a formality since they always travelled by the same road.

As they talked, a cheer rose up from some of the younger single men of the village. A pair of ravens, startled by the sudden noise, took to the air from their perch on the shingled roof of the nearby lychgate. All heads turned to the main road to see a small cart being driven from the yard behind The Swann With Two Knecks. On the cart, were several kegs and other provisions. Mr Carr, the landlord, gave a wave, stopped to allow Mr Keaton to load some covered trays from the bakery, and then drove on to set up the wares ready for the arrival of the villagers.

By this time, the stragglers were gathering about the wains, and a hasty discussion took place when it was realized that this year there would not be enough room for all those who wished to ride. Mrs Reeve, who was waiting close by in her carriage, offered the use of the windmill's flat cart as long as no one minded getting a bit dusty. A man was despatched and before long a third cart appeared.

A general re-shuffle took place so that the older children were accommodated thereon. Being low, with small wheels, it was deemed to be quite safe. Once that was settled, the Reverend Beckett and Ruth joined Mrs Reeve in her carriage. By the time everyone was ready, it had passed eight o'clock. The horsemen finished their pipes and went to their horses. A hush descended, loud laughter dying away, talk turning to whisper.

Through the now quiet village Rowland Henty slowly walked, approaching the gathering. Some turned to watch him for he was still an unknown to many in the village. As he joined the small group who intended to walk, nodding his greetings, there came the voices of the horsemen, strong and clear. The great horses took the strain, brakes were released, and the great carts rumbled slowly and noisily up the slight incline, dust rising in the morning air. Rowland made his way forward to catch a look at the horses in their show attire. Farmer Elam's shire, Samuel, had won many a prize at the County Show in Hamm.

As he moved through the gathering, Rowland began to pass Mrs Reeve's carriage where it waited for the other vehicles to pass. He looked up for an instant and Ruth, who had been watching him make his way toward the front of the procession, caught his eye. He smiled at her, hesitantly. She returned his smile and indicated the vacant seat by her side.

Shrugging inwardly, he nodded and walked forward. "I must first…"

"Come, Mr Henty," said Mrs Reeve, leaning towards him across the Reverend Beckett. "Today is a holiday. A rest from all things."

He stood for a moment, uncertain. Then, grasping the handle, he opened the carriage door and mounted, taking the seat beside Ruth.

"It will be a fine day," said Ruth, her pleasure obvious, their earlier conversation forgotten or perhaps discarded.

Mrs Reeve and the Reverend Beckett smiled at Rowland and to his horror he felt himself blushing.

At that moment, the carriage jerked as it began to move forward, following the carts onto the main road. Rowland looked across at Mrs Reeve's house as they turned the corner. Her late husband had built it with the profits from his windmills and the farm now tenanted by the Robertson brothers. It was a small house by town standards, built to serve a purpose rather than for ostentation. But for all that it was grand enough and certainly pleasing to the eye. Passing beyond the house they left the village and crossed Swann Brook. Through the trees on the right hand side of the road, Rowland could see up the slope to the field behind Mr Brigg's orchard. It was empty.

"Tell me, Mr Henty," asked Mrs Reeve, "what do you think of our modest gathering?" She was a practiced host and knew the worth of conversation in building relationships.

Rowland drew his gaze away from the hillside, satisfied that the caravans had gone, and turned to face Mrs Reeve. He thought for a moment, his head on one side. "I am puzzled," he said eventually.

"Puzzled?" asked the Reverend Beckett. He sounded somewhat surprised by Rowland's comment.

"As to its origin," Rowland explained.

"Ah." The vicar smiled. "Gloriously pagan," he said with some relish.

Rowland frowned.

"This is the thirteenth day of the seventh month."

The creases along Rowland's brow grew deeper.

"Do not tease, grandfather."

"Its origins, Rowland," continued the vicar with mock solemnity, "are to be found in the Newelm Man. Since before anyone can recall, and likely much longer than that, the villagers of Swann have gathered each year on this date, and travelled up to the chalk figure. That is," he continued, resuming his true voice, "they used to. The original function of the gathering was to scour the figure. Why it should have been the people of Swann rather than Newelm I do not know. There is no obvious connection between the two places, nor is there an obscure one that I am aware of. Over the years, however, the outing has turned into an annual picnic and the scouring of the figure has been forgotten."

There was silence for a moment. Rowland was picturing the chalk figure in his mind's eye. "Someone must still do it," he pointed out.

"Not for a long while now," said Mrs Reeve. "Not since the big fire."

The Reverend Beckett placed a cautioning hand on Mrs Reeve's arm. She bit her lip, a belated attempt to snatch back the words. Neither Ruth nor Rowland, however, had noticed.

"Why do you say that, Rowland?" Ruth asked.

He turned to her, already half lost in other thoughts. "It is so clean. So clear." And its shape was bright in his mind, sitting with its head in hands and gazing across at Wealden Hill. It too had some connection.

The happy procession of carts and pedestrians moved slowly and noisily southward along the road. The men, now, were beginning to relax and accept the prospect of a day at ease. The women and the children had had no such inhibitions to overcome and for them the day was well in its stride. As they passed through Lower Cross, the villagers there stopped their work to watch and talk and wave. The cavalcade then moved on to Dean, noise and colour swathed in dust.

Rowland withdrew into himself, sheltering from the small talk and the brash display which surrounded him. As they travelled along the twisting, uneven roads he kept a tight grip on the side of the carriage to prevent himself swaying against Ruth. For a while, he had searched for some excuse to leave and slip away, but there was none. Trapped, he shut away his longings, closed his inner ear to the half remembered strains of the dream song, extinguished his vision of the dancing lights, and stared out into a world that seemed less bright than it had a month before.

At Dean, they crossed the river and followed the road to Under Fore. From there they travelled along a seldom used cart track up onto the wooded southern slopes of the Beacon Downs. Finally, they settled on the south-eastern slopes of Fore Hill, overlooking Fore Bottom, a peaceful hollow clear of trees but surrounded by the green shade of young birch and beech. In the centre of the hollow was a small well, in good repair, the incongruity of which escaped Rowland. Here it was that Mr Carr had set up his wares.

*

Games, races, and other competitions had filled most of the morning and created large appetites. Having eaten, the villagers were now scattered in groups about Fore Bottom. Some sat under the shade of nearby trees. Others, mostly young, continued to play less formal games. The woods that surrounded Fore Bottom and crowned Fore Hill erupted constantly with the shouts and screams of children. Those more observant than others had noticed several missing couples, both young and not so young, but knew the unpredictable presence of the playing children would prevent serious transgression and were wise enough to leave it at that.

Rowland had settled on a comfortable carpet of thick, dry moss at the foot of a vast oak tree on the northern spur of Fore Hill. From there, he could see all that happened without becoming directly involved. He sat contentedly in the warm and spangled shade with the Reverend Beckett who had brought with him a battered but serviceable backgammon case.

Absorbed by the game against an opponent who played to win, Rowland began to relax deep inside where he had not relaxed for days. For a while he was able to close some inner door on the strange events that haunted him, that had stirred up strands of thought and emotions from unknown depths within him. And as they played, they talked. Of small things touching everything and nothing, all and none.

When the everlasting afternoon finally ended and the sun, bloated and red, eased down into a haze of its own making, staining the sky with heat blanched colours, the villagers gathered at the head of Fore Bottom. During the day a great stack of dead wood had been collected from the surrounding woods and piled there. The gathering was subdued, tired by the heat and the activities of the day. Exhausted young children sought comfortable places by their mothers and there slept. Older children sat, half sleeping, caught between innocence and experience. Lovers shared passionate hopes and glances.

Rowland, tired from his vigil of the night before, sat with his back to the trunk of the oak tree. His head was bent forward and his chin was resting on his breast. Slowly, regularly, and almost imperceptibly his head rose and fell as he dozed.

"Do you think you will ever love me?"

It was Ruth's voice, quiet in his ear and unmistakable. It provoked no dreams. Indeed, it woke him straight away though he was not at all sure it was meant to. Her voice had been soft and there was something about the way she asked the question that suggested she was talking to herself.

He looked up to find that they were alone. Swiftly he stood and brushed some twigs from his clothing. Oak, and ash from a nearby tree. His haste felt ridiculous. Slowly, in a conscious effort to appear unconcerned that served only to make him feel

65

all the more self-conscious, he removed his glasses, polished them, and put them carefully away.

"I will not cry, nor play the frail maiden, Rowland. But... I still wish to know."

He looked at her in the soft light. "Why?"

"I am considering my prospects." Rowland was silent. "Shall I tell you?"

"No."

"I am twenty-nine, Rowland. The granddaughter of a vicar in a small village. My parents have more interest in their calling than they do in me, if they are still alive. I am certainly not wanted in South America nor am I keen to travel there. When grandfather dies I shall have no home. Although I shall never starve, I have no fortune. Before long, I shall be considered to be too old for marriage and past the safe age for bearing children. I do not want to be an old maid, Rowland, but in my circumstances there is only one person that I could genuinely consider. If he does not wish to marry me, as seems to be the case, I must best prepare myself for a future on my own."

Having finished, she walked away. Rowland followed her. "Ruth."

She stopped, facing away from him.

"Ruth." And no more. He did not know what to say. He could not deny the truth of what she said, and he was curiously thrilled by the honest analysis of her position, but he refused to martyr himself, as he saw it, for her happiness. He took a step closer and she turned her face to him.

"No love for me then?" he asked, curious for the first time about her feelings for him. "Just the correct prospect? And why do you want to marry? Are you really so afraid of growing old alone?"

"Afraid? No, Rowland. I am not afraid." And she said it as if the fact that she was not afraid was a revelation to her. She looked slightly nonplussed for a moment but then seemed to find a new strength, a new conviction to carry her forward. "I simply want to marry. To have children. And I anticipate you. I know part of the reason is that it is expected of me. But remember, you are not exempt. You are not special." There was the beginning of anger in her voice now, enough to put a hard edge to her words. "I grant that your experiences are beyond the comprehension of us mere valley dwellers. We have not seen the Afghan. We have not been in a slaughter. But none of that is reason for you to hide from the world. Condemn it if you must - for that would be right and just. Fight it even, if that is how you feel. Do not..." Her voice trailed off as if she had lost the will to continue this particular battle. There was a wildness, now, in her eyes that bespoke a person he barely knew and had no right to reject. "Do not withdraw, Rowland." With a last look at him, she turned and swept away down the slope towards the distant gathering, leaving him standing alone and once more perplexed.

Shadows had lengthened and spread and darkened and finally claimed the day. The great pile of wood was ignited, blazing suddenly upwards, crackling wildly in the quiet evening. Sparks rose swiftly and faded to become deep red fading stars. And the fire became a new sun, gathering people about it like planets, each moving to find a comfortable position in the gravity of its warmth. And from the new and dancing darkness that the flamelight caused, a voice touched the air, soft and gentle, as Sarah Elam stood and sang.

They all listened, entranced, some linked by memories and others alone with their thoughts. Rowland stood beneath the oak tree where Ruth had left him, his eyes closed, sinking into a darkness that was achingly empty. Ruth's new found confidence had torn into his new found equanimity and opened the door he had managed to close earlier in the day. Whatever order he had managed to impose upon his recent uncertainties was gone. All manner of confusion and pain now beset him.

Who was she who sang in the early morning mists of summer? Who was it who danced starlike through the trees? He knew that he had not dreamed, could not have dreamed such things into being. Someone sang. And he knew from the voice he now heard that it was not Sarah Elam. And someone danced. A beautiful music teased his senses.

*

Only as the wains, cart, and carriage, led by the light of a lamp carried on a pole, drove along the road at the foot of Cobb Spur did Rowland come to realize his surroundings. The evening had gone. He had travelled a long way without conscious contact with the rest of the world. The jump back to the outside world frightened him with its sudden inrush of clarity. Around him people whispered. Somewhere a soft voice sang 'Mowing Down My Meadow', sleepy children joining in.

The lanterns on their poles swayed, shadows leaping crazily across the sleeping figure of Ruth Beckett. Her head lay on Mrs Reeve's shoulder. The Reverend Beckett gazed into the dark, trying to stay awake. He smiled briefly at Rowland as he leaned back against the corner of the seat. Soon his eyes closed as well.

Rowland looked out and up into the dark, wooded slopes on his right. They seemed dense and full of mystery. A shiver walked his spine. The music of the song was still in his head, half there, half forgotten, as were the words he could not quite recall - a mood more than a memory. A feeling of panic rose suddenly within him that he might forget altogether, that the song might slip away. His mind called out in desperation to the night and to the stars, to the trees and to the hills, to the earth and to the river, a formless call for help to the wild magic in all things.

And then the procession began to move away from the trees, crossing the valley towards the bridge close to the schoolhouse. As he twisted in his seat and stared desperately back at the woods, the starlike lights flared up and his heart beat suddenly faster, making him draw breath to ease the pain of his joy.

*

The wains and the cart were long gone, the horses were stabled and resting, children and their parents were long abed and fast asleep. The whole village was settled and quiet. A single light burned in Mrs Reeve's house. Beneath the stones of Swann Bridge the river talked in its sleep, whispering dreams for all who understood to know. Upon the bridge Rowland stood in silent rapture, surrounded by the gentle whispers, and watched the lights dance across the hillside before him. He was afraid to move forward towards them, he was afraid to stay still.

In his head, as he stood in his paralysis of indecision, there was a music, quick, bright, and lively. And the rhythm of the dance touched his body. At first he resisted, afraid of the vastness of the longing he felt. But the music played, insistent, tugging at the dormant joy within him. Finally he let the rhythm take his feet until he was running towards the wooded spur.

In his heart, the joy burst free of the bonds of the inertia of disbelief to become a bright and passionate flame. It flared within him and beyond him in a riot of wild emotions and then it faltered and died - as did his steps. Still and breathless he stood on the road. His eyes scanned the darkness upon darkness of the hillside where the lights no longer burned. In his head there was only silence.

(Friday 14 July - Saturday 15 July)
"Quiet!"

The word came large and hoarse, filling the room in an unpleasant complement to the warm, stale air. Stunned by the anger in Rowland's voice, the boys stopped their murmured comparisons of the previous day's adventures. Several brows creased in silent, self question at the unexpected and unlikely outburst. The older boys knew this type of anger for they had met it often in their previous teacher, but it surprised them now. Mr Henty had not before been given to such intolerance.

It surprised Rowland as well, left him feeling uncomfortable. He surveyed the bowed heads and sighed. They had done nothing wrong. They had worked as well this morning as any other and their desire to discuss the events of yesterday was quite natural. There was little else in their lives that ran counter to their settled, everyday experience. It was only right that they should have the chance to absorb that experience properly by talking it through with their peers.

He took his watch from his pocket and saw that it was ten minutes to twelve. For some moments he watched the second hand sweep round the face. He was very tired and the regular movement half mesmerized him. With an effort, he drew his eyes away and looked back at the silent class.

"Look at me, please."

All heads rose, faces stamped with doubt. The boys placed their pencils quietly on the tables in front of them and sat straight-backed with their arms folded.

Rowland looked at each one of his charges in turn. Not one of them looked away or dropped their eyes and he was glad of their confidence. When he finally spoke, his voice was quiet and steady. "It is very hot today and we are all tired, especially after yesterday. This afternoon we shall have a nature lesson on river life. You may go for lunch."

Without fuss, and with as little noise as possible, the boys packed their books away. Something of the greyness in Rowland's mind lifted when he saw the smiles on their faces as they left the schoolroom. They already knew about Mr Henty's nature lessons on river life. It was just the weather for swimming.

*

Although Rowland was the first person to the river that afternoon, it was one of the boys who discovered the swan. Rowland, who had been keeping careful watch over the boys from the bridge and talking quietly with John Elam, walked round to the river's bank. There, after peering through the dark lenses of his spectacles into the sparkled shadow beneath the bridge, he discarded his boots and socks and rolled up his trousers. After placing his jacket on the grass beside his other things, he climbed carefully down onto the cool, thick mud and into the water. He kept close to the edge and waded slowly to where the boy was pointing.

The swan lay beneath the bridge on the pounded rubble of the footings by the western bank. It was evidently stressed by all the noise and activity that had suddenly burst upon it. Rowland turned and signalled the boys to keep still and quiet. Without waiting to see if the boys had understood, he turned back to the swan and approached it more slowly. Its neck was back and the head trembled as if it were tired from the effort of keeping it upright. The feathers on its body were discomposed.

As Rowland drew close it turned to face him and hissed, but it was more a formality than a real threat. It was obvious that it no longer had the strength to translate its signal of anger into any form of action. Instead, it sat with an unnatural stillness as its eyes glazed in and out of focus. Gently, Rowland reached out and stroked its neck. The beak clicked, waving in his general direction, but the great, white bird made no other move.

Very slowly, without removing his hand from its neck, Rowland turned his head. Quietly but with strength in his voice, he called up to the gathered boys. 'Someone pass me my jacket, please.'

One of the boys gathered it up and slithered down to where he could hand it to his teacher. With care Rowland laid it over the birds back and then wrapped it about the creature to prevent its

70

wings flapping and being damaged. For a moment he looked at the bird, trying to will it to understand that he meant no harm. He then slipped his arms about it in a careful embrace and, with an ease that belied his frail appearance, he lifted it from its cold bed of river weed and hard stone.

With some difficulty, taking careful steps, he turned and carried the swan out from under the bridge. In an operation that took nearly five minutes, the boys helped him up out of the river and onto the top of the bank. There he stood for a moment, gathering his breath, cradling the bird. Sweat soaked his body and his muscles were taut and knotted. He looked at the boys and knew he would have to disappoint them.

"No swimming without me."

A chorus of quiet protests arose. He smiled them down patiently.

"Go home, all of you, and tell your parents that school is closed. I have a sick swan to tend."

"Do you want any help, sir?"

Another quiet chorus of voices rose, offering help and suggestions.

"All right, all right. Some milk if you will, Bobby Hall. I will also need bread."

With that, he began walking towards the schoolhouse. The older boys went off to fetch what Rowland had asked for. John Elam and the younger boys followed Rowland. With them they brought their teacher's belongings.

A bed was quickly prepared for the swan outside the house in what cool the shade of the building could provide. Its whole body was trembling faintly as Rowland put it down and removed his jacket.

Standing back, he watched the bird as it tried to assess its new surroundings. As he did so he heard the wing beat of the ravens as they came to inspect. They settled themselves on the corner of the roof of the house and looked down.

"Will it live, sir?" asked John.

Rowland hesitated before answering, trying to judge the health of the bird. He wanted to raise no false hopes. "I do not think so, John, but we can try. A little help is all it may need. A little love may ease the pain."

The small group stood in silence for a while, watching the swan, each praying in their own way for its recovery. There was an understandable affinity for the birds in the village that bore their name, an affinity which Rowland shared. Before long, the others could be heard in the distance, returning with the bread and milk.

*

The hot and endlessly long afternoon was nearly gone. The sun was now well into the west. Sapped of its strength by feeding the day, it was a vermilion glory lowering itself slowly from a nearly green sky. Rowland watched it, stunned by the overpowering beauty. Even behind the protection of his glasses his eyes were streaming.

All the boys had long since gone to their homes. John Elam, caught in some dread spell of fascination, had stayed longest, lingering in silence until his sister had come to collect him, and difficult to move even then. Now Rowland was alone. Almost.

He sat cross-legged in the dirt beside the bed of sacking on which the swan lay. The mud of the river had dried upon his legs and was now flaking like dead skin. His jacket lay dirtied and discarded behind him with his boots and socks. And when, at long last, the sun was obscured by the downs, he drew his eyes away from the horizon. It now seemed to be dark though the day was, in fact, still bright.

He looked down at the bird. Tears still clouded his vision. Removing his glasses he fumbled in his pocket for a handkerchief and wiped his eyes. He wondered again whether the bird would survive, whether moving it would prove too much of a shock to its system. He doubted the last, for it seemed to be easier in itself, its neck a little more erect than before, its eyes a little less glazed.

"How fares the swan?"

Rowland twisted around and looked up at his unexpected visitor. He replaced his glasses. "Miss Ruth." He stood, careless of his appearance, and looked back down at the bird. "It seems a little improved, but it is hard to say. I have known men to revive thus from sickness before they died." He was conscious of the slightest edge of bitterness in his voice. He had seen many more people die in hospital than on the battlefield.

"Have you eaten?" she asked briskly, clearly intent on preventing his thoughts from dwelling on the past.

"Eaten?" It had not even occurred to him that he was hungry.

"It is past eight o'clock, Rowland."

"I am all right."

Ruth pursed her lips and looked at him hard. "Meaning that you have not. And your clothes. Go in and change at once. I will watch over the bird until you return."

Her orders, though spoken softly, brooked no argument. It was one of the doubtless many facets of her personality he had not encountered before. Without comment, he gathered up his things and placed the boots on the cold grate and the other things on the easy chair by the kitchen range. He returned to pump up a ewer of water and then went back inside.

Stiff legged, he climbed the stairs to his bedroom. As he did so he heard Ruth call after him. "And bring that suit down with you. I will have it cleaned for you by Monday."

He shrugged to himself, making no attempt to understand her. This aspect of Ruth only served to confuse him further. Her seeming assumption of a role in his life felt horribly like a trap, one foot within the dread circle of iron teeth, poised in mid stride above the plate.

Having washed and changed, he returned to the bird, bringing with him a chair from the kitchen. If one thing was certain it was that he was not going to abandon the bird. He placed the chair close beside it and it looked at him with a certain, if feeble, curiosity.

"Where is your suit?" Ruth asked as he settled himself.

"It is in the kitchen." Despite himself he had complied with her instruction. It seemed the easiest way.

"Good. Now I will prepare you a meal."

"No!" he said, more loudly than he had intended, startled by the implication. The swan looked at him sharply. A raven 'prucked' its disapproval. He looked up to see that they were both still there.

"No?" asked Ruth.

"No, thank you, Miss Ruth." It was an automatic reaction from his childhood and it embarrassed him intensely. His cheeks flushed.

Ruth had quite evidently seen his embarrassment but spoke across it as if it did not matter. "Nonsense, Rowland. You must eat. And formality will not dissuade me. Sit easy."

"But..."

"What?"

There was a pause. Suddenly she laughed and he liked it. It was pure and natural, an honest laughter that shattered a whole defensive rampart of deliberate misconceptions within him. "Are you scared there may be gossip?" She leaned towards him, a smile in her eyes, touching her lips with the side of her forefinger. "Whisperings in the village?"

Embarrassed even more, Rowland looked at the swan. It looked back at him with an implacable stare. The ravens in their wisdom also decided to keep their counsel.

"Oh, Rowland. There will be nothing to talk of. I will cook your supper and then go home."

It sounded, to his ears, like a sigh. For a moment something stirred within him and he looked at her in a different light. She was not what he thought of her at all. She never had been. She was what she had made of herself, which was a wonderful thing. It was a moment of opportunity that caught him off guard. The moment passed. She turned quickly away and went into the kitchen.

*

Pale blue had long since darkened to night and myriad stars shone fiercely. Rowland sat on a cushion on his doorstep and gazed upwards. At his back was silken lamplight, turned low. He had moved the swan just inside the door after he had eaten. Ruth had helped him and then left. Those moments had marked a new understanding in Rowland. For the first time he had been able to view her as a companion, pure and simple. Yet even that had confused him. She had troubled his mind but briefly, however, before he had succeeded in shutting her from his thoughts. Perhaps that was one of the rewards of understanding.

As he watched the stars, one hand gently caressing the sleeping swan's head and neck, he once again tried to make some sense of all that was happening. He needed answers to his questions. Desperately so. As one might desperately need to know the name of a beautiful girl one had just seen. The answers might not solve anything but they would be something to hold on to. Yet even knowing can inflame curiosity. And it was not a girl. It was not love.

Or was it? The idea startled him as it crossed his mind and made him sit upright. Love. What did he know of love? He savoured the word, considered its meaning, thought of it as an emotion, tried the emotion on. No. Not that. How could it be? All he had was a dream. A song that had been sung. Lights on a hillside. Lights and music. Lights dancing. But what lights? What music? Try as he might, he could not properly remember how the music went, only that it was infinitely sweet and infinitely sad and that it cut painfully through him. Like the bullet that had torn his leg. Only this time he wanted more.

He leaned forward and looked to his left. His eyes searched the distant hillside and saw nothing but shadows in darkness. His ears strained and he heard nothing but the distant liquid ripple of the river, an even more distant owl, the embers of the cooking fire as they settled in the range.

Beneath his hand, as he gently smoothed the feathers, he felt or perhaps only sensed the slight and final rending at the end of the struggle. He could never afterwards say just how he knew, but the moment did not pass him unnoticed as the faint avian lifespark slipped suddenly and gently away to fly into the dark glory of the night.

Tears sprang painfully from his eyes and coursed down his cheeks. His whole frame shook with sobs as he gathered the body of the bird close to him. Why such death to a bird like this? It should have been with its own kind, its spirit safe in the great love of their wild magic. He cursed the unfeeling world that men were creating, knowing somehow that this death was a man made thing that would one day become a vast and callous slaughter.

Carried by such a sudden prescient bitterness, he went and gathered his garden spade and fork. With almost formal movements, as if this was some ritual he had performed before, he made straps of twine and strung the tools to his back.

With great gentleness he lifted the bird from the floor and settled it into his embrace. He walked in the night to the river, crossed the bridge, and followed the bank for a mile or so to the north, the tears still flowing - a dam burst with years of poisonous agony and uncertainty pouring from him.

The long, wild grasses whipped at his legs and tangled themselves, but he kept a marching pace that tore through them. And though the swan was heavy he did not pause until he came to the confluence with Cobb Reach.

There, he finally stopped, placing the body of the swan gently on the ground. And there he rested, searching the night until he finally saw what he wanted - a small rise of ground towards the foot of Cobb Hill.

Lifting the bird again, he walked across the springy turf of the wild old water meadow and climbed the slight rise to its peak. He set the great white bird down once again and, without pausing to rest, he began to dig.

Keeping a steady rhythm, he cut first through the matted turf and then bit deep into the rich earth and layers of silt washed there by centuries of flooding. As he worked he felt the reverent eyes of ancient folk upon him, watching from their barrows and ancient forts upon the heights.

He dug a grave broad and deep and there buried the swan, within the flesh of the planet. When he had finished, when the tears were cried out, when he was too exhausted to do more, he looked once more to the stars. As he did so a great blaze of light burst and then died upon the ridge above the head of the Newelm Man. A shiver coursed through his tired body. The blaze was answered by another flash of light from close to the summit of Wealden Hill. With the light he heard the music, the song, sung inside his head. And then there was silence.

Empty and filled with despairing wonder he stood beneath the stars alone.

(Saturday 15 July - Sunday 16 July)

Still only half awake, it was several seconds before Rowland realized why Bobby Hall and John Elam were trying to peer past him into the kitchen. Taking the milk can from Bobby, Rowland turned and went inside. He emptied the milk into a jug. At the door the boys stood silently with questioning eyes.

"It died," he said to them quietly as he placed a cloth over the jug and stood it on a marble slab. "At about two o'clock this morning."

Both boys frowned. There were no tears, however. They were much too much the sons of farmers. The death had happened and there was nothing that could change that. Death was part of the cycle they were familiar with. Taking the can from Rowland who had returned to the door, Bobby crossed to the pump with John. Rowland followed them to watch the can being rinsed and then strolled with the boys to the road. They stood for a moment by the low wall that surrounded the yard.

"I buried it up by Cobb Reach."

The boys looked quickly in that direction and then at their teacher. They were both surprised that Rowland should have buried the creature in the middle of the night but they nodded solemnly as if conferring their approval of the action. It seemed to them a right thing and a good thing to have done.

John stepped over the wall. "Goodbye, sir."

Bobby Hall did the same. "See you on Monday, sir."

They walked slowly and quietly back to the village without talking and Rowland watched them until they were out of sight.

*

The warm, heady scent of freshly baked bread and pastries was almost overpowering as George Keaton stacked the shelves in his shop with his second bake of the day. Mrs Keaton stood and watched her husband in silence, smiling with a pride in his skill that had not diminished in any way since they had married some thirty years before.

With a "Mornin', Mr Henty," thrown over his shoulder, George disappeared into his kitchen, the door closing it from view. Mrs Keaton selected a loaf of the type Rowland preferred and wrapped it for him.

"Now, Mrs Keaton," he said, "how much do I owe you for the bread the boys collected yesterday?"

"Well," she said thoughtfully, "that very much depends."

Rowland, in his tired state, wondered what conditions might attach to the purchase of bread.

"How did the swan fare?" asked Mrs Keaton as if asking after a favoured aunt.

"It died," said Rowland, his sense of defeat drenching those two words. He drew breath. "At about two o'clock."

"Ah. Bless its heart." She was silent for a moment. "In which case, Mr Henty, my George's bread was of no value and is not to be paid for." Rowland opened his mouth to protest but Mrs

77

Keaton shushed him. "No argument now, Mr Henty. 'Twas only the day's wastings."

He would have said more, but several ladies from Lower Cross came into the shop. Handing over the money for the loaf in his hand, he gave his thanks and turned to leave. She cast him a wide and warm beam of her smile and then launched into a bout of gossip with the new arrivals as Rowland closed the door.

On leaving the shop, Rowland walked tiredly towards the lane through the village. Outside Mrs Reeve's house, on the gravelled drive, stood her carriage. Ruth was sitting in it waiting for Mrs Reeve to appear. She saw Rowland and smiled and beckoned to him. Her action caught his eye and he looked in her direction. He could not, however, manage a smile in return. It would not have settled easily upon his face. He walked across to the low hedge that separated Mrs Reeve's drive from the road and looked across to Ruth.

"We are going into Hamm, Rowland. Would you care to ride with us?"

In trying to phrase a polite refusal he fell confusedly to stuttering and suddenly yawned, covering his mouth with his hand.

"I am sorry, Rowland," she said with real feeling. "How thoughtless of me. You must have been up most of the night. Robert Hall told me that the creature had died."

"Yes."

"Is there anything you need from Hamm? You should go home and sleep. I will get anything that you want."

By transferring his bread from one hand to the other he was able to take a list from his jacket pocket. He handed it to her along with some money. As he walked slowly on his way, he heard Mrs Reeve's voice.

*

Summer quiet pervaded the cool and refreshing green of the wooded slopes and bathed his troubled mind as he climbed upwards and away from the valley floor. Muted birdsong gentled his mood. The scent of flowers, wild garlic, trees, earth, all laced on the still air, fostered a gathering strength in his spirit if not a gathering joy.

Fully awake after his morning's deep and dreamless sleep, he looked around as he carefully picked his way between the trees. His eyes, quick and sharp, searched the ground and the undergrowth for signs. As a necessity he had developed some skill as a tracker in the Afghan. The old skills were still there though long unused. As he climbed the slope, he kept glancing back through the trees towards the schoolhouse. Finally he stopped.

"Here," he said quietly to himself. A small surge of excitement tingled in his stomach. "Here they danced."

For a while he could do no more. He had reached the goal he had set himself and now was uncertain about what to do next, if anything at all. The schoolhouse was easily seen from this spot. The rest of the village, though, was obscured by foliage. It was disconcerting to see the familiar from so strange a perspective. It was equally disconcerting to wonder whether this spot had been chosen for those very reasons of what was and was not visible.

He waited, crouched down into a position where he could rest and yet be ready to spring up immediately if needs be, another legacy of his military career. Yet even as he waited, he was not still. His eyes roamed endlessly over the scene. He was committing it to memory so that he might recall it at will, a real and tangible memory, the very first of all this strange affair.

Eventually he was satisfied that he would be able to recall it as he lay in his room and so he stood once more. Something, after all, had drawn him here. Perhaps, then, the thing to do now was to allow himself to be drawn further on.

With almost exaggerated care he began to move about the clearing, quartering the ground, scrutinizing the trees and the undergrowth. Yet, for all his skill, and despite his certainty of the location, he could find no trace that anyone had been here beyond his own clumsy scars in the carpet of wild flowers.

He stood still again, giddy with the fear that he might be wrong, that the whole thing was indeed some product of a fevered imagination. In sudden despair, he closed his eyes. And there, quite as suddenly, was a whole new world. He could sense a presence like the lingering in air of perfume after its wearer has passed. A perfume of exquisite subtlety, a perfume that was addictive. Savouring the feeling, he stood silently with his eyes tight closed. This was the place. He knew it with such calm certainty that he smiled.

Eventually he opened his eyes and looked carefully about him again. Still there was no physical sign. But it no longer mattered. There were other ways now he knew what he was looking for. Casting about, he traced the presence and slowly at first began to follow it towards the peak of the hill. Beyond the clearing, however, it soon faded away from his untrained senses and he was left wandering the greenwood with only his memories and doubts.

When he returned to the schoolhouse, the sun was setting. He found his shopping on the doorstep with a few coppers of change. Picking it up he put the money in his pocket and placed the basket on the kitchen table. He fetched a ewer and went to the pump to draw water, returning inside to cook and to eat and to wash his dishes. It was all done without thinking. He was drained of energy and battered by the emotional turmoil. Whipped up by his recurring dream and released when the spirit of the swan took to new and unseen skies, he had been turned inside out and shaken. Now he was empty and tired. Yet he was calm as well. Something was out there in the valley. A benign life. A gracious light.

The sky was darkening and the stars were afire by the time he went back outside. The world was still and, save for the lights of the village, might have been uninhabited. Yet the valley was alive. A sleeping hollow between the hills. But alive.

Limping slightly from the ache in the muscles of his bad leg, tired from his afternoon in the woods, he sauntered along the road to the bridge and sat on the parapet facing the east. He found peace here. The river sang in the background of his thoughts. Warm, scented air traced the contours of his face and was still. Colours of day gave themselves up to barely distinguishable hues of the night and distances faded, darkening shapes merging. The silhouette of the horizon, trees and hills, became the broken line that marked the edge of the night sky.

He sat waiting for the stars to dance amongst the trees, but they did not dance there. Only above in the sky where they sang out in their gorgeous millions, a song he could not hear.

"Is it to be denied me?" he asked quietly of the world. And with a sigh he berated himself. "Rowland Arthur Henty, this is folly. Songs. Lights. It is nothing but a dream."

But he could no longer truly convince himself of that. The turmoil of incomprehension was gone, replaced, for this tired moment, by a waiting acceptance. He knew it was more than a dream. He knew it would not go away and so he stayed there watching the hillside, obsessed by the haunting beauty that had captured the shadows of his mind.

TWO
(21 July 1883 - 23 July 1883)

(Friday 21 July)

With eyes stinging from lack of sleep and senses dulled by a persistent ache that had settled hard and cold into his shoulders and head, Rowland sat quietly at his desk in the schoolroom. The week had passed slowly. Each night had been spent at his bedroom window or on the bridge across the River Rushy as the hours stretched and twisted into a dark and timeless emptiness. Each day had been spent in the schoolroom struggling with the incessant problems of educating those in his charge, pretending he cared when the importance of his task now seemed overshadowed. But that responsibility, at least, was nearly over for the summer.

At that moment, the boys were outside in the yard. They had all helped to tidy the room and the work had been finished in less time than Rowland had allowed for. He had, as a result of their care and swiftness, given them leave to play outside before being dismissed. So it was that, with an energy drawn from some deep well of life and seemingly oblivious to the heat, they were whirring excitedly in a wild celebration of the holiday to come.

Rowland watched them through the open doorway. It was a rectangular picture of animated brightness, a classical landscape on a portrait canvas across which madcap children ran. But even in that world all was not well. It might seem at first glance a picture of rural joy, healthy country boys at play on a summer's day. Closer inspection of the background revealed the first signs of a valley and its people now weary of the sun and suffering its excess.

The summer was far too hot. Scrutiny of the expressions on the faces of farmers would have been enough to elicit that. Where at first they had been quietly pleased and talked of a good harvest, there was now an edge of worry to be seen, the slightest crease of a frown on the brow. More and more often now they looked to the sky as did many others. They looked for clouds. They looked for some signs of relief. But there were none.

People had become weary of the succession of long, hot days that gave them no respite. They had become sickened with sunlight that was forever so bright it made the air seem to glow with an all intrusive brightness, banishing most shadows. They were tired of breathing and re-breathing the same stale air. In short, they were becoming claustrophobic. And more, for their innate sense of the balance of nature was offended. Such a summer would have to be paid for. That was the common belief. And the longer the heat wave persisted, the greater the payment would have to be.

Rowland pushed his fingers up under his glasses and rubbed gently at his closed eyes. He, too, was bone weary of this unusual summer, wary of its apparent unnaturalness. It seemed to him, in some way he could not articulate, to be well beyond the bounds of rightness. He re-settled his glasses and looked through the open door again. It was as if something was coming to an end and the weather was the last glorious blaze of some power determined to ensure its final days were remembered.

Rowland knew that both his judgement and his vision were heavily distorted by his emotional state. But he no longer believed the pathetic fallacy to be a fallacy. The world, nature, all of creation had been humanity's tutor as it grew from one kind of thing to that which it now was. And it had learned well, coming to terms with a world in the ways the world dictated. Atmospheric pressure affected emotion, as did the cycles of the sun and the moon. It was no fallacy to attribute human emotion to nature for it was in nature that human emotion was nurtured.

For all his intellectual understanding, the constant daily round of stale heat and all pervading light was wearing him down. The patient acceptance he had settled about himself a week earlier had soon worn away. All was far from well. Quite simply, he no longer had the strength of mind to be the stoic. Within himself he could now feel despair like it was a flood welling up against the barriers he had tried to construct. The flood was growing and the flood was strong. The barriers were beginning to crack.

Desperate for some activity to delay the coming crisis, he stood, straightened his jacket, and strode to the door. On his way he picked up the hand bell, holding the clapper with his other hand so that it did not make any noise. And then he stepped out into the sunshine where, for a moment, he could do nothing but stand and adjust to the fierce impact of the day.

The boys were already beginning to flag when the bright ringing tones of the bell brought them to a standstill in the middle of their game. Rowland pointed to the meagre shade

86

offered by the shelter where John Elam already stood. Quickly the boys formed a line there. Rowland waited while they all caught their breath. When all were still and attentive, he took his watch from his pocket.

He had intended to send them on their way with a few well chosen words. He had not got round to choosing them, however, and besides he could not now trust himself to speak. Instead, he watched the second hand sweep slowly round. When all three hands were aligned he put his watch away and looked up at the expectant faces.

Forcing a slight smile, he managed one word. "Dismiss."

The boys stayed in line for a moment and then began to drift away. They were quiet, almost disappointed. Such longed for events are inevitably tainted by some sense of anti-climax, but they had also caught something of Rowland's mood. They soon shook it off, however, and Rowland could hear their cries as they picked up momentum and raced harum-skarum through the village.

And now there was nothing that could distract him from his thoughts for even a few moments. Turning his back on the receding noise, he went into the schoolroom and closed the door. The spirit had gone from the room, loosed into the village for the summer. It would return, changed on the surface but in essence the same. Yet that was not for another six weeks. He sighed and went through into his kitchen.

The barrier that held back his despair gave quite suddenly without any real warning. He was standing at the sink washing plates after his midday meal and staring out at the garden. One moment his mind was blank. The next, a flood of depression welled up from within and swept over him. It carried him, battered him, tore him, half drowned him, and left him choking as he sank into darkness. Finally, unconscious of his actions, he climbed to his bedroom. There, he collapsed on his bed, tumbling slowly in the dark and heavy depths, scoured by the crushing, poisonous fluids of his anguish.

Days had passed in a long agony of dull and endless waiting and nights had passed in an agony of empty loneliness. Not one note of song. Not one glimmer of light. It was something he simply could not understand. After first reasoning that they could not exist, he had finally accepted the song and the lights to be real things. And the moment he had accepted their reality, they had ceased to be.

The deprivation hurt him to the core of his being, and the hurt confused him more than had those strange, beautiful, elusive, and transient events. To have had a dream. To have come to accept it. To have, against all rational sense, believed it real. To have known it, finally, to be real. To have accepted it into his life. And then?

For a few days he had caught some elusive, tantalizing image of a happiness he had not thought possible. A feeling of belonging. A deep and abiding love of some... he could not say what. And now it was gone, known for what it was only after it had slipped away.

*

As the afternoon wore on it became too hot to stay indoors. The violent surge that had torn through Rowland and raged about him had long since passed by, leaving him washed up on some distant shore of quiet despair. Like the survivor of a shipwreck he finally rose, sluggish and beaten, instinct telling him to move on, weariness and hopelessness a check on coherent or sensible movement.

Wearily, he climbed down the stairs from his room to the kitchen below. There was little relief there. No place to settle. So he wandered into the schoolyard, searching there also for some relief from the stifling air inside the house. Yet again he was to be disappointed.

With the advent of late afternoon, the relentless sunshine had finally abated, giving way to an unhealthy atmosphere. It was as if the day itself had been adversely affected by the monotonous regularity of the sweltering heat. It had sickened until the sky now bore a sheen of slick ill-health. A pale and transparent sickly yellow lustre lay over the blue sky. The oppressive heat that bore down seemed to carry the promise of a storm.

Rowland crossed the hard packed earth to the edge of the yard. From the roof of the schoolhouse, where they kept their silent and enigmatic vigil, he was watched by the ravens. A vast silence and a brooding stillness had settled darkly on the over-bright world.

Rowland lifted his eyes. Around him the smooth, dry, downland squatted and seemed as if it was waiting. Waiting as it had for millennia for some thing unknown and unknowable. Watching, in its own way, as it had the rising and falling of the sea, the growth of the forests, the coming of man. The hills had a tale that they might tell, secrets that they would forever keep, buried beneath the rich grassland that was their mantle.

In the lowering gloom, Rowland sat himself upon the low wall, elbows on knees, chin cupped in his hands, staring at the dust. Impenetrable and impassive, ancient beyond comprehension, the mystery of the valley came to him, surrounded him, reached into him, and ran slowly through him. Who was it that had scarred the hillside with their image of a seated and despondent figure? Who was it that had buried their dead beneath the raised mounds and barrows that littered the hilltops? Who had toiled and left the pattern of their fields where sheep now grazed? Who else had sought the safety of the open palm of this valley and called it home?

He stirred uneasily and looked up at the ravens. They stared back as impassive as ever. Home. Did he have the right to call this valley his home? His family had lived here once. His great-uncle had admitted that much. Yet that was not the whole of it. His claim went further than that. There was a deeper pull than an unknown family connection. Yet his thoughts lingered on those unknown people and they worried him, thoughts that had never worried him before.

He sat upright and shook his head slowly, taking a handkerchief from his pocket to wipe the sweat from his face. It stayed clasped in his hands which did not move from his lap. What was the use of speculating? It had been a long time ago and those he might ask were gone. After his mother had died whilst he was still a babe in arms he had been taken in by his great-uncle and raised in Norfolk. From his home in Thorpe he had gone to grammar school where he had excelled and earned himself a place at Oxford. There he gained a double first in philosophy. There, too, he had attended many of the lectures given by the great men of the day, John Ruskin most notable and influential of them all. Rowland had once talked with him at some length.

Rowland's life at that point had reached a crossroads. Being rootless, having no strong family allegiance, he decided that he wished to see something of the world; finish his education by touching real lives; then return to Oxford and teach. But, as a none too rich young man, his only realistic option was a commission in the army. His uncle bought him in at the highest level he could afford and thus it was that Rowland became one of a select and often reviled band of officers who formed the Afghan arm of a somewhat rudimentary military intelligence service. He did not and could not have known then that the road he had chosen had no return path.

As one of an elite, he had travelled the dusty breadth of the Empire. He had, both as an off duty soldier and working under cover, savoured the many and various delights it made available to a man. He had also, with a growing social conscience fired by the rhetoric of Ruskin and others, come to know and be increasingly disgusted by its many injustices. Then there was what turned out to be his final posting. A return to the Afghan.

He arrived there not long before the Afghani onslaught that led to the defeat at Maiwand. Rowland had been on patrol, looking for any sign of large gatherings of hill tribes. They had been away from their base for ten days, had seen nothing, and were camped in a small, sheltered dell several hundred feet above a mountain road. It was their last night before returning. Rowland's orders had been for a nine day patrol but they had covered little ground and he had decided that an extra day would do no harm. It was not unusual for such patrols to be a day or so late.

Despite the heat, he shivered as he recalled the events. The following morning, the morning they should have been safely ensconced behind defended walls, that was when they had encountered the bandits. A 'minor incident' was how the Regimental Diary eventually recorded it. The ragged band that surprised them hadn't been part of the gathering Afghani force. They were nothing more than a bunch of outlaws looking for food and a bit of sport. After all, where 'civilized' men and women gather to conduct the serious business of settling disputes by organized violence, 'uncivilized' men and women will also gather to play.

Rowland lost every one of the seven young men in his patrol and took a lead ball through his left leg.

And all through that increasingly nightmarish time in India and the Afghan, especially when he lay wounded, he had held a formless dream, a hope of some better world. It was a dream that had been realized, in some equally formless way, on his coming to Swann. There was no other place to which, it now seemed to him, he could have come. The unknowing world of Oxford was out of the question. Even had his great-uncle been alive he could have gone to no other place than the one he did. And now he was in his dream. He had reached that 'better world'. And it was marred. Marred by other dreams and strange visions of some other reality.

*

As the sky grew less sickly and the sun moved into the extreme west, he stood and walked towards the bridge. A light breeze had sprung up and was clearing the stormy feel from the air. It was, as ever, comforting on the bridge, sitting above the river, insulated from the land. He thought briefly of the swan, but the images of mortality were swamped by the view before him. Dark shadows beneath the trees on the Spur, the multitude of tired greens and premature browns that cloaked the slopes of Wealden Hill. Through the sunset heat haze it seemed as insubstantial as the strange things he had seen there. A dream like the dream of the song.

After the sun had been eclipsed by the western hills he stood up and stretched. For a moment more he looked at the wooded slopes but decided it was all over. Deliberately he turned his back on it all and returned to the schoolhouse. He had taken a final look at those things that had come so quickly to dominate his life. He had made his decision and now he had said his farewells. That night he did not watch, for there was nothing worth the seeing. The emptiness within was complete.

(Saturday 22 July)

Wearing an impassive face to hide both his boredom and his discomfort, Rowland sat stiffly upright in a chair that had clearly been designed to ornament the room rather than accommodate a person. Before him stretched the polished expanse of a large table. Around the table were sitting, equally upright, in equally uncomfortable chairs, and with equally impassive faces, the rest of the School Board.

The room in which they all were sitting was deep within the town hall. In compensation for the discomfort afforded by the furniture, it was deliciously cool and dim. Rowland still needed his glasses, but enjoyed the comfort of the cool air.

The meeting had slowly picked its worthy and meticulous way through the long agenda. Each member had had much to say on each tiniest point of order. Although Rowland did not know it, the meeting had in fact taken much longer than usual. No doubt this was because of the temperature in the room. All those present were making the most of it. The meeting was now, however, drawing to a close. And, with no further need to concentrate on the events, his own small part long since played out, Rowland allowed himself to retreat into his thoughts.

He surveyed the others present. Churchmen, landowners, minor industrialists, gentry. They all seemed, to Rowland, very much the same as one another, even the Reverend Beckett. Healthy men in mind and body, clean of soul, bereft of much humour, self-satisfied. That, at least, was the picture they presented to the world, but it was a grey and overweening facade. Who knows, wondered Rowland, what murky depths were swilling beneath.

What have they, Rowland wondered, in common with the children whose education they are charged to oversee? What can they know of the world beyond the hedges that fence and protect their privileged lives? Yet, they have accepted me on the Board as a teacher representative, and I do not fit their pattern. Or do I? Sitting here enduring this meeting as they all do, dour of face, smart of dress, educated, and well respected members of the community. I am just like them. And are they just like me underneath? The implications of what he was thinking filled him with a sense of unease.

At the head of the table, the Bishop seated himself after making his closing remarks. The members of the Board relaxed. Except Rowland. His speculations were somewhat disfiguring to his ego and held him fascinated with their horror. Remorselessly, his thoughts went on. I am just the same as them. One of so many. A featureless cipher. No different.

And those brief flutterings of sweet scented petals on the breath of a song? He looked at his hands where they lay palm down on the table top. The relaxed posture was in direct contrast to the tension inside as he tried to deny their worth and their reality. Yet he was a traitor to himself. He might pretend a rational coolness, but it was just and only that - a pretence.

Why should I not believe? he asked himself. Why not? He looked at the others as they chattered, barely seeing them, not hearing them at all. In the last few months, he said to himself, I have dreamed and I have heard and seen such strange and beautiful things. And I was convinced. Yesterday I turned my back and began to move away from that along the stony path of convinced doubt, the path of the rational man. By Christmas I shall no longer believe it at all, if even I can recall it. But the pain was still there.

It was not a very convincing argument, yet it was often used by people to great effect. How else could they live with themselves when they made vast fortunes by impoverishing others? How else could they survive in society if they were not prepared to conform to its standards, no matter how deplorable? If there was one thing that so-called scientific thinking had taught people, it was how to be selective. Invent a theory and select only that evidence which supports it. Suppress all else. Discredit those who come up with counter arguments.

When a man employed thousands of women and children in conditions that ruined their health and offered them little compensation in wages or care, he would say as loudly and as often as possible that it was for the good of the nation. When another man asked, 'what is a nation if it is not those people who work in the factories?' he would be branded a trouble-maker, a revolutionary, an anarchist, someone whose sole aim was to bring society to its knees.

When a man became caught up in things that went against all established thinking, even if he had overwhelming evidence that he is correct, then he knows he is out and alone on very thin ice. Much safer to make back toward the shore where the ice is thick. Even if the thickness is made up of countless layers of lying and deceit. Safer. But there is more to life than safety.

"Rowland?"

He was standing, had done so with the others when the Bishop had left. Now the room was empty. He turned to face the open door of the committee room. There, the Reverend Beckett stood waiting, frowning.

"Are you not feeling well, Rowland?"

"I am all right, Reverend. I… my thoughts were wandering. I was pondering upon my mortality."

The Reverend Beckett smiled, almost laughed, and glanced quickly along the corridor to make certain they were alone. "I am afraid that once the Bishop starts talking, he has that effect upon most people." The remark was whispered conspiratorially and elicited a smile from Rowland, lightening his sombre mood. He picked up his papers from the table and then bent down and retrieved his satchel and a small parcel of books from beneath his chair.

They left the cool and dim calm of the Council Chamber, made their way through the gothic horror of the town hall interior, and went out into the heated mayhem of the crowded High Street of Hamm. The sun was, as ever, blindingly bright and the air of the town was stiflingly hot and dusty. A thin film of acrid chalk dust lay over everything. It coated shop windows and covered the wares displayed on benches, despite the best efforts of junior staff. It settled on the roofs and in the gutters of the buildings. It drifted against the kerb stones in the road, clogged the drains, and collected in corners. The source of it all could be traced to the faint sound of pounding hammers that reached them from the rail workings to the south of the town.

A small knot of sparsely clad and barefoot children ran by, chattering loudly as they wove their way between the other pedestrians. They dodged across the road in front of a brewer's dray. Loud curses from the horseman followed them on their way.

"Come, Reverend, I will buy us both some tea before we return to Swann."

Lemuel Beckett hesitated for a second, but no more than that, and nodded his agreement. Rowland led the way to the end of the High Street and then down the steep slope of School Hill. Part way down, opposite the Grammar School for which the street was named, was a dairy shop with fine stained glass in the door. In the parlour above the shop they sat at a table by the open window that overlooked the road.

For a while they sat in silence, Rowland watching passers-by struggling in the heat, the strain clear in their faces; the Reverend Beckett skimming the pages of one of the books that Rowland had bought earlier in the day. The silence was insubstantial, much invaded from the street below, and finally dispelled by Rowland with empty conversation as he tried to find a way to meet the need to voice his deeper thoughts.

"So, Reverend," he said, placing his now empty cup on its saucer. "How do you think my first year as the Schoolmaster of Swann has gone?"

The Reverend Beckett looked up slowly from the book where he had found a particularly interesting paragraph on the true nature of machinery. His face was shaped into an expression of surprise. "Do you really need to ask, Rowland?"

"I am not searching for compliments," Rowland added hastily. "It is just that I am anxious that the School Board should accept me."

"I know this will sound cynical, Rowland, but they are interested only in results. They care not who produces them, nor how, as long is there no scandal. Your results are good. There is no scandal. They are satisfied."

"I am relieved."

"Relieved?" He closed the book and placed it on the table beside the others.

Rowland noticed that it was the Matthew Arnold. He looked across at the Reverend Beckett. "The prospect of failing was not one I relished."

For a moment they locked eyes. The old man's face was now expressionless, his voice neutral. "Failure? This is peculiar talk. You surprise me, Rowland. What is behind this? Did you ever really consider that you might fail?"

"Oh, yes," said Rowland with feeling.

A slight frown momentarily creased the previously impassive face. "But why?"

Rowland thought very carefully before replying. He did not want to seem to be indulging in self-pity for it was not really that, yet he felt he must say something of what was on his mind. He was no fool and neither was the Reverend Beckett. The old man could hardly have failed to notice that something had been distracting Rowland for the last few months. Something needed to be said. "Failure," he said, still searching for a way into the maze and still uncertain about wanting to take on such a search in this way, "is part of my life." He was in now, but only so far. He could always step back.

"Surely not, Rowland. When have you ever failed?"

"Not me, Reverend. Although do not misunderstand me, I make no claim to perfection. You know me too well for me to try that. I have always striven to do my best. Yet, wherever I go there is failure. I do not mean incompetence. It is just that things fall short or die away. All around me things fail. My mother died when I was still a baby. My guardian, though he gave me security, was not a parent. My schooling, for all that it was good and that I was a good scholar, did nothing to prepare me for university. And university taught me nothing of life. My training as an officer did not prepare me for the realities I encountered in India. It certainly offered nothing that could have prevented the death of those seven young men under my command. And now..." He faltered. How much more should he reveal, if he had not, in fact, revealed too much already?

His eyes dropped to the napkin that was twisted in his hands, conscious that the Reverend Beckett watched him closely. Rowland let go of the cloth and picked up his cup. It was empty. He put it down again. Already he regretted his candour.

"Tell me, Rowland," asked the vicar softly, "what is it here that has upset you in recent weeks?"

He glanced round the room to make sure they could not be overheard before replying. "I really wish I knew." He glanced quickly out of the window at a passing cart and then continued. "I have thought about it. Too much perhaps." He shook his head. "Parts of it seem comprehensible. But all the time there is something... wrong."

What he wanted to say now struck him as being foolish, even though it weighed heavily upon him, in much the same way that a nightmare is not frightening when described in daylight yet carries with it, woven into its very being, the fact that it terrified the sleeper. Confession was meant to be good for the soul, but Rowland was finding it painful and of dubious worth. In the hope that it might clarify things, however, he continued with an edited version of his thoughts.

"All my life, since I can remember, but especially while I was in the mountains in the Afghan, I have had a sort of dream. No. That is not quite the right word." He tapped the table cloth in front of him while searching for a word. Inspiration was in short supply. "A vision, perhaps." It would have to do. "A valley.

Green and quiet. Hills. Trees. A village. It is, in the end, what kept me sane out there in that war."

"You are surely not alone in this."

"Oh no, of course not. But my dream, my vision was very precise. Not in minute and fixed details. In that respect it was vague, had many imprecisions and uncertainties within it." Suddenly he knew something about it that he had not known before. "Like a memory," he said slowly, the certainty of discovery in his voice. "Precise in that it was a true thing. It had happened. Imprecise as memories always are. Yes. That is it." He looked directly at the Reverend Beckett, pleased at the discovery. "I have always thought of it as a dream but it was not. It was a memory. A memory of something that happened a long time ago." The little exhilaration of discovery gave way to a confusion, for how could he remember something he had not seen. "Memory, dream, vision. Whatever it was, still is, a year ago, when I got off the train here, I walked into it."

The Reverend Beckett frowned, clearly not understanding what Rowland was trying to say. "I am sorry, Rowland, but I do not understand."

Rowland paused for a moment, thinking. "When I was shot, I thought I was going to die. Not from the wound, you must understand. I had seen men with much worse who returned to service. It was not that." He shuddered. "They came to us, you see. Our assailants came to make sure we were all dead. Young Alfred, a tough lad from the East End of London, who was perpetually scared so far from home..." Rowland stopped, shaking as he recalled the way in which the youth had been mutilated. "They cut some throats to make sure of their work. And other things. But when they found me, still alive, still conscious, bleeding into the snow, they looked at me and left. In a hurry. At first, I thought help must have arrived. But no. They just left me there. I was very scared. Unable to move. The corpse of my sergeant lay across me..." Again he faltered. He poured some tea with a shaking hand and sipped the tepid liquid. "There was a lot of blood. Flies, even at that altitude. Stench. Vultures. I was in a great deal of pain. It is difficult to remember now, that pain. The seemingly endless hours I lay there, unable to move, wanting desperately to scream. And through it all I kept seeing this picture in my head, comforting me. A valley. Hills. Trees. A village. It was so strong, so vivid, that I knew without any doubt that it existed. When I came here last year... Do you remember?"

The Reverend Beckett sat transfixed. He had never heard Rowland talk so vividly and at such length about his experiences before. Indeed he had never heard Rowland talk about anything at such length with the possible exception of John Ruskin. It was a moment before he was able reply. "Yes. Yes." He was thinking desperately. "Yes. I do. Very well. Ruth and I met you at the railway terminus. In Mrs Reeve's carriage."

"It was raining."

"Yes. Quite a shower as I remember."

"As we rode down the valley, the clouds broke up and the sun shone. I was very quiet."

"You were. Yes. We thought you very shy."

"That may be true. But it was not the reason. I was simply overwhelmed. There was the sun lighting up my vision. It was a doubted memory confirmed."

"You mean you knew what the valley-"

"Not exactly. It was not a replication of what I carried in my head, it was never that precise. I seem to recall it always contained a large lake, but it was close enough in essence that I forgot the differences."

"Remarkable." It was a conventional reply. It was clear from his expression that the Reverend Beckett had no idea of how to respond properly to what he was hearing.

"But it has all gone wrong."

"Gone wrong?"

Rowland could not bring himself to talk of his recurring dream, of the song and the lights, or of the strange longing they had instilled in him, nor yet of the emptiness that had ensued, his rejection of it all. He looked out once more onto the busy street. "Something is missing. There is an emptiness."

"In yourself?"

"Yes. To a degree. That is, I would suppose, inevitable after Maiwand. You cannot live through slaughter and remain unaffected. But there is an emptiness out there as well." He turned to look at the Reverend Beckett. "It seems to me that there should be... more."

"In what way?"

"It is nothing physical. It is... I... I just do not know. That is what truly worries me. I feel so helpless. For a while I thought the missing element might be found, would at least reveal its nature. Now I am not so sure. I am not even sure that there is anything missing any more." He shrugged and smiled apologetically. "It is all so unclear. I am sorry."

*

Although he was now hot and exhausted, the steady rhythm of his work had soothed him and his sense of achievement went some little way to filling the great emptiness. All around him in the yard stood the benches and desks from the schoolroom. They were drying in the sun after the scouring and rinsing they had received. Tomorrow they would all be given a layer or two of beeswax.

As he scrubbed with a brush at his own desk, he picked over the conversation he had had with the Reverend Beckett earlier that afternoon. It had solved nothing, opening his mind to another in such a way, yet it had, against his expectation, helped. Some of the mystery had been dispelled, edited out of the tale and cast aside. He had, however, found a new mystery for he could not now shake off the feeling that what he had always thought of as a dream or a vision was in fact a memory.

Going to the pump for fresh water, he saw a figure approaching from the village, instantly identifiable beneath the parasol she carried. Ruth Beckett. He was suddenly annoyed, filled with a desire to run away, to lock himself in his house until she had gone away. It was an infantile wish, he knew, and that annoyed him further. He went back to the desk and continued to scrub, more forcefully this time.

"Hello, Rowland."

Her voice was cheerful and Rowland could not understand how or why she remained so optimistic. He did not look up to begin with, determined to finish what he was doing. At the edge of his vision he saw her enter the schoolyard and select a dry bench. As she sat, he let his brush fall into the bucket, slopping water over the sides. He leant on the desk, his hands bunched into fists, and stared at her. He was a laughable vision of immature idiocy.

"You are busy."

The banality made him wince inwardly. She was predictable. Are you well? Will you come to lunch tomorrow? It had, of course, never occurred to him that she might be doing it on purpose to irritate him into some response.

"I have nearly finished. Just this and my chair."

She smiled. He waited. "Are you well?"

"Yes, thank you."

"Will you join us for lunch tomorrow after the service?"

It was expected of him.

"Yes."

He wished she would go away.

"Why are you upset?"

"I am not upset," he said tightly.

"Then why have you…"

"Please, Miss Ruth, let us not repeat our conversations."

She sat in silence for a moment and he saw her eyes turn to the bucket before lifting back to his own. "Until tomorrow, then." She stood and left the schoolyard.

Rowland watched her return slowly to the village, wondering just how close she had come to actually lifting the bucket and giving him the drenching he deserved.

(Sunday 23 July)

Cool shadow filled with the murmur of voices, a susurrance that chased into dark corners, followed there by the echo of slow footfall on stone as the congregation left the church. Outside they encountered the full heat of the day, swimmers in the lightness of mystery stepping heavy-footed on dry land. The Reverend Beckett spoke a few words with each of them as they passed, occasionally mopping his brow. When they had all gone he turned to Rowland who waited in the porch out of the full glare of the sun.

"You were in fine voice today, Rowland."

"I thank you," Rowland replied, as much embarrassed at having been noticed as by the compliment. He had not sung out of religious joy for he had no faith in the teachings of the Church and did not wish it thought that he had. Yet this morning he was happy. He felt suddenly and truly free of the strangeness that had reached out and touched him. He remembered it. He accepted it. Yet, this morning, it had no more hold over him than any other memory. It was a great relief and he felt disinclined to think too much on the subject lest it was a temptation to fate.

The Reverend Beckett smiled and held out his hand to indicate the path. A faint breeze blew, but it did little to make the heat bearable. They walked slowly along the lane towards the vicarage, the Reverend Beckett asking if he might borrow the book by Matthew Arnold that Rowland had bought the day before.

Farmer Hall, who had been absent from the service, appeared from the top end of the village, a worried expression on his face. When he saw them, he approached. "Good morning, gentleman."

They returned the greeting.

"And what is it," continued the Reverend Beckett, "that worries you so?"

"Fire, Reverend."

"Fire?"

"Has there been one?" asked Rowland, alarmed at the prospect.

"Aye. There has. Ralph, my shepherd's brother, come across from Kemp this morning. They have lost several acres down to wheat across that way. They beat it down at Kemp, but I've been up to see Elias Brigg. He be worried. Brook Down is nothin' but a hill covered be tinder. He have moved his sheep off and put them down in the orchard pasture. And now this hot breeze have come up..."

"Is there anything to be done?"

"Little that we can, Mr Henty. Elias have already informed the Fire Officer in Hamm for what little that be worth. Best we can now do is keep watch. I should little want us to have the like of East Fore again."

The Reverend Beckett pressed his lips tightly together, a grim and frightened look on his face.

"Well," said Rowland, not noticing the old man's expression, "if help is needed, I can be called upon."

"I thank you, Mr Henty."

"I will mention the situation during notices this evening," added the Reverend Beckett. His voice was strained and Rowland gave him a sideways glance.

"'Twould be a kindness to us all. Now, I must be over to Cross to spread the warnin'. Good day to ye."

They watched him on his way and then continued on their own.

"What happened at East Fore?" asked Rowland.

The Reverend Beckett stopped and bowed his head for a moment. When he looked up at Rowland his face was pale. Rowland was suddenly worried for the old man's health.

"There was a small hamlet there. A few cottages, a well, nothing more." He frowned. "In '47 there was a grass fire that swept up Fore Bottom, fanned by a breeze such as this. It destroyed all the buildings." He cleared his throat. "Four people perished there, Rowland. It was a terrible thing."

"Let us hope, then, that it soon rains."

The Reverend Beckett nodded and turned towards the vicarage. He seemed to have recovered some of his composure by the time they reached the gate. At the open front door, the old man stopped suddenly. "What you said, Rowland. Yesterday morning."

"Yes?"

The Reverend Beckett did not reply immediately. Rowland waited as the old man struggled with his words.

"Your pa..." He faltered and shook his head. "Is it still there?"

"Still there?"

"Rather, is it still missing?"

It was obvious to Rowland that the Reverend Beckett had started to say something else, but he did not feel inclined to discover what was on the old man's mind. He had had enough of cryptic mysteries. Whatever it was, if it was of sufficient importance, it would come out in its own good time. He was learning, at last, to take the line of least resistance. "No." He smiled reassuringly. "Perhaps it was the meeting that depressed me. I was carried away."

The cool shadow of the open doorway enclosed Rowland as he went inside, cutting off any further conversation. Shaking his head slowly at some private regret, the Reverend Beckett followed.

*

102

Bloated by his lunch, Rowland pushed back his chair, carefully folded the spotless napkin, and patted his stomach.

"Oh, Rowland. You hardly had anything."

He smiled benignly at Ruth. The irritation of yesterday was long gone. All feelings of threat to his independence had dissolved. He had come through whatever little crisis he had faced. It was behind him. He stood now in an absolute and golden calm of the spirit. "It was much more than enough."

"But you eat so little."

"It is an advantage, Miss Ruth."

"At least finish your wine," entreated her grandfather. There seemed to be a faint shadow of concern behind his smile, a hesitant conciliatoriness in his manner.

"Well..."

"Bring it into the garden."

"Very well."

They rose. There was a feeling of ease between the three that recaptured, in part, the earlier days of their relationship. It was a good feeling, something of that 'better world' that Rowland had thought of in his younger days. He smiled. With middle finger and thumb placed lightly on opposite sides of the rim, he lifted his glass from the table in a salute that was only half mocking and then turned towards the door.

Quite suddenly, mid way between the table and the door, he stopped, utterly transfixed. His face, pale at the best of times, had become deathly ashen. A complex pattern of interlaced and dancing ripples appeared on the surface of the wine in the glass he held in his partly outstretched hand. Ruth and her grandfather exchanged quick, worried glances. The Reverend Beckett spoke Rowland's name several times but Rowland did not notice. He had heard another voice.

A tense and expectant silence grew and filled the room. Rowland strained his senses. It came again, reaching deep within his soul. It was not louder, but it was more certain than the breeze-born fragment that had frozen him where he stood, so clear and so unmistakable.

The day-curtains of organdie trailed into the room, but no breeze reached them through the open windows. The Becketts looked at them in alarm. And then came the voice again. It was stronger now, sweet and low as it had been in his dreams, calling to him. Only to him.

The glass he held slipped slowly from his fingers. There was nothing he could do to stop it. The whole thing was inevitable from the moment he sensed it was happening. Helpless, he watched it as it seemed to drift down toward the floor where it shivered instantly with a dull 'clop' into a thousand, wine soaked flakes of crystal that folded downwards about the stem and slid outwards across the polished oak floor with a razor like hiss.

*

A sudden mist flooding in from the sea had engulfed the afternoon. A formless and colourless absence had settled, intangible at first but soon condensing into an uncomfortable damp, closing off the rest of the world. Rowland stood in the doorway of the schoolhouse. It had become his island in a foreign ocean. A place of shipwreck. A fragile sanctuary. A prison.

Denied the distraction of the sights of the valley, he stood and stared into the ever shifting vapour, but saw only into the equally obscure and swirling world of his mind. The slow, tumbling free-fall that had come after his seeming releases from the dream had filled him with elation. Now the bright, shattered jewels of that short moment lay scattered in disarray. Bright jewels. Windblown petals.

There were visions in the moist air that teased his sight, half formed shapes that came and were gone before they could do more than suggest something he could not quite grasp. Water pattered in a slow monotonous rain from the eaves. Sudden chill patches of air came and were chased away by the stifling heat. The dampness became slick and unpleasant.

Out there, he knew now without the slightest uncertainty, was something he could not escape. He had tried denying it, but it would not deny him. It merely worked in its own time and to its ends. Pretending it was not there had merely torn at the barely healing wounds in his mind. Accepting it opened him up to many other sensations. Feelings that he had suppressed and distorted. Now they were free to find their true form. Now he was free to explore them without prejudice. But it was not without an equally painful engagement with the world.

He felt as if he was being called and the idea frightened him, a fear that seemed to rise and cover his head, threatening to drown him. For an instant, through the mist, he fancied he saw a smooth expanse of deep, dark water all about him. Gasping in panic, he stepped backwards into his kitchen and slammed the door.

Through the rest of the afternoon he prowled about the confines of the house, both upstairs and down, his body driven by the restlessness of his mind. When he became tired, he sat some times in his chair trying to read and, at others, he stood at the windows, waiting in vain for a glimpse of the wooded slopes of Cobb Spur or of the smooth shape of Wealden Hill. The mist remained.

When night came, he retired to his bed and lay for seeming hours, unable to sleep. He turned this way and that, tangled in the sheets, still haunted by visions that never quite resolved before fading. Finally, he drifted into sleep, wrapped in song and lights that danced freely in the night air until, exhausted, he woke, standing naked beneath the stars. His feet were in the cool grass, his flesh wrapped in a warm embracing breeze.

THREE

(24 July 1883 - 6 August 1883)

(Monday 24 July)

Early morning misty shades were fading in the waking valley to be replaced by hard-edged daylight shadows as the sun cleared the eastern hills. Already the day was hot. Too hot. Those creatures that were not forced by necessity to be abroad lay panting under what cover they could secure. No breeze wandered to stir wilted leaf or dry grass or bring any relief. Yet the very air, still as it was, seemed to hum with the vast burden of heat.

Rowland felt it, listened with such care and concentration as would come, but he could not sense it thus. So he lay, caught again in the dreamwebs of a twilight sleep. Uncertainty about the state of his own mind, combined with a lethargy induced by the narcotic qualities of the incessant sultriness, left him confused about the boundaries of reality. It was a frightening experience, cast adrift from all the old, firm assumptions about the world. And so he lay for a long time.

Seconds piled with unheeded monotony into minutes which in turn piled to the hour. He might have lain there much longer had not the ravens, in quick succession, come fluttering to his window sill and broken his torpidity. Sluggishly, he rose and poured water from the ewer into his wash bowl. For a while he stared at it, not seeing, not hearing. It was even difficult to make the effort to summon up some simple and rational train of thought. Eventually, it was habit that carried him on. He picked up the bowl, carried it down the stairs, leaving the ravens to their preening. Once in the kitchen, he stood the bowl on the draining board.

The simple actions helped to release him from the dreamy and debilitating void and acted as an anchor to a familiar reality. From that familiar element, he was able to venture out to other familiar aspects of being. Slowly he connected himself to his everyday life until he emerged into an ever growing consciousness of himself standing in his kitchen with a bowl of water in front of him. His growing self-awareness then drew in the stiffness of his tired muscles. He leaned forward and dipped his hands slowly into the clear liquid. The water he brought up to his face, though tepid, was a shock that cleared the last of the clinging strands of the dreamweb and brought him fully awake.

Savouring the cleansing effect the coolness had on his whole being, he splashed his face again and then washed himself properly. After rinsing the lather from his face and with water dribbling and dripping, he reached for his towel and dried himself. As he was about to pick up the bowl to take it outside he stopped, let his arms fall slowly and loosely at his sides.

Behind him a presence inhabited the room.

There had certainly been no one there when he had come down - he had not been that locked into the drugged aftermath of a restless sleep that he would have missed someone standing in his own kitchen. Neither had he heard anyone enter. Yet someone was there. A palpable being. By the chair at the table where he sat to take his meals. Watching him. His heart beat faster, forcing blood through his veins with desperate pressure. His muscles tensed, ready for action. He turned swiftly on the balls of his feet. No one.

Frozen, he stood, his eyes wide and darting about the room. The feeling that someone was there had been strong. Very strong. Stronger, indeed, than if a person had actually been present. He shivered. It was as if he had been touched by an incorporeal hand, as if he had felt an insubstantial breath, as if he had heard an unspoken word. And yet, as soon as he had seen that the room was empty, the feeling had gone.

Expelling a long held breath, Rowland picked up the bowl. He crossed to the doorway and there he stopped. A delicate pattern of ripples covered the surface of the water. Rowland watched, aware that it was the shivering of his hands that caused the effect. It took a lot to unsettle him. But a lot had happened recently. Gripping more tightly to control his reactions, he walked out into the yard and from there into his garden, looking carefully about.

He had felt no real fear. He had not been threatened. Whatever it was, he told himself, it had simply been curious. He stopped at that thought and, once more, looked about him. The shaking had gone from his hands but not from his mind. And it was a quiver of excitement rather than fear. It? He wondered about that. Perhaps a something? Or a someone? And curious? He carefully poured the water along the line of potatoes and then went back inside to prepare some breakfast.

During the morning he worked steadily in his garden, hoeing the vegetable patch and the flower borders. When he had finished he stood quietly for a moment in the sunshine, resting his weight on the handle of the hoe. Sweat shone brightly on his face and soaked his shirt. A slight haze of dust hung about him, thrown up from the dry, powdery soil that he had attacked so vigorously.

As he had worked, he had been haunted by the same experience he had had whilst washing. He felt discomfited. He also felt, strangely, resigned. It was yet another event that had no place in his understanding of the world. One of the many that had plagued him in recent weeks. He had not realized how easily such an edifice as the human mind could be made to become so uncertain of itself. It should be the one certain thing in the universe. He wondered how close his was to toppling altogether.

While he rested and pondered, his gaze was drawn almost inevitably to Wealden Hill. Its presence was imposing and constant, out of all proportion to its physical size. Wrapped now in a haze that shimmered with the colours of sun scorched herb and scrub, it was a solid mass that seemed, more than all the others, to watch and know. Another enigmatic symbol, as much a question as any other in his life. Despite the heat, he felt cold.

He broke his stare and, first removing his glasses, wiped his face with a kerchief. Turning his back on the hill, he replaced his glasses and began to walk towards the corner of the house, intending to prepare some lunch. As he did so, a movement caught his eye. He dropped his hoe and ran, seeing a shadow flicker away. At the corner of the house he stopped. There was no one in sight.

Someone had been standing there watching him. He had seen their shadow quite distinctly if only for a split second. He removed his glasses again and rubbed at his eyes. Searching for some simple explanation, he wondered if it was one of his pupils, bored by the heat into spying on him. Yet he knew there was not one of the boys that would do that, even if they had the time. Besides, where could they possibly have gone? There was no way around to the other side of the house without climbing over a thick hedge of hawthorn at the side of the school. Still puzzling it over, he went to the pump to wash.

The feeling of being watched returned once again as he later sat at table. This time it was from outside, through the window over the sink. Yet he was sure that no one had passed the open door, not even in the distance. He had been facing in that direction, gazing out into the brightness as he sat and ate.

Having been caught with his knife paring a slice of cheese, he stared at the half finished meal on his plate, reluctant to look up. Even though his heart raced, he knew now with certainty that it was not fear. There are no ghosts, no spectres on a hot and sunny summer's day. It could only be human. And yet? Quickly he turned his head and looked up at the window.

A flicker of movement. A shadow dance within a shadow. Quick as light. A radiance. An aching sweetness. A face that was gone so quickly he could recall no detail of it. Again there was nobody there when he went to look. Just a quiet, still world between the hills. In the village a dog barked half-heartedly, venting its frustration with the heat.

Throughout that long afternoon the presence continued to be with Rowland wherever he went. It was more circumspect. No more did he catch sight of shadows or movement. There were just the sounds and that peculiar and overwhelming sensation that someone was present.

Seeking shelter from the intense, relentless afternoon heat, Rowland sat in the kitchen. Cooling himself with a fan he had bought in India he sat and read until the whispery noises from the schoolroom drove him to inspect. There was nothing there to be seen, of course, only that the book of ballads lay open where he was certain he had left it closed.

Later, there came the sound of cautious footfall from above, as if someone was inspecting his bedroom. He delayed his ascent as long as he could, no longer curious. He knew what he would see when he got there. In the end it was the beginning of irritation that drew him to the room. When he had finally climbed the stairs, he heard the sounds coming up to him from below. For a brief instant he caught sight of himself in his mirror, wide-eyed and tense.

For a long time after that he stood at the foot of the stairs, listening to the splashing of water from the yard. Only when it stopped did he go outside. The ground around the wooden trough was damp. The pump had not been touched. From the low wall bounding the yard by the road, the two ravens watched him with curious eyes. He retreated to the house, too confused to answer the questions rising in his mind. But he could not retreat far enough. With the questions came all the remembered horrors of his war, all the emptiness of the past, all the doubts, exhumed from their dark graves to flutter obscenely into the calm, dispelling the sense of identity he had fought so hard to establish.

Yet, deep within the malevolently slow storm that was brewing in his mind was the ever present feeling that it was not he who did not belong. It was the others. It seemed much clearer now, as if someone had been patiently explaining it to him. Over and over again until he understood. They all existed on the surface of the valley, but strong winds would fill the many tiny sails of their leaves and pull their poor roots from the thin soil. His roots went deep, tapped the very life-blood of the earth - but it was an ichor that was burning deeply into him.

Dusk finally threw the ashes of the day into the eastern sky where the first stars, like embers, glowed in the dying light of the sun. It stayed warm and still. Rowland sat on his step, his knees drawn up and embraced tightly in his arms. He was at the strangely calm centre of the wild turnings of his mind, listening to the sounds within the house, borne down and slowly giving under the weight.

He saw the first stars in the sky and watched. They had been constant to him those bright distances. Climbing slowly to his feet, he shuffled inside, feeling immensely tired. His vision began to swim with hazy dervishes of light dusted mist. At first he thought it was simply tiredness and he rubbed his closed eyes gently with his fingertips. But when he opened them again the faint luminescence was still there, milky colours weaving slowly in an enticing pattern.

"Leave me," his lips said.

The haze began to coalesce. Stars glimmered in the doorway.

"Go away!" he screamed.

Sudden silence.

Calm.

Darkness.

The busy rushing was gone. In the quiet, he was suddenly aware of the torment of the many days just passed, of all the whispering and laughing that had plagued him since he had woken and which now was hushed. The very clamour of the presence which had haunted him had contrived to conceal its existence.

He lowered himself into his armchair and felt the tension drain from his muscles. A great release bathed him, as if he had woken healthy but weak from a fever, and in his release he knew that his strange dreams and visions were a reality that had been distorted by that fever, a sickness that was the small world of men. Another threshold had been crossed. Another threshold across which he could never fully return. Drawing up, he stood and returned to the doorway, wondering at his new knowledge. Night had fallen fully and the stars glowed, pulsing their vast but evanescent and glorious life against the darkness.

(-   )

There was a movement. No form. No substance. Simply movement to which his eyes were drawn from contemplation of the stars. Inevitably, he saw nothing. But he no longer felt any form of apprehension, was no longer plagued by a debilitating dis-ease. He had come to a simple acceptance that some thing or some one was there. Somewhere.

It was a gentle presence that had been with him constantly through the long, tiring heat of the day. It was a presence that had been with him these past weeks.

Nothingness became visible, still without form, still without substance. It was there, in the corner of his eye as he looked elsewhere, was gone when he tried to see it directly. He experienced a moment of doubt. His acceptance was still largely intellectual and he had been subject to many disappointments in recent weeks. It passed swiftly, however, when he looked away again. In its place a belly tingling frisson of joy.

On the edge of his vision, from the corner of his eye, beyond all sensible reach, was the graceful movement of a faint cloud of transparent light over Swann Bridge. It was real and he came, as the evening lengthened, to accept it within his soul as well as within his mind, surrendering himself to the truth, taking into himself all that he had once learned to accept as impossible.

As midnight approached he was a man with a new vision. Possibilities opened brightly before him with prospects of dizzying uncertainty and potential. The world had become an infinitely larger place. And in it he was a free man - free of the blinkering preconceptions of the dull senses of humanity. The new revolution of the machine was re-arranging the world so that people no longer had the opportunity to touch it for themselves. Even here where they lived by the soil. It was putting scales over their eyes when it should be lifting them to the stars.

He turned his own eyes once more to the bridge. There, coalescing from the strange, luminescent mist, hovered a small constellation of lights. They were vibrantly alive, breathing an air rich with beauty. And he knew they could dance for they were the lights he had seen at a distance. Not similar, but the self same. His surrender had made him certain.

Glowing sweetly, they were, with an ever-shifting luminosity, colour, and form that touched him and teased him and enticed him. And within the light, yet somehow beyond and before, there was a hint of something other. A something that was the essence of what beckoned him. A something that had called to him these many days gone by. A someone who now waited for him.

Hesitantly, he stepped down from the doorway of the schoolhouse into a new world where he stood and listened. It was full of the vast and echoing silence of night noises; pervaded by the sharp clarity that comes with the immediateness of contact with all things as he reached out and they reached out in return. Magic shimmered and trembled in the night air.

There were lights burning yet in the village, he saw, faint shafts from one or two of the cottages. But they were veiled now in some way, merely the dull and fading lights of a humanity that shunned the night. He turned away from them and walked into his garden, an act that in some subtle way unknown even to himself was a shunning of humanity.

Above the bridge, its stonework illuminated as never before, the lights glowed brighter. They moved as if in anticipation, their golds and greens, deep scarlets and gentians, pulsing with life, splendid and calling still. He watched as they drifted and mingled, separated once more, illuminating that something other which was clearer now, more solid, like a drifting of organdie in stained glass moonlight.

A great and growing feeling of ecstasy washed over him, tempered with a gentle sadness. It sparked within him a deep yearning to be there and bathe in the light, a desire that overcame his faltering apprehensions. He crossed the yard, his eyes constantly on the condensing luminescence. At the edge he stopped for a moment and then stepped across the wall onto the road, crossing another boundary, this one more profound and permanent than he knew. The lights blazed in transcendent triumph and then swept away.

(-   )

From the bridge he could see the woods on Cobb Spur, picked out in starlight. Each leaf glowed with the faintest sheen of icy white, the whole ablaze with almost imperceptible light. Shadows danced with shadows and cast their darknesses about. The whole hillside was sculpted from a living and deep night, warm and alive.

The air he breathed was sweet, as if heavy with the scent of blossom. Yet it was more tantalizing than that. No earthly bloom shed such a scent to the winds. No flower could capture a soul in this way without also destroying the body. This that he breathed was a perfume that would haunt a man in his loneliness, into his madness, into his very death.

He reached out to touch the whole world and then stood relaxed, a deep calm within, content to stand on the bridge where they had been and share a common space. Even should he never see them again he felt he could find some level of contentment. He felt that his spirit would have some certain and unassailable base from which to foray into the brute world of man and his uncontrollable desires and his uncontrollable machines.

A faint breeze from off the wooded slope before him brought with it an exquisite music. It was so quiet as to tease his senses at their very limit. The breeze faltered. There was silence. Then again it came. Gentle to the ear. A catch. A phrase. Words that were indistinguishable but which he knew from his dreams. And that voice, so pure and so clear.

The voice, the words, the enchantment of the perfumed air he inhaled, the shimmering stellar illumination, were all of a piece - emanating from a common source, a single, ancient earth magic that had evolved and dwelt in the valley since long before the coming of man.

Slowly, entranced, but still in full command of his faculties, he left the bridge and cut across the sun withered meadow towards the foot of the spur. He knew there was no need to hurry for they had called him and now that he had heard, they would wait. Beneath his feet, the parched grass sighed an accompaniment to the music that grew gently ever stronger. It was a lilting tune, slow and stately to match the rhythm of his stride.

He came once more to a road and followed it southward. His eyes, however, were still on the slowly developing tapestry of coloured patterns that glowed so closely now in behind the trees to his left. Road, river, and trees eventually ran close together and he stopped, hesitant, as a child in the presence of great ones. The music that had accompanied his approach came to an end and there was breathless laughter. It, too, beckoned, called him into its company. All truly great ones welcome the child to their midst.

(-)

When he heard the voices, too soft to know what words, he smiled. It was impossible not to. They struck a deep harmony within him, ringing clear in the deep calm that had settled there. He savoured the sweet delight. He listened with a joyous incomprehension to their hushed conversation. He heard the intertwining voices of people who were not people. Tones of love and confidence. Undertones of some great and ancient sadness.

There came a pause in the talk as if they were waiting for him to join them. Leaving the road, he carefully picked his way up the rough grown bank and made his way into the star shadow beneath the trees. Night came suddenly close around him as the canopy of dry leaves cut off the sky. The soft darkness there beneath the thick layer of greenery made the waiting coterie of lights seem all the brighter, all the warmer.

With his heart beating fiercely, he walked on up the slope between the trees. His way was not difficult to follow. As he drew closer to the company, the lights finally resolved to familiar shapes within. Each was a bright and flame-shifting aura of life that surrounded the shape of a young woman. He could not tell the precise number and could never afterwards remember, save to say that it was a small company.

Again there was music, a harp and a flute weaving a simple tune and lively, bright and gentle spells sparkling their sound on the air. Before he could reach them, they had set to dancing once more. He drew in under the mass of an elm tree and watched in wonder. With the music was their voice and he listened. His foot began to tap, his head rocked from side to side, a smile of contentment transformed his face.

They danced bravely and lightly in the clearing before him, their bare feet hardly touching the ground. With them danced their light. Colours spinning in a wild fire of joy. Sparks like fireflies detached themselves and clouded the air with an evanescent life of their own. Shadows of many deep hues danced far into the woodland.

While they cavorted, he studied them each and all with great care. There was still something translucent about them, but they had corporeality beyond the dream of any spirit. These were substantial beings. They were real and they were beautiful. They were real... but they were not human.

He was, as they danced, able to catch glimpses of their faces beneath wild, flying hair. Of all about them that was entrancing and marked them as a race apart there was one especial feature. Simple and pure they seemed, but one more than the others. Though she was no more beautiful, nor greater in stature, her radiance outshone the rest of the company, her depth gave them gravity, and she it was that led the dance. In her footsteps the others followed, outshone but not overshadowed.

They danced until the breath was gone from his body and his mind span with delight. And still they continued to dance. He felt quite dizzy and had to lean, quite still now, against the tree beneath which he stood. The rough bark was cool against the flesh of his left cheek and the palm of his right hand and the ancient and slow spirit of the tree flooded through him and soothed him.

118

And then the dance was done. The dancers fell in a laughing heap upon the flower-carpet of the forest clearing. Silence burst upon Rowland's ears and it was some moments before he could hear them talking softly to each other until their voices, too, were silence, commanded thus in gentle tones by she whose soft, sweet and haunting voice had woken him so often from his dreams. One by one, where they sat against each other, they turned to face him. She who was the brightest then stood and reached out a hand towards him.

(-   )
Before he could respond, she had risen and come to him and her hand had touched his where it rested against the tree by his face, all without seeming to move. Her long, slim fingers folded gently over his thumb to touch his palm. Cool, dry, and soft; vibrant with a life that burned his flesh without pain and made him draw sudden breath. Her eyes watched him, steady and smiling, seeing deeper into him than he thought was possible.

And therein lay the difference he had seen, the difference that marked her and her kind as different from his own race. For her eyes were of rich green with flecks of gold. Her eyes were of the deep sea shot with sunlight. Her eyes with their vertical pupils. The eyes of the night dweller, devotee of stars and moon.

As if in living obeisance to that reverence, purest moon-silver hair framed her face, fell across her shoulders and down her back in a shimmering cascade of cool light. Barely concealed were delicate ears that tapered upward to gentle points. Her face was high cheeked and narrow, classically fay, with an expression in which could be seen a natural wildness wherein was mingled the strength of the tree root to topple mountains and the delicate beauty of the tiniest flower of the forest floor. She smiled like spring sunshine.

Pressure from her hand in the slightest of squeezes took his hand away from the tree. Her fingers slipped around and touching turned to holding. Into his awed acceptance came again a moment of doubt, as if he had heard something that might waken him from a dream. He held his breath and there was silence and the doubt left him, replaced by a blaze of life, of joy, of love that knew no possession. He was standing in the centre of immensities and was no longer alone. All around bloomed the lights of their life, running, shimmering, entangled with the light of the trees, playing now along his arm to unshutter the light that was within him. It was like plunging into cold water on a hot day.

Reaching out, he took her other hand and knew in that instant that the music would come. Someone he had not seen before, a small and wizened autumn-clad man, began to work the bellows on a set of pipes. It was faint at first, as if in some other and distant land, but it grew ever stronger, echoing through the darkness amongst the trees.

Hesitantly, following her unshod feet, Rowland took his first steps in the dance. They began alone, moving slowly into the centre of the clearing. Then, around them, as their walking steps became dancing steps, the others joined in one by one. All at first were stately and solemn faced, moving in a slow ring. Before too long, though, he found he knew where next to step, whereat he lifted his eyes and smiled into her smile.

Almost imperceptibly the tempo of the music began to quicken and they followed its lead, turning circles, moving slowly away from the glade. Light and free, they began to climb the slope, weaving faster among themselves, turning from tree to tree, crossing paths, and gliding lightly across wild flowers to cast their scent into the night air. Their shadows, dancing their own dance, burned bright as sun-fired dragonflies. The wild music of the pipes filled their ears. They gave themselves up to the dance.

Faster still they whirled, breaking free in wild delight to touch the byways with their magic, returning again to the circle. The myriad trees became a blur. Stars turned and blazed in great circles. The scent of countless flowers coursed through the air. Higher and yet higher they danced, faster and yet faster. Legs in a frenzy, feet scarce touching the ground, hearts wild, heads flung back, turning, weaving, circling, whirling, close to flying, finally bursting free of the trees to dance at last on the high hilltop, crowning it with the light and the power they had conjured.

And then it was finished. Silence echoed across the valley as they fell and lay upon the grass, laughing when breath came to spare. In the warmth of this ecstasy, Rowland lay a long time upon the hilltop and watched the stars burning in their own dance, idly counting their number, filled with joy at their celebration. So he would have stayed forever, feeling contentment and security as never before. So he would have stayed but for the cool touch of fingers on his brow.

She knelt at his head, his lady of the dance. He looked up at her. Her smile was gone, the time for ritual, for dance, and for celebration now passed into a time for reflection. Her expression was now serious, a sadness overlaying that essential wildness. He sat up, and they then stood. Once more she took his hand, this time to lead him from the hilltop. They walked down to the head of the gap that lay between their own crowned peak and Beacon Hill to the east.

Far below them lay Cobb Reach, a smooth ribbon of aqueous reflection, gliding gently southwards and westwards between low banks to where it was pulled into the flow of the River Rushy. Beyond Cobb Reach was Wealden Hill. He looked across to it and experienced a sudden, powerful, and totally inexplicable yearning that brought tears to his eyes. They burned as they blurred his vision and then ran warm and salty to his lips.

He looked away and down, brushing the tears from his eyes. As his vision cleared he looked down at the slope directly before him. There lay the great, carved figure of the Newelm Man that sat, head in hands, gazing sightlessly across the valley beyond. The chalk that was exposed by the deep scar in the turf was clean, free of weed and moss, and glowed faintly with the ancient power of the hills. Rowland cast his eyes back across the valley to where its sightless gaze had been directed for time out of mind.

From the floor of the valley a mist was beginning to rise, clinging thickly to the surface of the Reach but spilling over its banks and spreading more thinly across the meadows to the base of the hills. Isolated patches rose and twisted thickly in small dells. In the sky, one by one, the stars faded, blinked their last and were gone. The eastern sky grew ever paler, casting a thin, faint light across the slopes of Wealden Hill, turning the shadowy grey to a sun parched sage green.

While he stood and watched the beginning of the day, a gentle voice and sad, her voice, echoed in soft edged shivers through his soul and soared through the centuries that lay spread before him, borne on a lost breeze that had at last returned home, singing the song of his dreams, the song that had woken him and brought him here, a song in a language he had never before heard but which he knew in his heart of hearts.

"Rise and leave the shadows in the hall,
Shake off the dust of winter's yoke,
And sing abroad the songs that will call
To errant, lost, and half-bred faerie folk.
Come step in the dew of dawning
Before the sun shall rise
And sing the song of charming
To open sleeping eyes.

"Strong sun lights the kirtle all of green
That wraps the frame of summer's land,
Drink the perfumed air that bathes the scene,
See swimming swans and waves break on the strand.
Come step in the joy of morning
Along the ancient paths
And hear a whispered warning
That nothing ever lasts.

"Touch the eyes now turning from their home
And call to the deep memories,
Wake the yearning, for so long disowned,
As gently as the faintest summer breeze.
Come stand in the heat of noon's sun
Upon the shaded way,
And learn from the raven's song
That faerie folk are fey.

"Sweet the rose that burgeons in the bower,
Sharp the thorn that bites unwary hand,
And past summers are as plucked wild flowers,
Though precious they are dying in your hand.
Come rest you in the afternoon
And watch the petals fall,
Listen to this new made tune
The last one of them all.

"Man has laced his iron round the world,
Cut the roads of the faerie race,
So this season is the last unfurled
To witness our dance on the green hills' face.
Come watch the glow of evening
Before the sun has passed,
And learn the steps I'm dancing
This summer is our last.

"Rise and leave the darkness of your room,
Take my hand and dance brightly now,
Together we'll outshine stars and moon
And with the sun we'll take a final bow.
Come dance beneath the dark night sky
Between the green leafed trees,
For with the dawn I'll be gone,
As will the gentle breeze."

The last note of the song drifted away into the first isolated calls of the dawn chorus. Rowland stood heartstruck and transfixed. He had travelled a long way. A whole, new, and undreamed of world was here at his own two feet. For an instant, as he stood, he thought he saw, clear in the distance, a great open doorway just below the crest of Wealden Hill. A figure, bright against the darkness within, stood watching, lifted an arm to wave and all was gone. He turned and saw that he was alone.

(Sunday 6 August)
Dust turned in an endless, slow, falling drift through hard shafts of sunlight, undisturbed and silent. All else was motionless within the still and oppressive air. The room felt long neglected, left to its own devices, left and forgotten. Objects lay where they had last been used. On the table in the centre of the room were the remains of a meal. The fragments of food were clothed in circular growths of black and green.

Yet the room was inhabited. In the armchair by the hearth Rowland sat, his hands resting palm upwards in his lap. His eyes were focused on some far distant world in which place his spirit resided. Sounds from outside filtered into the room and penetrated Rowland's consciousness but they went unheeded. With great weariness he sighed and his eyes closed.

A knock on the door roused him and he looked up, focusing now on the room. Raising his hands to his face, he worked his fingers over the flesh, massaging the tiredness away, yawning widely as he did so. When he let his hands resume their place in his lap he looked round and saw the thickly settled dust, the untidiness, the mouldy food, and blinked to banish it from his sight. Standing, he stretched as if he had just woken from a deep and restful sleep.

Again a knock at the door. The sound was sharp and harsh. He turned to look at it, irritated at the noise, wondering who it might be and still far too drowsy to apply the simple solution.

"Rowland? Are you there?"

The wood-muffled voice that penetrated the room was filled with anxiety. Another sigh escaped Rowland's lips. With considerable effort of will, he dragged his feet across the floor. At the door, he placed his hand on the key in the lock. Brief sparks of fantastic memory burst brightly in his mind and were gone. Suddenly he was properly awake. He looked back at the room in puzzlement. More knocking. The key turned with a harsh click and he opened the door. Hot air pushed past him into the kitchen. Bright light burned at his unprotected eyes.

On the step stood the Reverend Beckett, looking old and crumpled, much bowed down by the heat. His pale, lined face was beaded with perspiration. The lines re-arranged themselves from anxiety into a frown. A single bead of sweat rolled down the old man's nose and hung at the tip before it was brushed away with a large handkerchief.

"You were not in church this morning." It was a statement without hint of accusation.

Rowland did not understand. His mind was still clouded, confused by a jumble of recollections that began, slowly, to order themselves but which nowhere contained the keys to understanding what had just been said. He groped in his pockets for his spectacles. "Church?" He was much agitated now.

"I know you do not believe, Rowland, but you always attend. I thought you might be unwell."

Rowland found his glasses and put them on. He looked past the old man, squinting through the tinted lenses as the bright midday sunshine penetrated. The valley was a vibrant green patched with fields of gold. "Did it rain in the night?" He could not remember it raining. Indeed, he could recall little of the past evening. Sitting on the doorstep, yes, but certainly he could think of no reason why he should have slept in the chair.

Careless of the Rev Beckett's presence, Rowland stepped past the old man and into the yard. The ever present ravens, perched on the pump, watched with black eyes. Slowly, Rowland looked all around, shading his bespectacled eyes with a hand. Everywhere, Rowland saw, was rain washed and green. It had been freed of some of the burden of the relentless summer with a gift of sky borne water. Already, though, the greenery was beginning to languish beneath the fierce sun. The onslaught had resumed.

The Reverend Beckett turned to watch him. A wistful smile replaced the look of confusion on Rowland's face as he ran his eyes along Cobb Spur and across to Wealden Hill. "Rowland?"

Rowland did not hear. He had remembered. He was dancing again, his head filled with the whispered memory of the song of his lady of the dance. The smile faded. Confusion returned. He turned to face the Reverend Beckett. "When did it rain?" he asked.

"Most of Tuesday and Wednesday," the Reverend Beckett replied. "Someone must have danced us up a considerable..." He faltered, looking intently at Rowland's face. "Surely you remember."

"Tuesday? Wednesday?" Rowland turned again to look at Cobb Spur as the Reverend Beckett nodded. Both men were now thoroughly confused at the turn the conversation had taken, although for very different reasons.

"And?"

The vicar could only shake his head. "And what?" he asked after a pause.

"I was not in church this morning." A strange chill ran through Rowland as he saw the slowly nodded reply. "Sunday."

"Come inside, Rowland."

After looking once more at Wealden Hill, Rowland followed the old man into the kitchen. The Reverend Beckett saw the state of the room, normally meticulously clean, saw the mouldy food on the table. He turned to face the schoolmaster. "Rowland, where have you been?"

*

Doctor Joyce joined them for lunch. His bulk was, judging by the way he approached his meal, the result of the prodigious amounts of food he consumed. He was not fat, but he was an imposing, overpowering man, strong in his frame and his convictions alike. It was the first time Rowland had met him for he had not ever required his services and the doctor was not normally a guest at the Beckett table. The reason for his presence today was all too obvious.

"Reverend tells me," the Doctor began as he helped himself to more vegetables, "that you are not well."

Rowland was angry at the comment and at all that lay behind it, but he controlled himself.

"I am well," he said curtly in reply.

The Doctor stopped eating for a moment and looked at him carefully. "You look pale."

"No more than usual."

The doctor grunted, putting a forkful of food into his mouth while he continued to stare hard at Rowland.

"You are not eating very well," said the doctor when he had finished chewing. He pointed to Rowland's plate with his fork. "Scrap of vegetables." He shook his head. "Poor appetite, pale, eyes sunk. Sleeping well?"

"I…"

"Thought as much," nodded the doctor.

Ruth and her grandfather ate in embarrassed silence, their heads down over their plates.

"Tell me, Mr Henty," continued the Doctor, "are you sickening for something?"

There was, perhaps, the hint of a leer in the doctor's voice, although it may have been Rowland's imagination. He flushed, though, and knew it would be misinterpreted.

"I have simple tastes, Doctor Joyce," Rowland said somewhat primly. "I want for nothing."

"I doubt that very much," came the reply. "What you need, Mr Henty, is a diversion. Something is worrying you. I care not what it might be, but it is undermining your health. For your own good, go away. Take a walking holiday."

"My leg…" protested Rowland.

"Leg?"

"A bullet wound."

126

"Nonsense. Exercise will not harm it. As long as you are careful. Lame excuse. Ha!"

Rowland could find no reply.

It occurred to none of them there that the doctor might also be embarrassed, that his bluff manner may have been an attempt to hide it. Consultations arranged in the absence of the patient are invariably awkward and few doctors approved of or enjoyed such approaches. Whatever his reasons, his behaviour was certainly likely to ensure he was not invited again to the Beckett table. "That is settled then. Excellent wine this, Reverend."

*

Rowland woke with a start. Late afternoon sunlight filled the study, splashing through the side windows, illuminating the rich, leather bindings of the books on the shelves. In the clock beat stillness, dust fell endlessly through the liquid bars of luminescence, winking into existence and winking out again. Before him, on a low table, was the unfinished game of backgammon that he and the Reverend Beckett had been playing when he had fallen asleep.

"I have brought you some tea."

He looked up. Ruth placed the tray she was carrying on the table beside the board and sat down in the chair opposite. Rowland leaned forward and poured milk into the cups.

"What time is it?"

"Nearly five o'clock."

As she spoke, the clock in the hall began to chime. He poured tea from the pot, passed Ruth her cup, and, balancing his own, sat back in the chair.

"Would you like to finish the game? Grandfather said it was your turn."

He looked at the board. "Why is everyone convinced there is something wrong with me?"

"You have experienced much."

He placed his cup and saucer on the table and took up his dice. He looked at them as they lay in the palm of his hand. Sighing inwardly, he closed his fingers over them in a loose cradle. It seemed a hopeless situation.

"Does that mean, then, Ruth Beckett, that there is something wrong with me?"

Ruth looked at him and he tried to discern her feelings from the gentle and impassive expression she wore, but her face gave little away. She turned her head slightly to catch a faint, freshening breeze that blew through the window. Could she dance? he wondered.

He looked again at the board and then rolled his dice.

"Will you go away, Rowland?"

"And follow the ancient paths?"

"Ancient paths?" She sounded almost frightened.

He moved his pieces and looked up. "It is your move."

The game was played. Rowland lost.

FOUR
(6 August 1883 - 3 September 1883)

(Sunday 6 August - Monday 7 August)

Unsettled, restless, Rowland moved about both rooms of the house. From chair to window, from window to stairs, from stairs to bedroom, he wandered, starting some task and then leaving it to take up something else, only to move on again some minutes later. Occasionally he would pause by the open door to try to gather a breath of freshness from the stale air that swamped the valley. What little there was brought scant relief and he resumed his restless wandering with renewed agitation, sapped by the humidity, driven by the desire to be doing something, lacking the concentration to commit himself for more than a few minutes.

He could not formulate any clear plan of action, could not resolve the conflicting desires within himself. He wanted to dance. Of that he was certain. He desperately wanted to be free of the narrow horizons of the life he had made for himself. There was a richer and wilder world to explore, but he had no way of knowing if that world was open to him. He knew it was there, had touched it, had been allowed to dance along its fringes. Knowing the existence of a thing, however, was no guarantee of becoming a part of it. But he wanted to dance. He desperately wanted to dance.

As night fell, he removed to the yard and, between more bouts of restless wandering in his garden, watched the distant hillside. It remained dark, a collage of many deepening shadows. Yet the fire of the dance was not completely extinguished. Long after the last lights of the village were doused, his own flame burned, fed by the endless fuel of the vivid memories of that timeless moment. Had he really danced for so long? Which sunrise had he witnessed?

The night grew darker and the close air became sonorously reverberant, full of the echoes of the life that was indifferently pursued by the nocturnal animals of the valley. Cry of bird, shriek of prey, call of mate, squeak of play, all slowly enclosed by the clouds that were blown by the high, hot winds from the far south. Fine desert dusts from Africa came with those winds to fall in parody of rain. And with the fall of dust came the subliminal and distant vibration of thunder, felt through the earth as much as through the air.

By midnight Rowland was exhausted. His nerves were frayed and he felt like screaming. He knew if he started, he might never stop. And his head ached abominably, a sick pain that drained the strength from his muscles. For hours he had fought against it with a stubborn determination. In the end, he realized, it had been the wrong thing to do. Some things can only be overcome by becoming one with them. He gave in.

Wearily, he locked himself into his house and, with trembling limbs, he climbed the narrow stairs. Slowly he undressed, folding the clothes neatly and piling them ready for the morning on a simple chair. Lodging the windows fully open, he lay naked on top of his bed, his body aching, his neck gripped tight, a heavy and sickening beat behind his eyes. Motionless now in body, his thoughts continued to tumble ceaselessly, eventually dropping over the edge of sleep into a thick mire of nightmare.

In sleep his body resumed its restless struggle. He turned and twisted, heaving himself from one position to another, as if trying to resolve his hectic dreams by outpacing them. Many times he brought himself to the edge of wakefulness in his agitation like a drowning man reaching the surface, conscious there of the turmoil into which he was locked, before sinking back into the depths. Finally, he woke himself in the early hours of the morning by falling from his bed to the floor, striking his face on the bare boards.

As he lay, groggy from sleep and more than a little stunned by the sudden blow, thick blood began to well from his nose. At first it was a tickling sensation that he could not ascribe to any particular cause. Then it dribbled into his throat where, as it made him gag, he tasted the iron. He felt, in the pit of his stomach, the familiar queasiness that came with the taste of his own blood. With a growing sense of panic he scrambled up to his knees. Fumbling in the starlight dark he found his matches and lit the candle at his bedside.

Smears of blood were on his hands and chest. Dark spots of it stained the bare boards of the floor. A drop fell and splashed warmth onto the ragged patch of scar tissue on his left thigh. For a moment he stared at it, all too conscious of the last time he had seen blood on his flesh. A year ago the sight might have unhinged him. Now, he sought out and found a kerchief in the pocket of his trousers and with it staunched the flow.

For a while, and despite his best efforts, he knelt, trembling with the recalled horror of the Afghan. It was many minutes before he had the sense of mind to take the candle and, kilting himself with a large towel, descend the stairs and open the door onto the yard.

Outside, the world was still and unnaturally silent. He could see very little in the thick darkness. It might have been the centre of a desert, did he not know otherwise, except that the air was unpleasantly warm. Lightning flickered in the far distance, casting a sudden transitory glow in the clouds.

The candle he held darkened the night around him still further and helped to fill it with the fears that had wallowed obscenely in his dreams. He went slowly to the pump, looking about him as he went, peering into the blackness. He saw nothing. There was nothing to be seen that should not have been there. But the darkness always reveals more than it conceals.

At the pump, he held the candle at an angle and allowed molten wax to drip onto the casing of the handle. When he had made a large enough puddle of the congealing fluid, he set the candle down on it, fixing it firmly in place. The flame flickered suddenly in an uncertain breeze. Shadows danced wildly. Rowland waited until the flame was steady once more.

Taking a deep breath through his mouth he began to crank the handle. The noise of its movement and the subsequent flow of water seemed to fill the dark as if it were intent on waking the whole village. But no lights flickered in distant windows. No dogs barked. Not one thing stirred. It was lonely in the night.

Soaking the bloody kerchief in the fresh, cool water that he had pumped up, Rowland wiped the sticky gore from his chest and legs. He leaned forward to let the continuing flow of blood drip into the small wooden trough. Occasionally he dipped the kerchief into the water and wiped his face. The ripples he made in the night-blackened liquid glowed like a smoky ruby in the candlelight.

For nearly half an hour he let the blood slowly drip from him, mesmerized and calmed by the quiet splash as it fell. Long after the candle expired, the flow gradually lessened and then stopped, blocking his nose with a hardening clot. He blew his nose into the kerchief to clear the mess and then breathed deeply through his nostrils. No more blood came.

Weak now, bathed in a slick sheen of sweat, he tipped the water from the trough onto the packed soil and cranked up some more. The noise did not seem so bad and his eyes had long since grown accustomed to the darkness. The fresh water was cool and reviving as he scooped great handfuls over his face and head. When he was finally satisfied, he stood and smoothed the water back through his close cropped hair.

With legs trembling from fatigue, he went back inside, closing the door carefully. Once inside he dried himself with the towel and then draped it over the back of a chair. Slowly, he climbed to his bedroom. Upstairs there was little evidence of what had happened. A new candle revealed only a few dark spots on the boards of the floor. His first panic had magnified the effect. He blew out the candle and, exhausted to the uttermost, climbed gratefully onto his bed and slept, peacefully and still.

*

The new day dawned dim. Thick, heavy cloud obscured the early sun. Rowland watched the gathering mass as he sat on his doorstep and ate his breakfast. It moved slowly and steadily from the south west, a vast procession of sculpted forms that showed no sign of breaking. He sat for a long while, eating and drinking more than was normal. After his loss of fluid in the night he felt in need of sustenance.

When he had finished eating, he put the sunless sky from his mind and set to work. The morning was spent washing dishes and clothes and tidying the interior of the house. He worked slowly, steadily, and methodically to conserve his energy in the enervating heat. By the time he had finished inside and all was ordered to his satisfaction, the clothes he had pegged out on the line were dry.

After lunch, another substantial meal, he washed himself, dressed in fresh clothing, and then filled his army pack. He had resolved to leave that afternoon on the walking holiday suggested by Dr Joyce, but in the heat the idea soon palled when he put it to a firm test. He put the pack to one side and returned to the book he had been reading the day before. The time would come right.

When he had read the first sentence of the next chapter some half a dozen times without actually taking it in, he closed the

134

book and tried to sit calmly and simply accept the imposed constraints of the weather. He sat thus for some while in a near transcendental state. The day, already dim, darkened further and from a great distance, out to sea, came a faint growling of thunder. The deep resonances in the air disturbed Rowland and he became conscious once more of his surroundings. Restless again, he stood and wandered into his garden. There, a degree of calm settled on him once more. In the darkening day he looked across the valley towards Cobb Hill.

Moving round to the front of the house, he felt the hot breeze as it blew along the valley from the coast. And there to the south, on the horizon, superimposed upon the high overcast, lay a heavy black line of thunder cloud. It was a vast and louring wall that seemed to fill the far end of the valley. Faint flickerings of light illuminated the interior of the dark mass. Rowland felt a sensation closely akin to menace.

With a sudden urgency born of some deep instinct that told him he should be elsewhere, Rowland entered the house. He closed and locked all the shutters on the windows. Leaving his pack upstairs, he left the house, locked the door, and began to walk with long, quick strides towards the woods on Cobb Spur. His ultimate destination was a mystery but he knew, without the slightest doubt, where the first steps of that journey should be taken. He felt a degree of ease return to his mind.

In amongst the trees, he gave himself up to whatever it was that now directed his life. He wandered, less hurried than before, peering into the shadows of now and of then, half lost in his memories of the dance and of the bright and captivating beauty of his partner. So he wandered until the night came, unheralded in the gloom. And still his feet fell softly on the ground, his eyes aware only of enough of his surroundings to prevent himself stumbling. But now his feet were falling upon an ancient path that took him onwards by its own route through the world.

Lightning seared the distance and thunder shook the darkness with long, rumbling, echoing concussions. Strong forces filled the night air in great swathes; a great slow storm of magic that caught at his spirit like the wind would catch at his clothes. It buffeted him and tugged him hither and thither across the path, but the path was not yet ready to release him.

Time was disturbed. Vortices shivering along the edge of the main stream broke temporarily free to become sudden and dislocating cross-currents. They followed him upwards, creating about him a new and relative temporal logic. As he climbed, so he journeyed with the magic of the wild place. He let himself be swept along by the currents there, kept buoyant by them, knowing they would tear him apart if he struggled against them. And at some point he was unaware of, he crossed the bounds from one realm into another, a new realm where he might be counted as one who belongs.

The storm of magic died away. Rowland was left standing with an inner calm and sense of being the like of which he had never experienced. His whole substance was in harmony with his environment. High above him, storm clouds had also closed off the new world in which he now walked. Ancient and ageless spirits stalked beneath the trees which whispered with the wind. The topmost branches sang a running water wind song but there was no dancing. Looking through the gaps, he saw down into the valley where water burned with a phosphorescent light, sparkling in the storm-laden air. Vague shapes swirled their immensities in folds and whorls at the very edge of vision. All the signs of men were gone.

Ideographic shadow forms jumped up and away, frightened into movement by the sudden incandescent flickering in the cloud. Rowland moved up the slope and left the shelter of the trees to stand in the wind and the thunder that beat upon the top of Cobb Hill. His eyes, attracted by the flickerings of light, were drawn up to the clouds. They ran like thick dye in slow water stirred. Within the heavy moving folds, lightning played back and forth in many subtle colours, creasing the air with the splitting crack of stillborn thunders. Great and multiform flickers of light crazed across the sky in interlocking webs that resolved into forks that struck the earth and sent out their noise in vast, deafening waves. Vulnerable, but uncaring, Rowland stood upon the hilltop, half suffocated by the heat, stretched taut by the tension of vast energies that crackled all around him.

(-)

An electric blue needle of blinding light pierced the air, coursing back and forth between cloud and ground in millisecond flickers, overloading Rowland's eyes with energy before he could blink. Simultaneously the sharp, explosive crack of thunder compressed the air in his ears beyond real hearing. He felt it assault his body in a sudden blast that stunned him as it threw him backwards through the air. As his senses began to return, the waves of a second blast of thunder battered him.

Rowland climbed painfully to his feet and staggered beneath the swift passing agony. His mouth was suddenly dry, his heart beat furiously, his ears ached, his whole body trembled. Yet, just as painful to his self was the sharp image that was etched brightly into his mind; of blue lightning in a great, searing, jagged fork that leapt downwards from the cloud and split into a double tongue that spanned the half league between the peaks of Wealden Hill and Cobb Hill; of the valley below painted in searing light and absolute darkness. A valley he did not quite know.

Blinking into the night, temporarily blinded, he could see only what had been seared into his retinae. Directly below, the valley floor was marshy, the river running through in a barely recognizable course. To the left edge of his vision had been the storm chopped surface of a broad lagoon, waves lapping at the shores of two small islands. Thick forest grew everywhere on the high surrounding hills except for Wealden Hill and the area directly beneath his feet. There, below, a carved figure sat with its chalk head in hands.

As his vision returned to normal, the worm-like coruscations of negative light slowly fading, so did the valley he knew. Illuminated by almost continuous flickers of light from the storm, the familiar features were revealed. There again the meadows and fields of the dry valley floor, the turf covered hills, the well defined course of Cobb Reach flowing into the Rushy. Thunder echoed across the downs. A fierce joy coursed through his body. The magic of storm and earth had empowered him.

He felt like a god in the act of creation. The worlds below him were his, part of his being, just as he was part of them. And the joy and the power came together within him. He reached out his arms and encompassed the world, drawing it and all its wild magic into himself. He raised his arms high to the heavens, reaching for the power there. Above, in the light torn sky, leaping, skittering spears of energy burned across the clouds, seeking the distant horizon. His head reeled, his fingers stretched.

And there was silence.

The sky was suddenly dark and the air was still. But he knew it was not an ending. The storm was by no means over. Some power had simply reached out and now held it in sway for its own purpose. Rowland held his breath, expectant. Time passed. Slowly, he lowered his arms and drifted back into himself, reducing to his essential self, shrinking without becoming smaller. And still he waited. Something more, he knew, was yet to come. Listening intently, he heard nothing. The darkness thickened.

His eyes moved through the night, searching, resting at last on the barely visible form of Wealden Hill. There, not far below the peak, a thread thin, vertical line of light appeared, bright and steady. Perfectly still now, Rowland watched as the line broadened and the light was thrown out, down the grassy slopes of the hill. The line became a rectangle and the thrown light a wedge, fading in intensity as it ran off down the hillside. A door had opened.

Again Rowland waited. There was a moment of repose, charged with an undercurrent of expectation. An errant bolt of lightning cleft the night and grounded itself away to the east, the thunderclap sweeping along the valley in a deep rolling growl. As the violent sound died, Rowland heard a faint music emerging from the air, a slow, regal march that conveyed a sense of dance. It grew no louder but, the longer he listened, the clearer it somehow became.

With the clarity came shadows. Inhabiting the depths of the light were dark achromatic shapes, vague at first but becoming more sharply defined the closer they came to the surface. Long threads of darkness ran before them, weaving along the ground. The number of shapes grew and the light, now shot through with so much form and shadow, took on a flame dance of its own. Slowly, the shapes moved out through the great doorway and onto the hillside. Small, flickering lights appeared in the darkness, flaming torches held aloft, casting their light onto those who held them.

In single and stately file, the inhabitants of the hill issued forth, moving in step to the music. As the line of figures moved across and down the dark slope and further away from the light streaming from within the hill, an astonished Rowland was able to see shimmering multi-hued light playing about the figures. It was faint, as if restrained or at rest, but it was unmistakable. These folk were her folk.

The line grew ever longer, curving down the slope and around to the east. The leader had disappeared around the edge of the hill long before the tail end of the procession emerged from the doorway. Rowland watched with ever increasing fascination and surprise. There were so many. Eventually, however, the end came in sight. As the last one finally emerged through the great doorway, the light from within the hill faded until it was a gentle glow.

As he watched them moving away, Rowland realized he was straining in their direction, filled with a desire to be with them. And suddenly, then, he was afraid. Afraid they would leave him behind. Afraid he would not be welcome amongst them. His first step was hesitant. His next took him onto the top of the steep slope of the hill where he had stood. From there, he ran.

Very quickly the momentum of his body took him beyond any hope of stopping, yet his feet fell sure on the rough turf of the hillside. Down the length of the head of the chalk figure, across the chin, between arms and over the knees he rushed, his eyes focused on the disappearing distant line of mingled torch-flame and fay-light that snaked around the edge of Wealden Hill.

In those first exhilarating moments he felt he was flying, although he knew he was closer to falling. The scarp slope down which he rushed had once had a gently sloping base and the transition from slope to level had been an easy one, but the valley had long since filled with silt. The valley floor rushed up towards him and his knees buckled with the sudden change of angle, pitching him forward. Somehow he kept his feet beneath him and ran on towards the river, moving to his right, trying to keep the procession in sight. Long grass whipped about his legs and the uneven, marshy ground kept trying to trip him.

As he reached the high bank of Cobb Reach, the last torch was eclipsed by the edge of the distant hill. Rowland slowed his pace, drawing deep draughts of the night air within him as he concentrated on his immediate surroundings. He trotted upstream along the top of the river bank, searching for a way to cross to the other side. A crude plank bridge built by shepherds served his purpose and he was soon across.

Close to the eastern foot of Wealden Hill he stopped, air burning in his lungs, a sharp pain in his left thigh. He squatted and rested, gathering strength for the climb before him. The faint light that issued from within the hill was just visible from where he crouched and, for a moment, he was tempted to make straight for it. Deep inside, though, he knew he could not enter until he had been invited, until he had danced with the others.

With shaking legs, he began to climb the eastern flank of the hill, following the direction so recently taken by the torch bearers. Rounding a slight spur, he expected to catch a glimpse of the torchlight but saw nothing. For a moment he was nonplussed. It had clearly taken him longer than he had expected. Now he no longer knew where the procession might be. And before him lay a choice of ways. He could carry on, to Green Down, a broad low hill to the north, or he could climb straight up, into a dip between the down and the northern slope of the peak of Wealden Hill.

He knew there was no way that he could find and catch up with the procession, so he had to hope that they intended to make a circuit of the hill and return to the door from the western side. Taking a deep breath, he climbed up into the dip and passed around to north of the crest of Wealden Hill. Here, tall grasses grew breast high and he wandered through them causing a faint rustle as he went. The clouds had thinned in places and a vague, weak moon showed, casting a watery and intermittent light. In the darkness, it was enough to give depth and solidity to the looming shape of the landscape.

Wandering on, he eventually drew level with the gap between Wealden Hill and Rushy Edge, the ridge that stretched away westward towards Hamm. There he stopped, uncertain, looking up to the moon washed slopes that surrounded him. All was silent and still. He could do no more than wait. Thick cloud crossed the moon and it became dark for a moment.

Out of the stillness, out of the silence, there came a sound. At first he did not hear it, but sensed only its presence. It grew until it touched the threshold of his conscious hearing and grew still more until it was music. He gauged the distance and direction. It was coming from Wealden Hill. He had missed them. For a second the strength went from his legs and he wanted to sit down and cry, but he did not for the music continued to grow louder. Hope that had so quickly guttered and died, sparked anew.

Whilst Rowland stood in the dip, still staring towards the crest of Wealden Hill, a light appeared over the crest of the western slope of Green Down, behind him. A flickering light, tiny tongues licking at the darkness. It began to move down the slope towards Rowland, followed by another and yet more. Rowland then knew the trick of the place. The music was echoing from the hillside before him. He turned and saw the procession approaching.

It was a great and stately dance that moved towards him, an act of living worship by those who knew the earth and her ways, and he watched in awe with joy in his heart. The flickering lights of the torches touched the sky and the woken auras of the dancers ran across the grasses, all casting dancing shadows that moved in empathic contrast. A great rustling of legs in grass complemented the music. A great beat of feet upon the earth pounded rhythmically through the frame of every being there. And the music was the energy that drove them on. Closer. Dancing. They turned and they wove, many individuals each with their own part to play and a whole people knit together, and suddenly they were upon him.

The procession began to pass by and Rowland's head turned back and forth in his anxiety to miss nothing. Faces turned to him and smiled and he smiled back, finding it difficult to keep still. Men, women, children, creatures all of some other world, danced about him. The very earth beneath him and the air about him were filled with the dance. And the dance was within him as well. Not quite knowing what to do, he stood transfixed until his dilemma was resolved by a hand that reached out to him. He looked and saw that it was she who had led him before. She embraced him and took him by the hand and led him once more, this time into the celebration.

By the time he was over the first flush of exhilaration and better able to take in his surroundings they were all on the crest of Wealden Hill and passing the great open doorway set into the southern slope. The music changed then from dance to march to slow walk and finally stopped. Silence swept over them with the force of thunder. All, including Rowland, were still, standing in a great circle about the crown of the hill. The excitement and elation of the dance faded.

At a single moment, all turned to face outwards to distant boundary fires that flared and died, and then inwards, whereupon the torches were extinguished. In the darkness that was silent, in the silence that was dark, a palpable wave of sadness broke over them all and slowly receded.

Rowland looked up to see stars in a clear, warm sky. Unfamiliar constellations burned with the bright and fiercely confident energy of youth over a strange but familiar landscape. A gentle wind sprang up and the stars were gone, cloud covered. Running across the assembly, the air seemed to blow away the last of the sadness. Gradually the circle broke up into small groups, some lively, others of quiet companionship, and they all made their way towards the great doors in the side of the hill where the light now blazed brightly again to welcome them home.

Hand in hand with his lady of the dance, Rowland lingered, moving in a shocked dream state. They were the last to reach the doorway and the first drops of rain fell cool upon their flesh. The power that had suspended the storm was now withdrawn. Lightning seared the sky and thunder rolled in great echoes across the land. As they came in under the doorway, the rain fell in strength, the scent of dampened earth following them in.

The roar of the rain was cut off as the doors closed behind them. The sound of the doors closing echoed deep into the heart of the hill. Rowland did not look back.

(-)

Just within the main doors, side doors opened onto what Rowland guessed was some form of gatehouse. Immediately beyond that, great tapestries lined the walls of the bright, broad, high tunnel. They were suspended from massive, age-blackened beams of oak. Worked with thread of vivid and natural colour they were broad panoramas, views from the hill by sun and moon. Rowland looked at them as they passed. They had taken many years to complete and were endowed with the craft and the natural magic of their makers for they seemed alive, capturing the life that was the valley as it once had been and as it was now.

Beyond the tapestries, passages branched off to either side, both curving gently away to the north where the great circle they formed was completed. In the dim recesses, Rowland could see stalls for horses, long empty but still well cared for. Gleaming silver on woven horse hair bridles, saddle cloths of velvet and finest linen, evidence of majesty and panoply, gone in a fleeting glimpse as he passed by.

His gentle companion led him firmly on down the tunnel. More side passages shrouded in shadow came and went. More wall hangings decorated their way. Scenes peopled with beings of grace, alive with exotic animals, great patterns of grand sweep and intricate detail featuring both sun and moon. Eventually, after what seemed an age, they emerged from the passage. It was, however, far shorter than Rowland ever after remembered.

From the passage, which had widened towards its end, they came out onto a huge, circular gallery that surrounded a deep shaft which sank into the depths of the hill and deeper still than that. A carved balustrade ran around the lip of the shaft, broken in the east and the west to permit access to two great curving stairways that descended in a double helix to the lower levels.

Globes of multi-hued light hung motionless in the air, banishing shadows with their soft effulgence. Looking all about, at the vast domed ceiling carved from the chalk, at the intricate designs in the woodwork, Rowland finally turned to face his companion. He had come thus far on the high crest of his joy. Now he was deep inside the hill and uncertain about what next to do in this new world. She smiled encouragingly and, with a gentle tug of her hand, led him to the western stairway.

Standing for a moment on the top step he looked down and saw the great sweep of the two staircases descending hundreds of feet into the heart of the hill. The carved balusters alone represented thousands of hours of craftsmanship, each one a unique design. The whole was a feat of engineering the like of which Rowland had not seen in any of the many exotic parts of the world he had visited.

His rapidly filling mind overflowed with new experiences and he could no longer take in all that was around him. The descent seemed to take a very long time but he could not, afterwards, recall how many levels they had passed. After they left the stairs, moving through many bright passageways was all he could afterwards remember. Entering and crossing a large hall, in which an enormous fire burned, occupied by groups quietly conversing, others alone, reading or quietly meditating. Up steps and turning to climb further to turn once more and descend deep into a broad thoroughfare, turning a last time through a door into a suite of rooms.

Of the woman who had brought him here he had no recollection at this point. Alone in a room from which opened several doors, he moved slowly to a large, tapestry covered settle that stood slightly to one side of a burning fire of rosewood. The confines of the room, its comfort, its atmosphere, all conspired to soothe him. Sinking gratefully into the cushions on the settle, he rested his head against the back. The exhaustion of his body and the exhaustion of his mind brought him swiftly to the edge of sleep where he drifted, surveying the room.

Pale oaken walls, finely but simply carved with decorative knotwork; a curious alcove high in the wall to his left where a window might be, lined with a carved relief composed of many native timbers, depicting a river bank with swans and lit by some hidden source; appended to the corner and reached through an open arch between fire and alcove, a small sanctum whose details he could not see for it was in deep shadow; in the corner on the other side of the fire a curtained doorway with the curtain drawn back and the door ajar. As he looked, his eyes closed for a final time and he slept.

Once, stirring, he woke briefly to see the small sanctum brightly lit, the illumination a faint green that complemented the grassy richness of the floor covering. More of a large alcove than a room, it was octagonal, seven walls lined with books, the doorway where the eighth should have been. On a small circular seat in the centre, his lady sat reading. Her head was bent over the large book that rested upon a small lectern. He felt he wanted to rise and join her, but sleep overtook him once again.

When next Rowland awoke, it was to a darkness more complete than he had ever known. He lay still, exploring the peculiar memories that surfaced in exotic bursts within his mind. His body conveyed messages that confounded him. He was not in bed; there was no starlight at any window. No starlight. Still cloudy, perhaps. And the storm? What had become of the storm? And such a dream. So vividly beautiful he could not but believe it was real. Except, of course, it just could not be. A thought that set a sudden and piercing ache in his heart.

Sitting slowly upright, he eased his aching muscles. He was devastated by his sense of loss. She had been so close. He had touched her. He had danced with her again. He had seen her in a private moment, reading. All as if their lives were deeply entwined. A stifled sob escaped his lips. For a moment he had forgotten the strangeness of his surroundings.

From his right came the rustling of a heavy curtain. There was now light in the darkness. He looked about. All he could see were the embers of a fire he had not lit. And through the darkness, following the sound, there came a movement. He was confused. The great storm. The procession. The long and confusing journey into the heart of the hill. It had been a dream. Nothing more. A dream that had touched his innermost and longest hidden needs. But only a dream. Only a dream. All his being rebelled, denied the possibility of it having been anything else.

A faint, quick light blew into the room and illuminated its dream detail. He closed his eyes. The sweet, clean scent of wild flowers teased his senses. A hand touched his and he opened his eyes again.

"What do you fear?" she asked gently.

He looked into her eyes of green and gold, but fear would not let him answer.

She searched his face for a clue. "You danced," she said as if that could be dismissed.

Still he was silent.

"You came to the call," she added.

"Why?" he croaked.

"Why should you not?" For her it sounded simple. For Rowland it was all impossible to believe yet equally impossible to deny.

She climbed to her feet from where she had knelt before him and moved away in a swift and graceful flow. From the shadows she returned with a tray on which were goblets and an ampulla of the finest iridescent blue-green glass. Placing the tray on a shelf by the fire, she sat on the settle. Carefully she poured some wine for them both. Rowland took it hesitantly and then sipped cautiously, watching her over the top of the goblet.

Her beauty affected him deeply, discomfited him to the core. It was a thing of purest nature for she wore no powders and paints. Nor was her hair styled by hand. It grew as its nature dictated, long and of palest silver, and was simply gathered in a ribbon of green velvet. There were no lines of worry about her features although a sadness seemed settled there no matter how much she smiled.

Her eyes, cat-like in form, and her ears with their gently pointed crests, though the most alien of her features, seemed to disturb him the least. What did disturb him was the knowledge that she was not human, something he knew without any shadow of doubt. She was, deep in her blood, of another race. Small of form though by no means diminutive. Glowing with light, dusted with the fragrance of wild flowers, gentle, a creature of utmost grace with a voice that spoke vibrantly to his soul.

"You sang," he said finally, of all the things he could have said or asked. "You woke me with your song."

She smiled and his heart ached with yearning.

"I couldn't see you."

"Nor could you then. There was still too much of the man in you."

He did not understand.

"Was it the same song?"

"It was."

"I was not sure. I could not remember it at first. It came only in my dreams. I only knew that I had heard it. That it…"

"Your ears were as your eyes."

He frowned.

"It will come clear, Rowland." She smiled a gentle smile. "Let all be still within you and the doubt will settle out, the shadows of unknowing will pass."

He sipped at his wine, unnerved by her use of his name. Of all that had come to pass, that unsettled him the most. In the end, he could only fall back on convention. "You have the advantage," he said quietly.

She made no reply, waiting calmly for an explanation of his remark.

"My name. You know my name."

Her answer was a laugh, a soft and soothing sound that quelled his fears. And he was amazed. He knew her laugh. She knew his name. They had, he now realized, been constant companions for weeks.

*

Rowland watched her with a growing and all too familiar feeling of unease as she moved about the chamber in her calm, precise manner. She had led him there without a word and he had followed passively, too confused even to think of refusing. He had long since stopped trying to question what was happening for he had joined a game, the rules of which he did not know. But he had, he conceded, joined it willingly.

The chamber was warm and bright, filled with the faint murmur of the water that flowed into a large and deep basin in the floor and thence out through the wall via a small, carved stone conduit. The whole room was lined with quartz that reflected the sourceless light. An array of crystal bottles was ranged on a stone shelf, along with herbs and hanging bunches of dried plants.

As the purpose of the room became clear to Rowland, his understanding prompted by the scattering of a handful of aromatic herbs on to the surface of the water, his discomfiture had grown to the beginnings of a mild panic. She turned and smiled. He felt his face grow hot for she was making no move to leave. At the same time he became aware of the stale odour that emanated from his body. Desperately, he looked for a screen. There was nowhere to hide.

It was a ridiculous situation. He had visited many bath houses during his time in the army. Indeed, they had proved to be a considerable source of intelligence. To say nothing of enjoyment. And not once had he ever felt embarrassment at the thought of being naked in the presence of women. Yet there was far more to this encounter than had ever been the case before.

He looked at her intently, silently pleading for her to leave. She was beautiful. She was, indeed, desirable. Yet he had been taught that those women you loved were respectable and those women who showed interest in pleasures of the flesh were not respectable; that the two kinds of women could not be embodied in one person. The hypocrisy was tearing him in two. He had already placed his lady of the dance on a pedestal. But she knew nothing of that.

She came to him and he backed to the door, feeling trapped. For a moment there was stillness and then she reached up to undo the buttons of his shirt. He brought up his hands sharply, but stopped himself from dashing hers away. Instead, he held them in his own. Their eyes met and he was at once confused and elated by what he saw. It was a feeling he did not understand. Her hands turned in his and their fingers twined and then slipped apart.

To hide his confusion, he undressed quickly, throwing his clothes into a heap near the door. Keeping his eyes to the ground, he sat on the edge of the pool and slipped as fast as he could into the water. Surprise at its warmth momentarily distracted him from his extreme embarrassment, but it reappeared when he turned at a splash. She had disrobed and was now walking carefully down into the water on steps cut into the rock at the other end of the pool. She waded slowly towards him, the surface of the water rising up her body as the floor of the pool became deeper. He tried not to stare but it was difficult. He tried to prevent his body from reacting, but that was even more difficult. His embarrassment turned to misery.

"You must not," he managed to say as she came close to him.

She stopped directly in front of him, her head cocked slightly on one side. Her hair was beginning to float out behind her. "Why?"

He could think of no sensible answer, and in the confusion of his situation fell back on the most absurd of conventions. "We have not been introduced."

*

Rowland was alone when he woke. His sleep had been deep after a night in which many paradoxes had been resolved, and now that he was awake again he felt he had at last come home after a long journey. His body ached sweetly but he was content.

He lay on a soft couch beneath a quilt of swan's down and enjoyed the luxury. There seemed no reason to rise so he just lay where he was and let himself wake fully. When he eventually sat up, the room grew lighter. By the couch was a table on which stood a bowl of apples. The one he chose was large and firm and juicy and sated the first pangs of his morning hunger.

Stretching, he rose and, from habit, turned to straighten the pillows. Something rough brushed his fingers as he did so. On lifting the pillow he found an acorn on an oak twig and a piece of ash with its keys, laid side by side. He looked at them for a moment and then replaced the pillow. Unable to make sense of it, he pushed it from his mind.

On looking round, he found fresh clothes which he donned without too much thought, comfortable apparel which fitted well. It was not the conventional dress that he was used to, but such considerations no longer played a part in what was happening. This was a different world. Different standards applied. That was something he now knew all too well and was happy to accept.

Dressed, he moved from the bedchamber to the room to which he had first been brought. He had half expected her to be there waiting for him, but the room was empty. His first reaction was disappointment, but he was also glad of the opportunity to explore. There was so much here and he did not know for how long he would be welcome. The thought that he might have to leave was a depressing one. It was a place where he felt comfortable.

He looked about. Despite being deep underground, the living area had the same feeling of any room in the early morning. The air was dawn fresh and the light seemed just like early morning sunlight. In the fireplace, the ashes from the night before had been cleared away and fresh logs had been piled ready. The settle was pushed back away from the hearth and the cushions had been straightened.

He wandered past the fireplace and through the arch in the corner. The small sanctum was octagonal, one side being its entrance. The remaining seven walls were lined with books, just as he remembered from his brief glimpse. Carefully he took one of the large, heavy volumes from its shelf and laid it on the lectern in the centre of the room. Opening the pages revealed a work of art. It was written in a language he did not know, flowing letters that pleased the eye and spoke of wisdom. Illustrations and illuminations of delicate beauty and vivid colour decorated the text and displayed the skill and vision of those who had woven the tapestries that lined the entrance to the hill.

Perplexed by the familiarity of the strange script, he turned the leaves slowly hoping for some understanding. It came, in part, for it dawned on him that this was the written version of a language he already knew. Yet it did not help and with reluctance he closed the book and replaced it on its shelf. There would, perhaps, be time to learn, but there was so much else to see.

He crossed the living area and went out into the passageway. On the threshold he hesitated for a moment. It was a vast place and he wondered if he would not simply wander, forever lost. The notion was absurd, and it soon passed. Trusting to some inner knowledge he turned right and made his way to a broader thoroughfare where he stopped. All was quiet save for a faint music which he thought to search out.

Listening carefully for a while, he chose his direction. Through passages of opulent simplicity he wandered, climbing stairways and crossing halls, passing doors both closed and open. Throughout there was an atmosphere of patient and loving care, of a half deserted building - kept repaired and ready by the devoted few for some long expected return.

At his first encounter with another being he stopped. The faerie smiled warmly, bowing his head slightly in greeting, and continued on his way. After a moment, Rowland moved on in the same direction, overwhelmed by what he was trying to assimilate. This world, he had thought, was of children's stories and folk tales. Faerie folk beneath the hill. A people who must have been here for centuries. The implications were beginning to paralyse his thoughts once more.

He managed to keep walking, however, and before long, he found himself at the foot of a wide spiral staircase. Slowly, step by step in a wide curve, he began to climb up towards the music. Close to the top he heard a voice, her voice, singing again the song, in a language he knew not but whose meaning he understood. The shivering beauty pierced his heart.

Quietly, almost on tip-toe, he reached the top and found himself in an ante-chamber that led into a truly cavernous hall, the hollow interior of Green Down. Long and wide, its walls were lined with vast buttresses that curved upward to merge in sinuous patterns with the roof of carved chalk. But the architecture, breathtaking as it was, was not what held Rowland's attention, for the hall was filled with folk who sat at long tables and listened. And the tables were laden for a feast.

As he stepped from the ante-chamber and into the vast open space of the hall, those nearest turned and smiled, greeting him as if he were their dearest friend. He returned their smiles and then sought out the songstress. As he scanned the ranks of gentle folk he became aware that many of the places there were empty. The harder he looked, the emptier it seemed. At the far end, all the seats at the high table were vacant. No places were set there and they seemed long abandoned.

Rowland continued to scan the assembly and soon found her. She was directly across the hall from him, standing by a table. Sweet and low her voice, filling the great space; sad the well-known song. There was silence when it was finished and he came to her through the assembled throng to find tears on her face which he brushed away with his fingertips.

All the folk there gathered lifted their glasses and drank a silent toast, turning their attention then to the food. Rowland sat with his hostess and ate. Conversation grew in gentle waves and some of the sadness was dispelled. The wake feast was taken with a dignity that said much for the peoples who gathered for, as Rowland was later to learn, it was their own end that they feasted.

When the meal was finished they all descended to the smaller moot hall that Rowland had passed through when he had first come into the hill. There, the gathering arranged itself, some in a circle about the walls, some upon benches and chairs, others content with cushions on the floor. In the centre of the hall was a clear space. Rowland sat on a comfortable settle, hand in hand with his lady. Through the swift passing hours they remained together as tales were told and enacted, as songs were sung and joined. And through it all the enchantment cast by the great gathering of folk, living here unknown to the other world, never left him.

At some point of the day, after many hours had passed, the trance was broken as his lady left him to sit at a great harp of ancient and polished wood that stood behind them. She settled herself at the instrument and a deep silence fell upon the gathering as she began to play. The rich tones of the harp struck clear in the hall and reverberated from the ceiling with great but restrained power and sweetest clarity. The tune she played was one that Rowland knew from his own world as 'The Faerie Queen'. It played solemnly in his heart and he felt some vast and sparkling span of time within him, green and wonderful and so lately despoiled.

From somewhere across the hall the clear tones of a pipe joined the resonant sound of the harp and many heads turned. Rowland saw his lady smile to herself and he looked across the hall. The music continued, pipe and harp together. Rowland could not at first see the other musician. Finally, however, he saw him sitting cross-legged on the top step of the dais at the foot of one of the empty high chairs that stood there. He was a small fellow, child sized but unmistakably ancient, dressed in the colours of autumn. Rowland felt that he knew the diminutive creature, but was unable to place him. As he played his pipe he looked up, straight at and deep into Rowland.

When the music finished and he had taken his pipe from his lips, the small man bowed his head at Rowland in most solemn fashion. He then turned his head slightly and, smiling now in a way that betokened the thanks for a liberty taken and forgiven, nodded to Rowland's companion. She smiled in return and rose from her harp.

(-   )

Through the darkling and star-filled night they had wandered together, hand in hand, she sometimes turning about him in slow, almost absent-minded steps of dance, returning to his side and to his arms. The path they had taken led them through the orchards, the gardens, and the wild places of the Summer Land about the skirts of Wealden Hill. Descending from the high downs they had wandered through sacred groves and on to a place where the trees sang the softest of wind songs. Beyond that, and lower still, at a place between high banks covered in night-scented flowers they stopped to listen to the screeching call of a tawny owl that watched them, half-hidden in the branches of a tall tree. Then on, talking softly around and around, wandering hither and thither, all the while falling hopelessly in love.

Down sloping ways they went to the valley floor where they came at last to the shore of a great lagoon. Two islands, dark on dark in the cloud-clipped moonlight, were visible in the distance. The water's surface was still and smooth, yet unmistakably liquid. They stood at the water's edge and looked across to the far shore. A peace surrounded them; within them was turmoil. Each reached for the other, he searching for a way to bridge the gap that only he saw between them.

Stepping back eventually from the shore, they walked on to the north. Fields of wild grasses stretched away to their right and there, sitting on the trunk of a fallen tree, they stopped awhile to watch the sky lose its stars and see the high cloud glow in the first light of day. Rowland felt a fire burn bright and fierce within him and he folded his arms about her, held her tightly to him, lost and desperate. The years of loneliness and the shell they had created could easily be shattered, but he hesitated, still on the edge of an unknown world, safe, he believed, in the familiar.

As the new day grew, they turned back, walking slowly, still hand in hand. Their steps led them on to a point they could not avoid, yet still they stopped, embraced, kissed a long and tender kiss. By the lagoon, on a pebbly beach, they stopped again and stood awhile as the day grew yet brighter. From there they watched the birds that emerged from their nesting places in the reeds and swam across the water. In the distance, several black swans cruised silently in their majesty.

In sudden rage at all he could not understand about his life, which was most of it, Rowland lifted a stick of driftwood that lay on the ground and hurled it out onto the water. It sailed silently through the air and then fell with a muted splash. The ripples spread and died and they turned to look at one another. She reached up and he felt how cold her hands were as she touched his face. He took them and tried to warm them with his own.

Tired by the long walk in the cool night, they returned slowly to the place beneath the hill and lay quietly in the warm; she gazing into some world and past he could not know and could not share, he close to tears from the emotional turmoil that had erupted so violently and with such little warning within him. He wanted a hand to hold in the dark. We are islands and this fire in me is a signal, he thought, but is that all we can do, light beacons?

*

He woke with his arms about her. In the faint light he could see that she, too, was awake. Slowly they unravelled themselves from each other.

"What is this place?" he asked.

She turned her head toward him. "It is your home."

"My home?" He was surprised by her answer.

"It is where you belong."

He felt, on certain reflection, it was true, but he could not trust the feeling and shook the notion from him. Too many years of rational scepticism and hypocrisy had poisoned his intuitive heart. "I do not belong here," he said after a pause. "I am not of this world. Not of your people."

She did not answer. He turned to her and tried to read the expression on her face. It was one of infinite sadness. The face of a child that has found something precious only to lose it again, has reached out to catch it but had it slip, inevitably, from her fingers. Yet her expression was also tempered with an understanding he felt more than saw. She was guided by a wisdom that had long since enshrined free will and eschewed force. Perhaps to an unwise degree. It prevented her from saying more.

"I do not understand," he said. It was as much a plea for enlightenment as a statement of fact. Indeed, he knew that he had never understood. Locked inside himself, never certain of what others felt, building what he now knew were dreams about a certain look or a gesture, but never seeing if what he thought might actually be the truth. Always looking back. A life of standing on the edge.

"Why me?" he asked quietly.

She did not reply because the answer was obvious, deny it as he tried. But he must, he knew, come to the answer for himself.

He turned to her again. "Why am I here?"

"I called. You came."

"But why did you call?"

"To bring you home."

"Beneath this hill? Home beneath the hill?"

"Yes. To this valley. To this hall. There was no other chance."

"These are but riddles to me," he lied.

"Soon, Rowland. Soon…" she faltered.

Rowland felt the great weight of her sadness, felt it, he now realized, throughout the heart of the hill. She took his hand. "Soon we will no longer be able to leave our hill. The gifts that Gofannon gave to human kind have been abused. The world is laced with iron. It is that that keeps the children in. By Samhain, men will have threaded this valley, our Summer Land, with their poison."

He thought of the sweating gangs of navvies in Hamm who sliced deep into the earth, forcing a way in preparation for the railway.

"When this summer is done," she continued, "and when our harvest is in, we will close the doors and sleep."

"Sleep?"

"Yes, Rowland."

"But why sleep?"

"The iron rails cut The People from the Land."

"Is that all? Surely you could be content with this other world."

She looked at him. "Have you strayed so far?" she said quietly, almost as if to herself. "We are part of the natural order. The Summer Land as it was is part of the world as it is. We are one with the world. We cannot be divided from it or within it. Any more than humanity can for long pretend it is some thing separate from the rest of the world. Not without desecrating and ultimately destroying it." She sighed heavily.

"But are the railways really so bad?"

"You know they will be. You feel it yourself."

That much was true. They were a creation of man. The potential was in them for great good. The potential was in them for great harm. Of themselves, perhaps, they were a neutral thing. But the railways could never be a thing of themselves for they were the creation of human kind and inextricably linked with them.

"Not in and of themselves, Rowland," she replied to his thinking. He was startled, but had no time to express his astonishment for she continued talking. "They are one of the first and minor symptoms of the disease. It will run its course through the whole of human kind - and it may well kill them. There is much worse yet to be."

"You can see the future?"

"No, Rowland, there is no need. The future has already been. In our past. We know the disease. We know of the greed and the warfare, we know of the atrocities and the lack of compassion. We are an old people. Much older than human kind. We know what symptoms will manifest. We understand what suffering that will cause. Only the scale will be different. There never were as many of us as there are humans. We never embraced the material."

"So you will hide?"

"We are powerless to change it, Rowland. Our magic is of another kind. And who, of humanity, would heed what they are so confident cannot exist." He blushed at that. "No, Rowland, the power lies with human kind alone. It is their magic. Only they can control it. And such a power it is. It has broken ours to a degree we did not think possible." She paused for a moment, looking into some secret distance. "What the consequences of that will be we can only guess." She stopped, gazing once more into that secret place.

"But there can be change?"

"Yes."

"Then what is there to worry about?"

"There can be change, Rowland; it is not too late for that. But the will to change does not exist, except in a few, those few who have vision to see the full dread of the disease, those few who can see the coming of the storm clouds. Perhaps that vision can be made more accessible. Perhaps. We do not think so. So, we shall sleep."

"Can you sleep forever?"

"Not forever." She rose from the bed. "It need not be forever. There will come a day when we will be free to walk our ways again, pay court to the swans, look once more upon the sea."

He stared into the half-light of the room, watching her as she dressed. When she had finished she came back to the bedside and sat beside him, taking his hands in hers. "Will you," she asked, "be with us then to dance that first dance of a new age? Would you dance with me again?"

(-)

The rough, squalid details of his bedroom jumped into focus before his eyes and he sat up, staring wild-eyed and uncomprehending about him as if it were a nightmare. Poor, rough-cast walls; wood worked against its nature; crude designs on the badly made china-ware. None of it had been built to last nor had any of it been made with love. He closed his eyes, took a deep breath, and then opened them again. Understanding slowly dawned, dispelled the mists of uncertainty.

He rose from his bed and drew on shirt and trousers. Dust lay thickly upon everything, even the floor, undisturbed. Stale air and an evening dimness hung in the room. Slowly, uncertain of his movements, he opened the windows and shutters to admit the warm, evening breeze. In the distance, he could see a line of men working in a field, bringing in the last of the harvest. Beyond them, a pale dust haze hung in the valley about Hamm.

As he moved about the room, he probed gently into his mind, desperate to remember yet also scared that he might succeed. It seemed to him that although he needed to know, there was a sense of sweet and unbearable pain and he was not certain if he wanted face that. He shook his head, conscious only of an area of his memory into which he could not find his way. Still searching cautiously for what he knew to be there, he moved to the head of the stairs. There he stopped. A faint scent of wild flowers was in the air.

Downstairs, to his surprise, he found food laid out on the kitchen table. Moist, dark bread of many grains; fresh ripe fruit; sweet cake. But he did not heed the provender. The dark, uncertain area of memory was now uncompromisingly bright and certain in his mind. Beside the food, resting on a square of rich green velvet, was an acorn on its twig of oak, and a piece of ash with its keys.

(Sunday 3 September)
Only when he saw the villagers going to the church did Rowland know what day of the week it was. He waited until the service had begun before emerging from the schoolhouse. Everywhere were signs that the harvest was nearly over. Only a few fields, on the northern slopes of Brook Down, were still to be mown and even there men were already at work. Soon the last stoop would be cut and the dollies made to hang in their places until next year. And where, then, would he be?

To distract himself from the intractability of the problem, he set about restoring order to his parched garden. The sun burned hot on his sweating torso as he dug and weeded, carried water that was more difficult to pump up than before. He tried not to think of what had happened, of what might be, but there was no way to prevent it. Several times during the morning tears streamed down his face as he worked.

While fetching water from the pump, he had seen people of the village watching him from a distance. One had waved, Ruth Beckett, and he had lifted his arm in vague reply, forgetting her almost as soon as he had turned the corner of the house. From the garden, Wealden Hill seemed to loom large and his time there lay in his memory in stark contrast to the world now about him.

By mid-afternoon, he had finished restoring a basic order to the sun scorched patch of land and he could find no other excuse for putting off what he must do. But a decision would not come. There were too many unanswered and unanswerable questions. Too many questions he did not even know how to formulate. For an hour or more he stood staring at Wealden Hill until his overworked muscles, trembling already with fatigue, threatened to give way.

He left the garden and walked slowly to the river, conscious always of the hill behind its veil of heat haze, conscious too of the great doorway near its summit. On the river bank, careless of who might see him, he stripped off his remaining clothes and dived into the cool water. The shock revived him from the stupor into which he had drifted and he surfaced fresh bodied and, for the moment, empty headed. With strong strokes he swam upstream and into Cobb Reach, stopping only as he approached a wedge of swans. There he rolled onto his back and floated, allowing the slight current to carry him back home.

His world of river bank and sun-bleached blue sky moved slowly by unseen. It was only the shadow of the bridge that brought him to himself. And as he climbed out onto the hot, dry grass, the thought crossed his mind that he might have drifted on, further and further away, out to sea until, too tired to cope, he would have sunk gratefully beneath the waves. No decision would have been necessary then.

The anguish within him welled up and overflowed as tears.

*

Long shadows grew steadily longer, crossed the valley, and climbed the eastern hills. A cooling breeze played across the garden and bathed Rowland as he sat on the grass with his back to the north-eastern wall of the schoolhouse and watched the night come. He longed to leave it all and return to the hollow hill, but his longing was tempered with fear and with sheer disbelief. Sitting here, despite all that had happened, he could not know, could not be certain in his mind, that it had not been a dream. It was all too perfect. All too much of exactly what he wanted. And even if it were real, could he really commit himself to that long sleep to wake and walk into a world that the centuries had changed? If indeed it was a sleep from which a mortal could wake.

His thoughts turned to his companion, nameless to him, for he had never asked, had never gathered sufficient courage to ask. Her voice was clear in his head, the weight of her body a pressure he could still feel in all its detail. The silken gentleness of her hair lingered on his fingertips. A breeze ran across his face and he caught a hint of the scent of wild flowers that made him look up with heart beating wildly, but it was a memory, and nothing more.

His home she had called it. His home. A hill now awash with shadow. A vast, underground city and a world that was young, untainted by the stain of human kind. As he watched, a wedge of swans flew across the valley and dropped down towards Cobb Reach. With them came the night.

159

The first stars punctured the deepening darkness, sparkling bright, flickering as if flames were blown by a silent wind, a wind that blew across the desert in his skull. A crescent moon rose above the hills. With the faint extra light of the moon, Rowland was able to distinguish more clearly the outline of Wealden Hill. It was his home, she had said. The place where he belonged.

Absent-mindedly he rubbed his left thigh while he tried to dismiss from his mind all the peripheral thoughts stirred up by the enormity of his experience. He had, after all, only one thing to do; only one decision to make. He could stay, here, at the schoolhouse. Stay and watch the disease progress, perhaps speak out against it. Or he could leave and walk up the valley to join the sleepers beneath the hill.

Shadows in the darkness closed around him and danced between images of the valley he knew and those of the valley he had seen from Cobb Hill, the valley he had walked in so short a time ago. The valley seen with other eyes, eyes that were fay. Her valley. He shuddered. It was insane. How could he possibly believe what had happened to him? How could he possibly deny it?

FIVE
(4 September 1883 - 24 December 1883)

(September)

It was not immediately obvious to most folk in the valley, but by the end of August the weather had changed. Indeed, the change came quite suddenly. On the high Downs one or two shepherds stopped to stand and stare at the sky as they made their way along the old paths in search of their flocks. Their dogs, too, felt something, sniffing the air and walking with an air of canine contemplation. Few others but the wild beasts recognized the change and they were keeping their own counsel.

During the last night of August a great mass of high, thin cloud had begun to wheel across the country, covering the south and moving slowly northward. It lay, a pearly and almost luminescent grey in the sky, the underside rippled by high altitude winds until it resembled the sand of a beach rippled by the retreating tide. But they were the only winds. And they soon died away. All was then still, and stayed so for many days.

Beneath this high, dull ceiling a small group of boys with fresh, scrubbed faces straggled through the village of Swann, growing in number as they approached the school. As a group it was much the same as last year. Some were new, some were missing, and all were silent at first. The prospect of a new year at school cast its own high grey cloud of seriousness over them. Soon, however, they were laughing as one of their familiar schoolyard games got underway.

Last to arrive, as always, was John Elam. Walking slowly along the lane he watched the others gathering in the yard. A smile, devoured at the edges by pain, hovered across his face. He alone was unreservedly enthusiastic, in his own quiet way, about returning to school.

John Elam was no great scholar. He knew he was not. But he found a quiet and deep satisfaction in work in which he could compete on equal terms with others of his age. But more than that, he had a love of learning for its own sake. A love that had been allowed to flourish over the last year.

By the time he entered the yard, the others were already chasing full tilt in a game of tag. They smiled and waved at him as they raced by. He was the eldest now and much liked by the rest of the boys. Skirting them, he went to the pump and stood, waiting patiently for Mr Henty to appear with the brass hand bell.

As if under the influence of youthful high spirits, the high cloud began to break into vast whorls, glowing a sickly peach colour in the places where sunlight began to penetrate. John watched the sky with the experienced eye of one who has never been able to do much else in his spare time, but he felt uneasy, knew something was wrong. It was, to begin with, past nine o'clock. He turned his gaze to the schoolroom and the house. Both parts of the building seemed to be dead, uninhabited.

His uncertainty had an infectious quality that spread across the schoolyard and the game going on about him slowed and eventually stopped. The boys, flushed with exertion, gathered in a loose group about the pump where John stood. Despite his physical frailty, he was their natural leader now that Bobby Hall was no longer with them. In the silence, puzzled faces turned to one another and then to the schoolroom. No one spoke, for no one quite knew what should be said. No one moved, for no one knew quite what should be done. So they waited.

It was John who finally decided that some action should be taken and what that simple action should be. He moved, unspeaking, through the small crowd which parted to give him passage. Slowly, he crossed the yard and went to the schoolroom door. He looked back at the others for a moment and then turned to the door and knocked. He waited for a few moments, leaning with his ear close to the wood. When he was certain there was to be no response, he tried the handle. The door was locked.

Stepping back several paces, he stared at the door, confused. He knew what the situation was, but it was so new to him that, try as he might, he found it difficult to understand. The schoolroom door was locked. It was past nine o'clock. He shook his head and rejoined the others who were still gathered about the pump. They, too, were puzzled.

"What should we do?" asked one.

"Oughtn't we to fetch someone?" asked another.

"Perhaps he did not come back," said a third.

"He did," said John with quiet authority. "I did see him yesterday. Digging his garden." Little was missed by John Elam of the comings and goings and the goings on in the village of

Swann, though a great deal of it was beyond his understanding. But he knew pain and bewilderment and he knew it when he saw it in others. And he had seen much of it in Rowland Henty.

"I'm going to get the Reverend," said Albert Trickett.

"No," said John. "I shall try the house first."

Slightly awed by John's courage, the others followed him in a shuffling bunch keeping a few, safe paces behind. John stopped at the door, noticing the milk can on the step, untouched since Bobby Hall had delivered it earlier that morning. He knocked, more softly than he had intended. They all listened intently. After a long pause, John knocked again, more loudly this time. The silence that followed lengthened until the boys began to move slowly away, John Elam last of all and greatly hesitant.

It was the sharp, harsh, metallic clack of a key turning in a dry lock that stopped the boys in their tracks. They all turned back to face the door, John still the closest. For a moment nothing more happened. Some of the boys exchanged glances of puzzlement and doubt. Then there was a second clack as the catch was lifted. More glances were exchanged. Slowly, the door swung inwards and Rowland stepped onto the threshold, his pale face drawn, deep shadows beneath blinking eyes that burned red from lack of sleep. He stared wildly at the boys, uncomprehending, almost frightened. Finally, he focused on John Elam whose swan-dark bright eyes stared back at him.

*

The dead-weight heat of the long day had slowly lifted the last of the moisture from the land so that, as the day came to an end, it hung above the valley in a fine and mystic haze. In the distance, the landscape dissolved, drifting skyward in livid hues, backlit in the west by the tired and setting sun. A weary silence hung over the still valley.

All through the slow, hot hours of daylight everyone in the village had been conscious of the approaching storm. The day's business had been conducted lethargically and with an edge of irritation. Those who had no business to conduct sat quietly and waited in limbo with varying degrees of patience for some form of relief. School, too, had been unusually sober. With their energy sapped by the closeness of the weather, the boys had simply been too enervated to work with enthusiasm or even to lose their tempers.

But many hours had passed since the boys had gone and Rowland sat alone on the edge of his bed in the deepening gloom, staring at the floor. Several weeks had passed since his return, since his mortal fear had overcome his desperate longing and left him stranded. Several weeks had passed and only now was he beginning to come to terms with what he had left undone. The harvest had been gathered in both worlds. The granaries were filling. And the great doors in the crest of Wealden Hill were closed and possibly locked. He was now truly alone.

During the long evening hours he had spent in his room, he had reached into the depths of his mind and dragged his thoughts and emotions out into the open. Once there, he had examined them with meticulous care, ordered them, re-arranged them to better suit himself, begun to tell himself that he had made the correct decision. He had even dared to comfort himself with the notion that at some point in his future he would look back and know it had all been a dream, a sweet dream to balance the nightmare of Afghanistan. It had all been done with great care and a severe lack of conviction.

The schoolhouse bore small physical signs of the changes he had wrought within himself. Attempts to establish a new outlook. Attempts to link himself more strongly with the mortal world. In the schoolroom, for example, he had hung a framed photograph of himself with his unit, taken in India before the long, final trek northwards. It was a constant reminder of a terrible event. Of the fourteen men in the picture, he was the only one now alive. All the others had died in violent circumstances.

This evidence of Rowland's past had excited the boys so strongly, he had been forced to tell them something of his experiences to restore order and bring about an atmosphere in which the routine work of the school could continue. Telling the tale, and having to tell it on more than one occasion to the same audience, had helped greatly in exorcizing that particular demon from his soul.

The story had soon passed from the boys to their parents and thence right round the village. Very few of the villagers knew the exact circumstances of Rowland's past for the Reverend Beckett had respected his desire for privacy. Once the story was out, however, and once it had been quietly verified to the satisfaction of those who heard it, Rowland became conscious of a subtle shift in the relationship he had with the folk of Swann.

Far from satisfying their curiosity, what little he had told had merely fed the smoky fires of the mystery that had surrounded him. And in such a closed society as a village, the slightest flavour of the exotic is much savoured. The more exotic it becomes, the more it is taken to the hearts of the people. Even the dour Farmer Hall had been affected, explaining at great length his reasons for taking Bobby from school, seeking Rowland's approval.

A second photograph, a portrait of Rowland standing stiffly in uniform before the backdrop of his billet in Kabul, face proud and innocent, stood on the dresser in his bedroom. The photographs were some of the few possessions he had clung to on the long march that came with the collapse of the British presence in the Afghan.

Whenever he looked at the picture now, he found it impossible to recall the pride that was so obviously expressed in his whole demeanour. What he had seen and learned in that foreign land had sickened him. Yet, for all that, he derived a strange comfort from that image of the past. It was something he could easily understand and to which he could relate. It fixed him securely within the framework of his understanding of the world. It chained him securely to his humanity.

*

Echoing from hill to hill as it travelled, the sound of the explosion reverberated through the still air of the valley, dispelling itself eventually into the distance. When he heard it, whilst sitting at table for lunch, blood drained from Rowland's face. Normally pale, it became deathly white. For several minutes he sat unmoving, rigid with fear, his breathing erratic.

When the second explosion came, he left his lunch and went quickly out into the yard. The echoes were confusing and he slowly scanned the entire horizon before spotting the source of the noise. A dispersing cloud of pale smoke and dust was the marker. It hung about the chalk river cliff just to the east of Hamm. Rowland stood and watched the cloud slowly dissipate, unaware of the presence of the Reverend Beckett. The old man, who had been watching from the churchyard, had strolled across when he had seen Rowland come out of the schoolhouse.

"Quite an explosion, eh?"

Rowland span round, trembling. The Reverend Beckett frowned, somewhat taken aback by Rowland's sudden reaction.

"What is happening? What are they doing?" asked Rowland, his voice tight with anger.

"Clearing the base of Rushy Cliff for the railway. They will be using the rubble for an embankment further along, to keep the line above flood level, I believe." He looked at the schoolmaster's expression of incomprehension. "It was in the newspaper, Rowland. And notices were posted."

Rowland remembered, then, reading the notices to which the Reverend Beckett referred. They had been everywhere, but they had meant nothing to him at the time. Little did any more, if truth be told. "I... I must have missed them," he lied quietly.

Unhappy at the intrusion into his confusion, unhappier still at the cause of his confusion, Rowland returned to his kitchen. The Reverend Beckett followed. They sat in the cool and shady room while Rowland pushed the remains of his meal about his plate in an attempt to finish it. His appetite, however, had gone. The silence between the two men grew to an uncomfortable length and finally the Reverend Beckett rose.

"Well," said the Reverend Beckett, as if dragging himself reluctantly away from an interesting conversation and convivial company both, "I should be going. The boys will soon be back and I must not keep you."

Rowland looked up on hearing the old man's voice, emerging somewhat from the turmoil of his anger. "I am sorry," he said. "It was such a shock." He desperately needed to tell someone what had happened, but knew it was not possible. Who would believe? Instead, he played the old game. "I was taken by surprise. It is just that... The last time I heard a sound like that..."

"Do not worry, Rowland. There are some wounds that take much time to heal."

Rowland looked at the old man, nodded, then rose, walking out to the road to see the Reverend Beckett on his way. And there he stayed, waiting for the boys to return.

Through the afternoon the talk returned constantly and inevitably to the railway and Rowland answered what questions he could, struggling to keep the hostility he felt for it from tainting his voice. The mechanics of the system were familiar to him for he had travelled much by railway in India, and had seen much construction work done under the guidance of army engineers. Knowing the system, however, did not endear it to him. Even before he knew of its effect on the folk of faerie he had felt an instinctive dislike of the railways. They had suddenly taken travel well beyond the pace that had existed during the evolution of human society. He did not believe they could do anything, in the long run, but harm.

When evening came, he felt the need for solitude but was not able to bear the thought of crossing the river. That would take him far too close to the memory of what he had let slip from his fingers. Instead, he wandered in the opposite direction, across the corner of the water meadow to the church and sat in the tall grasses at the edge of the graveyard, hidden from the Vicarage. In the evening shadow beneath the trees he rested, looking down the valley towards Lower Cross and Dean.

Sapped of vitality, he stared empty-eyed across the meadows. Many were the slow changes that had been wrought through the long centuries to bring about the landscape before him. A gentle evolution that had stripped the trees away from most of the hillsides and allowed much of the soil to be washed into the lagoon, creating this fertile valley. Now, though, the violent hand of industrial man tore at its flesh, intent on rape. And what was all this that he could see? This victim about to meet its fate. The dream of some god? The work of blind nature? What did it matter? Humanity was awake and could see. Humanity had no right...

He let the confused thoughts drift away and sink without trace into the dark futility of his beliefs. How could you possibly fight it, this monstrous greed and fury that drove people to dominate? What could be done to make people see that they were abusing their gift of creativity? But their abuse also dulled their own senses, destroyed their ability to recognize what they were doing. He could not fight that, but only dream. Dream of the valley, green and quiet, and drink in the peace that would soon be driven away, was already being battered, by the grinding noise of the mindless machines that man had set running and could no longer control.

Dream. He tried to hum the tune of the song but faltered. What point in dreaming? What point in caring? He looked about him at the stones that littered this little field of the dead. All these here beneath the earth where he sat had dreamed. Of what use had it been to them in the end? Had their lives been free of fear and pointless toil? Had they regained paradise here or sold themselves to slavery in expectation of some future glory?

Rousing himself from the dim emptiness of his black frustration and despair, he turned to study the grave stones more closely. Even in death, the will to dominate was clear. The headstones of the rich stood tall and ornate. The markers of the poor were huddled at the edges of the field. For all that, it was the graves of the poor that were mostly better tended. Some, however, like the ones he sat beside, were long overgrown and uncared for.

He twisted round into a kneeling position and pulled large handfuls of tall grass away from the simple stone that was closest to him. It was done with no urgency. He simply felt the need to even the balance. When the grass had been cleared back from the stone, he dug with his fingers into the spongy cushions of moss to clear them from the letters carved thereon. It began with a dispassionate need to expose the stone once more to the common view, but he felt compelled to continue by the stunning momentousness of his findings, moving then from the first stone to that which lay beside it. When he had finished, nails broken, knuckles scraped, he read the simple inscriptions over and over, as if such repetition might answer the many questions they posed.

ARTHUR HENTY
1811 - 1847

MARY HENTY
1813 - 1847

1847. Not, then, his parents. Yet, he bore that name. Henty. He shared a first name. Arthur. Rowland Arthur Henty. They tantalized him. Simple inscriptions in slabs of stone. Simple, yet entirely obscure as far as he was concerned, for they told him nothing.

Eventually, he stood, seeing then the smaller, flat marker tucked away in the grass beneath the tree whose shadow covered him. More carefully this time he pulled away and prised off some stubborn moss, splitting the skin of one of his fingers so that it bled.

CHARLOTTE HENTY
1835 - 1853

A daughter of the others? So young. Yet, not too young. He had been born in 1853. At last, and so suddenly, here was a possible answer. A counterweight to the mystery that had already torn him. It was then that he felt the pain in his hand and looked down to see the broken and bleeding flesh.

*

During the week in which the blasting took place, Rowland visited the graves every evening. He cut the grass around them properly with shears and cleaned the stones with a stiff bristled scrubbing brush. As he worked at his task, he rehearsed in his mind the ties he had created with these long dead people and the subsequent objections that rationality sought to impose.

Why, after all is said and done, should graves in a village he had only recently made his home have any connection with him? He knew there was some family link, but his great-uncle had always been vague and Rowland's curiosity had always been satisfied. Would be still, he supposed, had he not danced and walked and slept beneath the hill.

It is your home, she had said to him. It is where you belong.

The memory of her voice was sudden and painfully distinct, as if she stood there with him. He sat back, discomposed, and looked across to the distant form of Wealden Hill. It was more than he could bear. He turned his eyes to the nearby bulk of the church and shivered in the cool breeze that had come with the last days of the month. The long, dry grass beyond the graves shifted uneasily expelling a dry and painful sigh. He felt the summer dying.

Five days had passed since he had found her. Charlotte Henty. Kneeling, he reached out and gently traced the name with his fingertips. She had died young and he could not put the year of her death from him. It was a tantalizing figure which, in his present state of mind, had all too easily grown to haunt him, had all too easily become an obsession. In the end, even after such a short space of time, he could no longer bear the uncertainty.

That evening, instead of leaving the churchyard and cutting back across the meadow to return to the schoolhouse, he strode swiftly along the lane to the side gate of the vicarage. He was anxious to put his questions before his sudden courage, born paradoxically out of fear, deserted him. The setting sun was eclipsed by cloud as he stepped up to the porch.

It was Ruth that opened the door to Rowland's excited knocking. She frowned when she saw him. He wore no collar or tie. His hands were dirty. All about him was an air of great distraction and neglect, far worse than she had ever seen before. Stepping back, in an instinctive display of 'good manners', she let him into the dim hallway of the vicarage, closing the door behind him.

In the gloom of the hall they stood in silence, frozen in tableau. Ruth regarded him with an expression of hesitant worry, clearly aware of the unseeing eyes behind the green lenses of his spectacles. She seemed caught up in a powerful surge of emotion she did not understand, but which emanated strongly from Rowland. He stood, transported suddenly and for some unknown reason to a darker lighter world. A smile haunted his lips for a brief moment.

And perhaps they would have stayed thus for much longer, each caught in the strangeness of the moment, had not Ruth's grandfather come to his study doorway to see who had called.

"Rowland?" The stillness was set a-shiver and Rowland turned slowly to face the Reverend Beckett. "What is it?" continued the old man, as taken aback by Rowland's appearance as Ruth had been. "Why are you here... and so dressed?"

Rowland said nothing, but pushed gently past him and went into the study as the Becketts exchanged worried glances.

"Some tea, I think, Ruth, if you would."

As Ruth turned to the kitchen, the Reverend Beckett went into his study and pushed the door to behind him. Rowland had crossed the room and was standing at the French windows, his attention fixed on Wealden Hill, which was partly visible through the trees. The old man called his name softly thrice before he turned his back to the outside world.

"You must tell me," he said staring fixedly at the old man. Rowland's mouth was dry with a fearful excitement and he spoke quietly with a broken voice.

The Reverend Beckett stared at the dishevelled schoolmaster. "Rowland, please sit down," he said sternly. "You are over excited. You must first..."

"Tell me." Again the words came low and broken voiced. Yet, despite that, they were insistent with an intensity that brooked no denial.

Silence, however, was all that followed and it settled with growing darkness in the room. The Reverend Beckett went carefully through the elaborate ritual of lighting the great oil lamp by which he worked in the evening.

As he put the match to the wick, eliciting a flame of golden orange silk, Ruth knocked on the door and entered the room carrying a tray. She stopped just inside the doorway, held by the tension between the two men. Her grandfather gave her a reassuring smile and motioned for her to leave the tray on his desk. She did so and withdrew, leaving with an anxious glance at Rowland who still stood by the window.

When the door had closed, the old man poured the tea and took the cups to the table that stood between the two fireside chairs. He sat down and looked across to Rowland. "Come and sit down, Rowland. Please."

Rowland did so. He settled into the chair and sank into a tired slump. On his face was a confused mixture of expressions that conveyed little but a strong sense of confusion. Something there also of a lost child, something of a very frightened man.

"Now," said the Reverend Beckett, taking up his cup and saucer as a kind of talisman of the calm and normal world to protect him from what was to come. "What is it that I must tell you?"

"Who was Charlotte Henty?"

The vicar sipped cautiously at his tea. His face betrayed no surprise. Carefully he returned the cup to its saucer. He looked at Rowland warily. "How much do you already know?"

"That she died in 1853, aged eighteen. That she is buried next to… next to her parents?"

"That is all?"

Rowland nodded.

"Surely your great-uncle…"

It was then that all the half-guesses that Rowland had made in the past few days began to fall smoothly into place. All the deceit of silence that had been contrived to conceal his past began, at last, to crumble away. He looked down at his hands, turning them slowly. They still bore the marks of his first cleaning of the graves. "He told me nothing," he said quietly. Then, more forcefully, he added, "Tell me about my mother."

"She…"

"Why did she die?" Rowland asked, looking up from his hands.

"She took a fever."

"Not how," he said, suddenly angered by the years of identity and memories that had, for some reason, been denied him. "Why?!"

The Reverend Beckett pushed himself back into his chair. "Because it was God's will."

Rowland looked sharply at the worried face of the old man and breathed deeply to control his growing anger. It was not the Reverend Beckett's fault. He had been kind, had presumably tried to redress the wrongs as he saw them. Rowland sat still and silent. Finally calm, he responded. "No."

"Rowland, do not presume-"

"I presume nothing." He cut in quickly, having no desire to continue on the obscure and circuitous path that others had chosen to impose on him. "My mother died, did she not, because she had a bastard son. She died of shame. Not a shame she would have felt herself," the whole truth beginning to dawn with a burning certainty, "but of a shame imposed upon her, no matter how inadvertently, by this narrow world. And the whole thing kept secret, even from me."

"You cannot know this." There was the slightest edge of desperation in the old man's voice and to Rowland it was nothing more nor less than an admission.

"But I do." Rowland looked directly into the old man's eyes as the truth of the revelation blossomed brightly and painfully

174

within him, adding harsh colour to the spare tale. "I have listened. Been taught. It is in the very earth." He paused for a moment, deciding how much he really wanted confirmed, and then continued. Anything less than all would never now be enough. "And what of my father?"

The Reverend Beckett put his cup and saucer on the table and sat back in his chair. He suddenly looked very frail, his hands trembling lightly. "Your mother would never say who he was. She ran away…"

"Ran away?"

"From the Reeves' house. She was in service there."

"Ran away?"

"It was August."

Rowland sat upright. It came upon him like a physical blow. Powerfully. Painfully. To the solar plexus. He felt like screaming with the accumulated frustration and anger and bewilderment, but smiled suddenly instead at the certain knowledge of a great and good beauty shared. It was something he had in kind with his mother though he had never known her. He continued to smile, but felt now like crying. "Yes," he said at last. "Yes. It would have been."

The Reverend Beckett looked at Rowland with a frown of puzzlement creasing his brow. "Why?"

There was no reply.

The Reverend Beckett tried again. "Why do you say that?"

But Rowland had turned in his chair as if listening to some distant thing outside the window. The anger and the pain had gone from him now, as quickly as it had come, replaced by a vastly dark and empty well of sadness that echoed with the sudden knowledge of a great and forever lost chance. He could see in his mind's eye the shores of the lagoon where he had walked hand in hand with his lady of the dance. He shut it away and turned back.

"August," he said quietly.

"Yes?"

"And she ran away?"

And out it came, the story he had for so long wished to tell. "Mr Reeve came to me himself. Very fond of Lottie. They both were. He did not know what should be done. Early one morning, knocking on the door. He babbled on but I finally got it from him that your mother had gone for an evening walk and not returned."

"Where?"

"I beg your pardon?"

"Where did she go?"

"I do not know. It was thought afterwards that she must have gone to the horse fair at Green and taken up with some gypsies. Then, two weeks later, the Reeves found her one morning laying the kitchen fire as if she had never been away."

Rowland was in something of a dream, so much had been recalled of his recent journey to that other world. "Horse fair?" he asked finally, simply to keep in touch with the conversation.

"It was banned the following year. But your mother insisted most strongly and consistently that she had not been there. It was most perplexing. I remember..." the Reverend Beckett's voice faltered and he looked at Rowland as if realizing something for the first time.

"What?"

"Something that your mother said." The two men looked at each other in the silken light of the lamp. The flame had turned the lenses of Rowland's spectacles to dark mirrors. "She was most adamant about it. She said that it was not possible to walk to Green and back in a single evening. No one understood what she meant."

Rowland nodded. He understood only too well. "And, on the first day of May of the following year..."

"You were born."

*

From the enclosing light of the house, Rowland moved into the darkness of the evening. Beyond the grey clouds the sun had long set. Fine drizzle, which had begun to fall as they talked, became rain as he crossed the back lawn of the vicarage. A cold wind gusted down the valley, stinging his face. The smile that had kept back the tears was gone and he wept openly and bitterly for all that was lost.

By the time he crossed into the darkness of the graveyard, the rain drove hard into the earth and he was soaked through to the flesh and shivering. In the dark he knelt and once more traced the letters of his mother's name with his fingers. The sound of

176

the pouring rain filled his ears as it beat against leaf and tree, grass and earth, hair and flesh.

Later, dry and warm, he lay in his room and listened to the steady beat of the heavy rain on the roof and windows. He was a person caught inside a person, trapped and looking out through strange eyes, utterly bewildered, for his captor was not malevolent. Just himself. Yet it was beyond his power to set himself free.

And into the prison, into the darkness, clear despite the sound of the rain, a voice. It is your home, she had said. It is where you belong.

He could conjure her so clearly in his memory. Her form, the scent of her flesh, the gentle and intense passion of their lovemaking, the sound of her voice in the darkness. Why had she not told him everything else? Why had she left it to him to find out? Now. When it was too late. He fought his exhaustion, but eventually he was left with no strength at all. With the monotonous sound of the rain still in his ears and a nightmare struggling horror growing ever more potent in his mind, he drifted into a restless sleep.

(October)

As the days passed by, the warmth of the sun and the chill of the wind were the only things that seemed able to touch Rowland directly. Nothing else seemed connected. It was all a hideous and painfully consistent dream. He directed the schoolwork of the boys as if from some great distance deep within, in control but no longer in touch. The joy was gone from his life, the spark all but extinguished.

With increasing frequency, when the commitment of school would allow, he would take himself up on to the broad hilltops. There he wandered in the many twilights of his being as he sought out the ancient trackways that crossed the land. He became a familiar sight to the shepherds who kept their hard vigil upon the downs. They would watch him from their special places and shelters or from beneath their great umbrellas as he walked, careless of the weather. They would watch him and wonder.

There, too, on the high top of Cobb Hill he would stand and watch the progress of the narrow embankment of the railway as it curved its venomous way along the base of Rushy Edge towards the foot of Wealden Hill. The incessant pounding of the work gangs and the bright cruel gleam of the newly laid rails were painful to him. When it finally became too much, as it always did, he would stride away with his memories, regrets, ghosts, and anger flurrying after him like a cloak stitched painfully through his very flesh and into his heart.

By night, he would sit alone staring into the darkness, slowly massaging his leg where the pain had now become a constant companion, a dull and sickening ache. He would sit until sleep came and the spark burned brightly in his dreams. Even there, there was no real respite for he slept uneasily and would often wake. Then the spark would flicker and die and he would sink back into the cold mist that was his future.

One Saturday, as his reason fell increasingly into shadow, Rowland was walking slowly back to Swann after visiting Hamm. He was in a trance-like state as he shambled along, unaware of his surroundings. And as he walked, he was overtaken by Mrs Reeve in her carriage. She had seen him briefly in the town and had been shocked. Closer observation did nothing to allay her fears. His face had an ashen pallor and the flesh had collapsed. He looked a sick man. Sick unto death.

As the carriage passed, unnoticed by Rowland, Mrs Reeve asked her driver to stop. He took the carriage on for a short distance and pulled it in to the side of the road. Rowland, aware only dimly of some obstacle, began to walk round the stationary vehicle. When she realized that Rowland had taken no cognizance of the carriage and was likely to walk right by, Mrs Reeve called to him.

Rowland stopped abruptly and looked up. He took a sudden deep breath and then let the air out slowly. He rubbed at his forehead in a distracted way, his eyes fighting to focus on what he saw. Recognition came at last. "Oh," he said. "Mrs Reeve."

"Would you share the rest of the journey with me?" Rowland stared at her passively. "The weather..." she said, finding nothing more to say despite the desperate need she had to explain all she knew.

Rowland looked up to the sky where heavy clouds were gathering. He then looked back and forth along the road, searching for something unknown, shaking his head with a puzzled frown. Finally he looked back up at the elderly lady. It seemed as if he were looking for some lost landscape, that the world he now found himself in was not the one he had set out in earlier in the day. The impression was so strong that she found it disconcerting, as if she too were lost between worlds.

The strange feeling was a fleeting thing. She opened the door of the carriage to reinforce her request. After a moment's further hesitation, Rowland climbed up, settling himself with his back to the driver. With the door closed, the carriage continued on its way.

The swaying motion of the vehicle rocked Rowland straight back into his reverie and he sat unaware of his surroundings. Mrs Reeve watched him as they rode, clearly disturbed by what she saw before her. When they arrived at her house, they alighted from the carriage and Mrs Reeve guided Rowland indoors. She took him into the small back parlour and sat him before the fire in the chair that her husband had favoured. Rowland was its first occupant since he had died. Few visitors were invited into this room. For formal occasions there was a much more spacious and now rarely used front parlour. When Rowland was settled, the maid was sent to prepare an afternoon tea for two.

Rowland sat staring into the bright, dancing flames. Eventually, without turning his eyes from the fire, he spoke. "Why did you bring me here?" he asked. It was the first indication that he was in any way aware of his surroundings. When he received no reply, he turned his attention from the flames to Mrs Reeve but she did not answer until tea had been laid out on a small trolley between them and the maid had departed. Mrs Reeve passed him sandwiches and cake. A strong gust of wind blew suddenly and rattled the windows, startling them both.

"I really do not know, Mr Henty," she answered finally. "Perhaps to explain," she offered, although there was nothing to explain. Just a story to pass on. "Your mother worked here. I feel… responsible."

Rowland scrutinized her face keenly, suspicious of such concern. Mrs Reeve returned his fixing stare with one of honest certitude. It was the truth that she had spoken. Rowland relaxed and sat back in his chair. "There is no need, Mrs Reeve. You were not responsible for what happened."

"But I am. Your mother was in my care, Mr Henty."

"Your care?"

"Oh, yes. Although she worked here. I..." She faltered and Rowland could see the distress, unexpected and poignant, that these long suppressed memories were causing. "We had no children of our own, you see." She looked straight at Rowland and he saw a sudden comprehension spark in her eyes. Of what, he could not say. "Her parents were dead," she continued as if in answer, "and-"

"Arthur," he said, interrupting. "Mary." He did not so much simply say the names as read them from the gravestones.

"Why, yes," said Mrs Reeve, gentle surprise in her voice betraying a memory recovered. "I believe so."

"How?" he asked softly.

"I beg your pardon?"

He was lost for a moment in the new and chartless world he had entered, trying to find some bearing. "How did they die?"

Mrs Reeve sighed. "In the fire."

Rowland searched his mind for the small hammer of memory that had just struck a chord. "East Fore." Where they had gone earlier in the year for the picnic.

"Yes. They lived in a cottage there." She paused for a while, clearly entering an unknown world of her own, a landscape of memories all too well charted, yet still laid out in a wider and unknown world. "Poor Lottie." Rowland looked down into the flames in the hearth and watched them dance as Mrs Reeve continued. "It had been a dry summer," she said slowly, "much more so than this, though by no means so sunny or hot. Your mother and grandmother were walking back home from church, here in Swann, one Sunday morning. Up through the woods on Cobb Spur. We saw the smoke here long before they did. Most of the men from the Swann hurried over in their Sunday clothes. Some on horseback and in carts, others running. Lottie told me later how they had reached Fore Hill before they realized there was a fire. They heard the noise first, she told me. A terrible roaring that they could not understand. Smoke began to drift their way. Then, through the trees they saw that the pasture in the Bottom was ablaze, the flames moving up the slope before a breeze. Moving up the slope to the cottages. There were only a few. They were all timber buildings. Fore Hill Farm property. Your grandfather was a shepherd there. He had always refused to go into business with his brother." Having lost the thread of the story for a moment, she stopped and sipped her tea.

After putting her cup down, she sat for a while staring at Rowland, but it was clear she was not really seeing him. Rowland waited. He drew his gaze from the flames and picked at a piece of cake. Rain spattered the windows noisily and then stopped. Somewhere a clock measured out the moments.

"Your grandmother, it seems, told Lottie to stay where she was and then ran to their cottage and went inside. She had said nothing more to Lottie, had given no reason. Perhaps she thought her husband was there. He was, in fact, with the rest of the men who were trying to beat out the flames. When he saw his wife run into the cottage he called out to her but she did not hear. He ran up after her and into the cottage. There was a sudden gust of wind. The buildings were engulfed. Tinder dry, they exploded into flame and burned fiercely. By the time help arrived from Under Fore and Swann, the cottages were completely destroyed and two others had also perished. Lottie was hysterical with grief."

They sat for a long time in silence, lost in their visions of the tragedy that neither had witnessed but which both felt so keenly. More rain was blown against the windows and it began to fall steadily. The day was passing. Mrs Reeve tried to persuade Rowland to stay for dinner but he declined and made to take his leave. In the dim light of the hallway he turned to the old lady.

"How did she come to work here?"

"My husband, God rest his soul, arranged it with Lemuel. The mills were flourishing and we needed a maid. It was better than that she should go into the orphanage at Hamm." She paused a moment and then, quietly, almost as if to herself she said, "Oh, she was such a good girl."

Rowland raised an eyebrow. "Am I not proof of something else?" he asked gently.

"No, Mr Henty, you are not." She said it with quiet conviction. "Do not ask me how I know for I have no evidence, nor did your mother ever talk of it, but I have thought of this a great deal over the years. She loved your father dearly and had, I now believe, known him for some while - whoever he may have been. And my husband and I were both agreed that she should stay here with you where you could both be looked after."

Rowland wanted to know more but let it rest. The day would come. "Thank you, Mrs Reeve."

"Before you go..." Rowland looked at her in the shadowy quiet of the hallway, a small, pale creature dressed in her habitual black. "Lottie... your mother..." He waited patiently for her to continue. "She did not speak of what happened."

"It would have been difficult," he said.

She did not look at him. "Yes. We did not make it easy. Not out of spite or anger. It was the way we were, and probably still are. I do not know." She lapsed into silence once more and Rowland was not sure whether there was any more to be said. As he was about to turn to the front door, Mrs Reeve spoke again. "She kept a small box. Her only treasure. I had forgotten."

"I beg your pardon?"

"Your mother. After... Afterwards. She kept a small box. I have it still. Come. I will give it to you. It is the least I can do."

She turned and began to climb the stairs, beckoning Rowland to follow. They went slowly up through the darkening house to the top floor. At the far end of a narrow corridor, Mrs Reeve opened a door. Tucked in under the eaves, the room was small but light. It was bare now, just a bedstead with a mattress, a chest of drawers, and a wardrobe. On the floor a rag rug. He stood in the centre and looked around, moving then to the window. The rain had stopped and in the failing light he could see across the rooftops of Swann to the dim form of Wealden Hill. He shivered. A faint rainbow stood above the peak. Tears formed in his eyes and he took off his glasses to brush them away with his fingertips.

As he stood watching, the silence was broken by the sound of a drawer being opened. He turned to see Mrs Reeve take out a small box. She brought it to him. It was of oak, exquisitely made, with a swan carved on its lid. "It is all that is left."

He took it and opened it. Inside, resting in a fold of faded green velvet, was an acorn on its twig of oak, a piece of ash with its keys.

*

The afternoon was passing swiftly. The lesson was nearly finished. From the older boys at the back of the schoolroom where they were clustered there was a soft buzz of noise as they worked together on a task. The younger boys were gathered around the blackboard, helping each other to solve the problems of long division that Rowland was setting.

He had turned to the board to clear it for fresh work when the pain came. It was sudden and all consuming. It reached his whole body from a small and fiercely intense centre. It was a sharp spike of iron driving through the wound in his leg. It brought tears to his eyes and sweat to his brow before it faded, leaving a sickening ache and a tiredness in his limbs. Slowly he put the duster down.

Turning carefully to the boys he forced a smile and said, "That will be enough for today, I think."

Overjoyed at their sudden and unexpected release from their struggle with the slippery numbers, the boys did not notice what had brought their lesson to an early close. Only John Elam, who knew pain, had noticed and he said nothing because he understood that for some, pain was a private thing.

After the boys had tidied their books and things away and gone, Rowland locked the schoolroom door and limped slowly into his kitchen. A terrible and sick ache had settled behind his eyes and he moved slowly in order that he might not aggravate it further. He sat awhile and picked at some food, attempting to delay the inevitable. He did not want to go any more to see the hill. He did not wish to be reminded of his own stupidity, his arrogance, his deep and fatal ignorance. He was tired to the very depths of his soul of the whole hopeless mess. So very, very tired.

Eventually, though, he left the house and made his way across the river to Cobb Spur. There was no escaping what he must do. No escaping the role he still had to play. He tried, however, to delay it. Beneath the autumn trees he sat awhile on the cold, damp ground and massaged his leg but the ache would not go.

183

Nor the sickening pain behind his eyes. Nor the compelling need to move on.

With a terrible sense of foreboding, he clambered to his feet. As he stood, the dampness seemed to have become a chill part of him. It clung and hung about him as he climbed slowly and painfully through the trees to the top of Cobb Hill.

Up there, the air was crisp and clear, sharp in his lungs, and the distance could be seen in great detail. The raised chalk scar of the railway embankment had lengthened, heading off to the east, broken only by Cobb Reach where a large gang of men was working on the construction of a bridge. The sound of hammer blows on stone and the pounding of rubble throbbed in the air and set up a pulse in the pain behind his eyes. It was not the bridge, however, that held Rowland's attention.

Gleaming in the westering sunlight were the steel rails on which the trains would eventually run. Already they had reached the foot of Wealden Hill. And there, its flatbed trucks backed up close to the end of the line, a greasy locomotive stood, a wisp of sulphurous steam rising from its stack. All around it, like a colony of insects, a second gang worked in a well worn rhythm born of long practice, laying the rails and hammering in the spikes that would tie them to the sleepers. They worked hard and fast, weary as they must be, in order to achieve their quota before the sun set.

As Rowland watched, the track grew. The pace was steady and inexorable. Long since set in motion, there was no way in which it could now be deflected or made to stop. Its creators had little or no control over the process they had formed and then deformed. And now it drove into the heart of the Summer Land, the jagged and poisoned magic of man polluting the fragile flower of life that had slowly grown of its own will to exist beneath the once unclouded sun. The pounding of hammer on spike beat deeply in his head. The sharp pain returned to his leg, growing worse and worse, as if the metal spikes were being driven into his very flesh and bone.

Transfixed by the pain, Rowland could only stand and stare with growing horror while the lines were slowly extended rail by rail. When they were set down directly between himself and the hidden doorway, the hammer blows beat at his whole body, echoed his cries as he felt a vast and agonizing rending within.

His breath came in ragged gasps. Some bright, lively, vital thing was withdrawing from him as it died, tearing at his inner flesh as it departed, and there was not one thing he could do to save it.

About him the world began to swim and spin and, as he fell into a swoon, he caught a glimpse of that other world, rent by a storm of terrifying and apocalyptic ferocity. The waters of the lagoon chopped and whipped into waves and pouring across the land, trees ablaze, the hills crumbling, a sky of unnatural colours swirling into muddy darkness. Or maybe it was his own world, burning up under a final paroxysm of the poisoned hatred that mankind had for his planet.

When Rowland regained consciousness the world was deathly silent and still. It was cold and night was falling. In the dusk sky, high clouds were shot through with the last of sunset colours, but not the reds the shepherds welcomed. Instead they were lurid and coppery. Rowland sat up and winced at the pain in his leg, his head still throbbing. He tried to stand. A wave of nausea swept through him and he vomited, heaving out the poisons and corruption of his dying soul.

Crawling away from the mess he had made, he headed gingerly to a nearby round barrow and sat with his back to its grassy slope while the sky grew dark. For nearly an hour he stayed there watching the dark and ragged forms of rooks in their thousand pass overhead with a grinding clamour as they returned to their rookeries for the night. Eventually the pain faded to little more than a dull ache. With care he stood. Then, feeling much battered and broken, he picked his way by familiar paths down through the woods.

The world was a different place. Rowland sensed it as he descended into the valley. The tree covered slope seemed quiescent now, bereft of the magic that had once sparked there and drawn him into the Summer Land. That magic was now beyond the iron lines, drawn deep within the hill and wrapped in protective layers about those who slept. Birds had finished their day without song and the nocturnal creatures dared not venture forth. The gentle and protective magic was gone from the land. The balance was disturbed.

*

185

Heavy rain beat loudly against the kitchen window, running down the panes of glass in beaten liquid dimple. Wind rattled the sashes and whined down the chimney stack. Rowland sat in his fireside chair, warmed by the heat of the range, listening and thinking. His mind was clearer now than it had been for many weeks, focused on the previous evening he had spent on Cobb Hill. Pain could do that - clean away the detritus of the mind. His leg still ached and his body still felt sore.

In his lap, cradled lightly in his hands, was the carved box that Mrs Reeve had given him a week earlier. Its hinged lid was open and, as he thought of all that had come to pass, he looked down at the contents. Oak and ash. He had laid his own tokens therein and kept them all carefully wrapped in the new piece of deep green velvet on which his own tokens had been left. It was all that was left now that the rails had been laid.

Rowland was quiet now that the storm had come. Not with the peace of contentment or even of acceptance. He simply lacked the will to do anything more. He had witnessed the end of it all. The day had, inevitably, been slow and long. It had dawned with the eerie silence that had fallen the evening before. The sun had appeared briefly as it rose, a misty lamp behind the high yellow cloud, before being obscured by thicker layers. No birds had sung to herald the day and the sky, yesterday filled with southward migrants, had been empty.

As the afternoon had drawn on, he had wanted to scream, had wanted to bang his head against a wall, anything that might drive the sweet, tantalizing visions from his mind. The anguish had driven him to a complete standstill. To have tasted of such beauty and then refused it for no reason other than cowardice. To have held and let go. Now he was adrift in his despair.

The storm became steadily stronger. Its gathering fury reached him and eventually calmed him. It was a blind rage out there beyond the walls of the house where none could exist within. Vast and violent, it was a natural magic released from the gentle power that had once soothed it and held it in thrall. Now it tore at the sky and maimed the peace of the valley as he, in his own rages, had wished. He felt peace in his empathy.

Closing the box, he stood and put it on the table. With meticulous care and no motivation but habit, he banked the fire in the range. Taking his candle, he went to the back door and fastened the lock. He could hear the wind shrieking in fierce gusts, felt the door shudder in its frame, and decided it would be prudent to close all the shutters.

When he had finished securing the schoolroom and the ground floor of the house, he climbed the stairs to his room. With the shutters there also fastened, he undressed and sank gratefully into his bed where he read for a while by candle light and then slept deeply without dreams remembered, a dull, dead man.

It was still dark when he woke. The rain had long since stopped though he could not hear whether this was so. A tremendous, endless screaming filled the room, gave solid voice to the void, engulfed him entire. It was all-consuming in its volume and the pure energy of its existence. The intensity of experience overwhelmed his ability to make sense of the cacophony.

With the sound was a deep vibration. The whole house, a solid structure of brick and flint, trembled. The floor shuddered and with it the bed. Perhaps even the very ground on which the house was built shook. He lay and listened, lay and trembled also, frightened by the intensity of the onslaught. Outside, he began to realize, it was the wind that roared in all its glory, pouring across the world unfettered, sublime, and supreme.

Rowland became frightened in a way he had never before experienced, not even when he lay bleeding with his leg in shreds. That had been a very personal and inward fear. This sound and vibration was so vast, so impersonal. Beneath the all engulfing volume of the storm he was a nothing. It could blot him out in an instant, tear him to shreds, and by its very nature it could neither care nor know.

As he forced himself to listen, the howling storm began to reveal other noises. Above him, the roof tiles were grinding one against the other as the wind pushed them against the roof and tried to tear them away at one and the same time. That was the only noise he could properly identify, but there were many more. Some, like the sharp cracks, must have been very loud for him to hear above the wind. The juddering thumps, along with other anonymous reports and explosions served only to add a fear of the unknown to his growing terror of the storm.

Worse still, perhaps, was the movement. His bed continued to shake and judder. And although it was not to any great degree, it was sufficient to be felt. It was an unsettling sensation to feel fluidity in what one had always taken as solid and dependable. To know that some force of nature could invade and upset one's certainties was to become exposed to the fact that humankind, for all its so-called progress, for all its marvellous and burgeoning technology, for all its intellect, was still an insignificant entity that could be smeared into a greasy stain across the face of the planet without the slightest loss to the rest of the living world. Rowland shivered. He was close to panic.

Above the howl of the wind with its accompanying dissonance of anonymous noises there came a loud hammering. For a while Rowland took it to be another part of the storm, but its regularity and persistence began to worry him. He began to wonder if the storm was trying to work its way into the house. Listening to the endless scream outside he was easily able to imagine what it could do if it gained entry. Like some frenzied and demonic beast it would tear everything apart in a matter of seconds.

With something specific to focus on, his mounting terror was held in abeyance. Rising swiftly, he dressed in the dark, finally pulling on his greatcoat. Lighting a candle, he moved about the room to check the shutters. Satisfied that they were all still well fastened, he made his way down the stairs. The shutters there, too, were fast and he felt puzzled. He turned towards the connecting door, intending to check in the schoolroom in case the wind had breached the windows there, but before he reached it the hammering came again. At the door to the house. Turning back, he stared at it in disbelief. Who, he wondered, would be out in such weather?

Hesitantly, he put the candle on the table and went to the door. He did not open it immediately. He did not dare. For in his breast his heart beat wildly with a sudden and ridiculously unfounded hope. Then, in his breast his heart beat with fear.

Gripping the handle tightly, he turned the key in the lock, and lifted the latch. Despite the awesome noise and the shaking of the house, he had totally underestimated the strength of the storm. The wind wrenched the handle from his grasp and the door swung wide open with a crash. The edge of the door caught Rowland on the shoulder, knocking him backwards. He cried out, more from the shock of the blow than from any real pain. Darkness came suddenly as the candle was extinguished and blown to the floor. The ceramic candle holder smashed. A chair fell on its side. A book on the table was whipped open, the pages tearing as they were fanned.

The room filled with the howling wind and Rowland had to fight against it to stay upright. He maintained his balance only by clinging tightly to the door frame. Outside, one on each side of the door, two figures were pressed hard against the wall by the wind, their faces ashen in the feeble light of a storm lantern that one of them held tightly. They peered in at Rowland who could only stare back in continued amazement.

The two men, Mr Keaton and John Wedland, the blacksmith, were shouting at him but he could hear nothing of what they said, their words torn to shreds. Mr Keaton tried speaking again. Rowland shook his head for he could not hear, despite pulling himself closer to them. John Wedland pointed wildly towards the river, his arm blown in the wind. Rowland pulled himself even closer to the two men and, gripping the door frame even more tightly than before, he leaned out.

It was extremely difficult to breathe. The wind was moving so fast that it was trying to pull the air from his lungs as it whipped past his mouth and nostrils. He had to work hard to draw breath as he stared out into the darkness. Finally, as his eyes adjusted to the night, he began to see with increasing clarity the reason why these two men had put their lives at risk in venturing across the open ground to the schoolhouse.

For a moment Rowland thought perhaps he was seeing the Summer Land once more. But only for a moment. The truth came to him quickly as he made sense of what he could see. The River Rushy, for some unknown reason, had burst its banks and was quickly flooding the valley. The school, although built on comparatively high ground at the edge of the old beach of the lagoon, was at the lowest end of the village. Flood water was already two thirds of the way up the slope between the bridge and the edge of the schoolhouse garden.

Rowland went back inside. He picked up the small carved box which he stowed carefully in a large inside pocket of his coat. He had no fears for his books for they were all kept upstairs, but the box with its tokens was more precious to him than anything in his life. After a quick check to make sure the toppled candle had not set anything alight he joined the other two at the doorway. They struggled against the wind to close the door but they finally managed it and Rowland turned the key in the lock. Then, supporting each other against the wind and making use of several ropes that John Wedland had secured on their outward journey, the three men made their way through the treacherous conditions back towards the village and higher ground.

By the first cottages they had to climb over the smashed remains of a great oak tree, strong in its heart, that had fallen across the road. Three hundred patient years of life destroyed in an instant. All about them, objects hurtled through the screaming air. Other debris littered the road, rolling and billowing and crashing along in the nightmare. Tiles. Branches. Farmyard flotsam. Personal belongings. All faintly visible in the strangely luminescent darkness.

Lightning flickered across the whole of the sky in great branching webs and lit the clouds from within with a flickering glow. The faint light cast equally faint shadows that jumped and combined in a disconcerting fashion. And it presaged the signs of fear that the wind had brought. The world had descended into Hell.

As they hugged the garden wall of the corner cottages at the lower end of the small village green, they came across a tired and shivering bundle of fur blown into the scant shelter afforded by a garden gate, set back, as it was, a meagre few inches from the rest of the wall. Indeed, they nearly missed it. But John Wedland's hand touched the fur in passing and he stopped to look. It was a dog, exhausted almost to death with fear and the fight against the overwhelming wind. John Wedland bent to it, his head against the fur, and then scooped it up. It made no struggle, merely moved to push its muzzle against the thick and protective neck of the large blacksmith. Rain began to fall once more, hammering their already beaten flesh.

The journey from one end of the village to the other, normally a gentle uphill stroll, took thirty painful and exhausting minutes. Eventually, all four of them soaked to the skin, bruised and weary with the noise and continual pummelling of the wind, they reached the sanctuary of The Swann With Two Knecks where many folk from the lower end of the village were sitting huddled around the roaring fire.

As they entered the large public room, Mrs Keaton ran across from the far side and hugged her husband, holding him tightly, pressing her face against his sodden clothes to hide her tears. John Wedland took the dog to the fire and laid it down. It looked up at him with wide eyes. No one there knew where it had come from and no one ever came to claim it. From that day it never left the blacksmith's side.

Across the room, Rowland saw Ruth Beckett and her grandfather, both wrapped in blankets. She smiled from a pale and worried face. The Reverend Beckett did not look well. John Wedland approached and guided Rowland into another room where Mr Keaton joined them. Mrs Carr had some of the Inn's towels warming in front of another fire that also roared fiercely from the updraught created by the storm. Mr Carr came in with a bundle of clothes and blankets and placed them on a table.

"They will be an odd fit," he said, "but get you changed."

"I've some broth ready when you are," added Mrs Carr as they both withdrew.

Dry and changed, the three men joined the others who sat quietly in the Inn's main room. Conversation was not easy above the continual scream. Rowland sat in tired silence and pulled his blanket tightly about his shoulders. His mind already dulled by recent events was further numbed by the force of the storm as it made even the solid structure of the Inn tremble. All through the night they sat in tired, silent, and wary wakefulness, praying for the tempest to blow itself out.

*

By mid afternoon the rain had stopped and the worst of the storm had passed on its way. Heavy grey rags of cloud sped in torn shreds across the stormy sky, revealing occasional glimpses of washed out blue. The villagers emerged cautiously from the relative safety of the Swann With Two Knecks into a wind blasted wilderness. Most were already numb from their night of fear; the sight that greeted them induced a state of shock. Their whole world was devastated.

Rowland had gone immediately to inspect the damage to the school. After a first attempt to make his way through the village had been thwarted, he doubled back and crossed Farmer Hall's lower meadow. As he came clear of the backs of the cottages and the tangle of fallen trees he got his first good look at the flooded valley. The sad, grey swill of water with its scum of wind torn flotsam did not hold his attention for long.

Damage to the schoolroom was minimal, mostly broken glass, wind scattered books, and a few missing roof tiles. He straightened most things within an hour and swept away the fragments of glass. His kitchen, too, was soon tidied after the short blast it had suffered. The house was, miraculously, unscathed. All the shutters were still closed and undamaged. All the roof tiles were still in place.

The garden had fared less well. Most of it was under flood water and that which was not had been salt burned by the wind beyond recovery. The large hedge to the north of the schoolroom was torn and full of large holes but it would recover with some careful re-laying. The great climbing rose that had graced the wall around the kitchen window had been pulled away from its trellis and the roots were badly damaged. It had been a little wonder and was now destroyed. Rowland looked at it with regret knowing that it would have to be removed. He decided, however, to salvage the sturdy main stem. The wood would make an excellent walking stick when properly polished and shod.

Swann had fared much worse on the whole than had the schoolhouse. Many windows were blown in, several barns were completely destroyed, and not a single hayrick was still standing. Tiles were scattered everywhere and those roofs that had been thatched were badly disarranged. Several were stripped completely bare. Elsewhere were scattered many rags of cloth and other mysterious objects torn apart by the winds. Where the wind had found its way into a building it had wreaked havoc. News came down the hill that the orchard at Brigg Farm had been completely destroyed, every last tree had been uprooted, even the old flint walls were gone, piles of rubble. Farmer Brigg was heartbroken.

There had, in Swann, been no serious injuries among the human population. Some livestock was missing and no doubt many days would be spent by the local shepherds in seeking out strays. Other creatures seemed to have been badly affected by the storm as well. There was very little bird song that day and for many days to follow. The ravens that had adopted Rowland were nowhere to be seen. Had anyone had time to look they would have remarked on the absence of swans from the swollen river. No one had time to look.

Having satisfied himself that all was as well as could possibly be expected with the school and his house, Rowland set out to gather news. He walked along the flood line to the sea, often finding it necessary to make some sort of detour. As he walked, he soon came to realize that the main victim of the storm was not human. Everywhere he looked there were trees that had been torn up by the roots and cast to the ground. Whole stretches of woodland had been felled overnight. The long familiar horizon was irrevocably altered for a whole generation of people. Thousands upon thousands of trees were gone. New vistas had appeared, things long hidden were now open to view, but that was no compensation. People grow and their landscape grows with them at the same pace. An injury to the land is an injury to its peoples.

As the numbing shock induced by the storm began to wear off, Rowland felt a growing pain as the true impact of the devastation grew within his consciousness. The trees, centuries old and gentle watchmen of the Summer Land, some of them remnants of ancient forests, denizens of the magical world that he alone alive now knew, eternal and graceful citizens of the world, home to millions, companion to many more, were laid waste. The Summer Land had been stripped of its greenery, the great pillars and the broad sheltering canopies were devastated. Fallen and shattered. Blasted to splinters. The litter of their destruction covered the world.

Had she but been awake and in this world to see. Rowland grieved for them both for he knew how much this would have caused her pain. As he walked, he no longer knew which way to look. The destruction was everywhere. Some places, for reasons it would never be possible to fathom, had escaped with barely a leaf lost from a branch. Other places had lost everything. Not a single tree remained standing on all of Cobb Hill. His heart, twisted by all that had happened to him, was now utterly broken. It too lay like the trees, uprooted and lifeless. Blasted apart by a force he could not comprehend. All seemed lost to him, all seemed so fragile and beyond his ability to help and protect.

By the time he reached Meeching he felt tears upon his cheeks. Slowly picking his way through the debris of the fishing village, he climbed the hill to Rushy Head. Near the top he passed two cottages that had been torn apart. Their walls stood barely a foot above ground level. The rest was rubble, neatly sorted into piles. Three wreaths, weighted down with stones, were laid on the path by the gate.

Passing on beyond the pulverized cottages he continued up the slope until he reached the Church of St Michael. The spire had gone and lay in a long, jumbled pile of wooden shingles and cracked beams across the remains of the lychgate. Rowland picked his way carefully over the mess and went on up into the graveyard from where he was able to see the whole valley stretching inland, flooded with river water as far as the railway line at the base of Wealden Hill.

What he saw laid out before him was a deadly travesty of the serene and beautiful lagoon he knew from that brief and haunting time. The islands were there, in the far distance, but blasted clean of trees. Wealden Hill stood grim and grey, somehow shrunken, in the windy daylight. The hills were stripped bare, trees stretched on the earth marking the direction of the storm. And the water, now slowly receding, was leaving behind a grey scum of silt and many dead things.

It was from this vantage point above Meeching that he was also able to see the reason for the flooding. In the night, whipped into a tidal surge of vast strength, the sea had scoured the seabed clean and thrown up the shingle into a vast bank, nearly thirty feet high. It had piled across the shallow mouth of the river and on beyond for several miles along the shore of the bay. The shingle beach that had for centuries lain directly beneath Rushy Head had been completely stripped away. And it was there that the river now ran, finding for itself a new exit and draining the valley.

Rowland joined a group of men from Meeching who stood at the edge of the graveyard. They were mostly fishermen who had left their boats above the tide on that same, centuries old shingle beach. Now they stood watching the tide ebb and the river cut its way into its new channel. Despite the loss of their boats, there was excited talk amongst the men. Rowland exchanged news and learned of several fatalities which had little effect on his overworked sensibilities. The talk eventually turned back to the new course of the river and Rowland lost interest. He knew it was not a new course. The river had simply returned to its original outing, blocked a long time since by the slow force of the tides washing shingle into its mouth. How he knew he did not question.

It was dark when he finally made his way home with a borrowed lantern. Stars were beginning to appear between the rags of cloud. He cared little for them that night.

(November)
The power in the land was broken. Violent proof lay in the chill, grey light of November's first morning; in the grey, oily sheen on the foul water that flowed through Meeching to the new river mouth. A steam hammer filled the dead air with the monotonous percussion of its working. Men, too, were at work, cutting a new road along the river's bank which others were shoring with great timbers. Others still, in boats, were sounding the channel under the direction of surveyors from the railway company. A steam dredger lay at anchor off shore, a great pall of dark and greasy smoke drifting lazily from its filthy funnel and across the surface of the water.

In the weeks since the storm, there had been rumours in the valley that had reached even Rowland's sense dulled ears and filled him with horror. It had never occurred to him that vultures would come to pick over the carcass of the Summer Land. Now they were here, he found it difficult to believe the speed with which they had appeared. And so he had come, while the boys had a mid term holiday, to see for himself if the rumours were true.

The new channel was deep and wide between Meeching and the sea. Having found its original course - long since silted up and now scoured out by the force of the released flood waters - the River Rushy was being prepared for a new role. It was, it seemed, deep enough to consider dredging as far as the northern limit of Meeching and establishing a considerable safe harbour, the only one for many miles on this stretch of the coast. The railway was close at hand and a branch line could soon be built down the valley. The village of Meeching would become a town and men would grow rich. The earth would die a little more.

Rowland turned his back on the noise and the activity at the riverside to thread his way through the almost frenzied activity in the village. There was a sense abroad of good times to come. The most oft quoted phrase concerned ill winds. He did not stop in the village, could see nothing to celebrate, thought it an ill wind, indeed. Instead, he climbed up behind Rushy Head onto the cliff top. He knew rape when he saw it, no matter what others about him might call it. The rape of a corpse was particularly sickening.

Exposed now to the wind, he huddled deeper into his coat. Nothing more had been done to the two cottages destroyed by the storm. There was too much to be done elsewhere to worry about piles of rubble. The wreaths that had been laid on the path lay there still, rotting. But that was progress. No one could be found to help replace the toppled spire of the church. A path had been cleared to the door. A tarpaulin had been tacked over the exposed upper room of the tower. Shattered gravestones lay untouched. That, too, was progress. Instant gratification and quickly in search of something else. That is how rape of the land had replaced love for the land. That is how salving of conscience on a Sunday had replaced a respect for the spirit in all things.

Restless, angry, despairing, Rowland moved on once more, joining the track that took him through Bollen, a shabby collection of long deserted cottages surrounded by salt-withered trees that seemed to have suffered little in the storm. Overhead ran clouds as grey and as chopped as the sea. Only the stiff breeze, sharp and cool, made any noise, the opening refrain of its hoarse, winter song running along the wiry grass of the open cliff top. Standing quietly he was just able to feel the background vibration of the sea as it piled endlessly onto what the storm had left of the beach below. Wind and sea. This was their world now and they would take a ceaseless toll of any invader. People had no place here, but they would come. No matter what the cost.

Breathing deeply, tasting the salt in the air, Rowland sighed. He felt so desperately tired. Every part of his body ached. Yet there was much more to his malaise than physical tiredness. He had fought for so long, won victories that had turned sour, had made decisions that led him further and further from the simple peace and contentment he so desired. Perhaps those things were not ever to be had. Perhaps they were things that moved further from your grasp the more you sought for them. But you could come close. Close enough to see. Close enough to be tantalized.

A sudden gust of wind pushed at him where he stood and he turned once more to look out to sea, moving down the grassy slope to the very edge of the cliff. He looked down, the wild updraught striking his face, making him sway. The roar of the breakers, a creamy, swirling turbulence four hundred feet below, was audible now. The tide was in.

Standing on the brink with the wind in his face, he forgot the world behind him. The memory of it was not worth holding onto, the grief of it too much in need of being forgotten. He became conscious only of the great drop beneath his feet. It seemed a clean thing. Vast. Empty. Free of memory. Free of pain. A single step.

Sudden light caught his attention. He let his eyes rove out across the vast expanse of water to see a gentle orange glow that covered a small, distant patch of the sea. It rippled with the motion of the waves, bright against the pale slate grey, some errant shaft of sunlight too weak to be seen against the hazy atmosphere. Another appeared and then a third as the first one faded. More, further out, barely visible, joined the display, moving slowly to the eastern horizon.

Stepping back from the brink, he turned and strode for home. In his mind he carried the chance wonder of the scene. It was a last image of the raw and natural magic of the world to take with him into the fast approaching winter, a last image of the magic that had sustained a land that was now being laid waste by the hand of man.

And the days drew on, shortening ever towards mid-winter. They remained relatively mild. The old magic had been strong and had lasted millennia. It would take some time to fade completely. Rowland settled back into his old routine, sufficiently numbed by the pain to continue his life, sealed up inside himself behind defences that he would not lower. They were not the clumsy ramparts he had erected once before, they were merely the deadness of his feelings. He had finally lost contact.

*

With the stove burning well to take the slight overnight chill from the air inside the schoolroom, Rowland opened the door, stepped out under the shelter and into the yard. Just beyond the pump, the boys were huddled into a small group that bustled towards the yard wall and back again in some new game that they had invented. He watched them for a while, trying to count heads. There was only one missing. He looked towards the village and saw, shuffling along the road, the huddled figure of John Elam.

Rowland placed the bell on the ground and strolled to the corner of the house, content to wait for the latecomer. It had been another mild night for late November, yet, as he looked north towards Hamm, Rowland could see a well defined edge to the clouds. Beyond them was blue sky, a thin and cold blue, the sort of sky he had seen in the high mountains in Afghanistan. The edge of the cloud moved swiftly southwards as the cold air ran down from the north.

Turning back to the yard, he saw the boys lined up along the wall, waiting for John. They called to him good naturedly and he waved in reply. As they all stood, the cold front swept across them on its way to the sea. A sudden cold wind gusted and the temperature dropped suddenly by several degrees. There were loud, laughing complaints about not being allowed into school and for that few seconds all the boys in the yard were turned towards Rowland. He did not hear them. Nor did he see them. He watched in the horror of knowledge as the sudden cold air hit John Elam's lungs.

John began fighting to draw breath. Once in, his eyes widening with a knowing surprise. The other boys, seeing their teacher's expression turned in bewilderment and fell silent. Twice in, John's head lifted. Rowland began to run. Thrice in, John's head was thrown back and his chest was thrown out as his heart gave under the strain. Rowland was over the wall, tumbling boys as he went. Before he had covered the distance, however, John flailed his arms weakly, twisted slowly round, and fell backwards stiffly onto the hard road.

Rowland slid to a halt beside John, losing his balance. He went down hard on one knee beside the boy, his trousers were torn by the gravel and the flesh of his knees was grazed. Grit embedded itself in the palm of his left hand and stung. He paid it no heed but struggled, in his half kneeling position, to remove his jacket. Angry and frightened, he turned to his petrified pupils.

"Move! Move!" He shouted as loud as he could to prevent them from sinking too deeply into a state of shock. "Fastest runner to Elam's! Bring his mother. Don't dawdle, boy!" he screamed desperately at the running boy's back. The boy responded by increasing his speed.

"Next one to the Reverend Beckett! Tell him we need the doctor!"

Another boy scurried past with desperate speed. Rowland placed his jacket about John to try to keep him warm. Somewhere, excited by the shouting, a dog began to bark frantically.

"The rest of you! Here! Now!" For a split second they hesitated but then some collective will brought them to life and they gathered quickly about the two figures on the road. Rowland spoke more quietly now, judging that they now needed calming. "Arms under him and lift him as quickly - be careful you ass - and gently as we can."

Forming a stretcher with their arms, they lifted John Elam from the ground, his head cradled by the strong and suddenly certain hands of Rowland. He turned to one of the younger boys still hovering uncertainly. "One of you spare bodies run ahead and get the schoolroom door open." Then he looked for a moment down into the dark eyes of John Elam and saw there the eyes of a swan. The boy blinked slowly. Rowland looked away, silently cursing all the gods and powers he knew.

Walking backwards, he led them carefully towards the warmth of the school, knowing that it was important to keep all those terrified minds occupied to prevent them from slipping back into shock. Death was no stranger to any of them, but this was one of their own age, one of their best beloved.

As he walked, Rowland talked to them, guiding them step by step. "Over the wall. Carefully. Steer east or we'll collide with the pump. Mind the step as we go in. Get the door closed.

Gently to the floor with him. You - upstairs in the house. Fetch my bedclothes and pillow from the bed. You - go with him. Don't gawk - do it!" For a long moment there was silence. He felt the fear grow into it and knew it must be dispelled. "There, John, no need to fuss. Your mother is coming. We'll soon have you..." Rowland let his voice fade away. The boy's eyes closed tiredly.

He turned to the others. "The rest of you into my kitchen and keep quiet. Someone warm up some water. And be careful. Now where are those bedclo...? Ah, good."

Whilst the bewildered boys retreated to the kitchen, Rowland made up a make-shift bed about the blue-lipped, ashen faced boy. Confused dark eyes looked up at Rowland. "You can ring the bell now, sir, I'm here."

The outside door opened and Mrs Elam came scurrying in, breathless, chalk-faced. For a second she could not see her son. Bewildered, she called his name. "John?"

"Mam?"

Her moment of disorientation passed. She knelt beside the cocooned boy and brushed his hair from his forehead. Once more the door opened and the Reverend Beckett entered. He, too, was pale, having never properly recovered from the fury of the storm. "There are men out on horses looking for the doctor," he said, breathlessly.

"'Tis too late," said the boy's mother in a whisper.

A silence descended upon the group. The suffering, for one of them, was over. The waiting for the inevitable was at an end. With some difficulty, the Reverend Beckett knelt down beside the boy next to Mrs Elam. Gently he closed her son's eyes and began to minister to his spirit. Rowland withdrew and went through into his kitchen. He closed the door quietly behind him.

The boys were standing in a small group by the range, quiet and uncertain. A pan of water released a wisp of steam. Rowland spoke to them quietly. "Now, listen carefully to me, please. I am sending you all home. Tell your mothers that John Elam was taken ill." He paused to let the tremble leave his voice. "Go quietly through the house door."

As they left, filing silently out into the cold morning air, he could see by their eyes that they knew John Elam was dead.

When the last of them was gone, the doorway was filled with the bulk of Farmer Elam and his shadow was Sarah.

"Come in," said Rowland. He stepped back and pointed to the connecting door to the schoolroom. "Your wife is through there."

*

Cold air and dampness filled the church. It was struck through with pale shafts of hard, lifeless, November light. The rest was empty winter shadow. The whole village sat quietly through the sermon, unable to add warmth to the stone interior, unable to draw much in the way of comfort from the Reverend Beckett's words. Every person present knew that John Elam had lived beyond his expected years. Every person present was deeply affected by his death. No hymns were sung for no one had the heart.

Rowland for once sat with the rest, but he was much more alone, lost in a great darkness behind his eyes, wandering, drifting. Men had broken the very tap roots of nature in the valley. And in tampering with nature there are always consequences to be considered. Nature had broken the boy. One of the early victims in a long conflict that humanity must ultimately lose.

In the dimming eyes of John Elam, as he had carried him into the schoolroom, Rowland had seen what humanity had chosen for itself. He had seen what he, too, had chosen. Mortality. The end, no matter how it might be put off, was inevitable. Rowland felt it moving slowly towards him, a starving dog in the night that had his scent and knew his fear.

When they went out into the graveyard, the vicious winds that had killed the boy, now running from the east, moaned around the mourners as if in an ecstasy of perverse pleasure. Rowland hung back and stood slightly apart from the others, close to his mother's grave. The thin voice of the Reverend Beckett was small and somewhat lost in the cold as he presided over the lowering of the coffin into the hard, cold ground.

In the distance, running before the keen wind, heavy clouds clipped the heads of the eastern hills in a broad, dismal line that billowed as it ran towards the exposed graveyard. Rowland looked up and saw it coming. At first, he thought it was mist. Then he saw a snowflake. Other heads turned as the muffling

201

wall crossed the valley floor. Soil was thrown onto the coffin, a hollow rattling sound in the cold silence. And then they were engulfed by the snow storm, cold and wild. Sarah Elam began to cry and Rowland wished in his deepest being for a song to heal all the pain. But the source of those songs was now choked with a poison that would kill so many young men.

(December)

Pale and with painful haste, the weak winter sun settled down to the horizon. The world gave up the day's struggle and came to rest beneath the many, deep, frozen layers of snow. Cold silence settled and only the ghostly woodsmoke that hung in the frigid air betokened continuing life.

Bruised still by the death of John Elam, the villagers of Swann had shunned the world and kept themselves close and sad in their homes. The only thing that moved in all the valley, dark against the bleached background and shrouded by a cloud dirty steam, was a distant, amorphous shamble of a railway work gang as it headed along the track towards the shanties outside Hamm.

With his head moving in the small jumps and shakes of a growing nervous disorder, Rowland watched them until the shadow of the world and a freezing mist dissolved their form from his sight. When they had gone, he let the curtain fall across the window. Slowly, he turned and limped across to the fire that smoked thinly in the bedroom hearth. There he removed his glasses and placed them on the mantelpiece. He stood then, grim faced and listless, watching the fire until it died. He let the charred wood lie unburned, careless of the cold that would come. He wanted the winter to lay its hand deep into the earth and never loosen its grip.

He had turned from the window. Now he turned from the hearth. To stand. Incapable. There was nothing of any purpose or worth in his head. It was a hollow vessel, cold and unknowing; a cup that had for an instant been filled with a gentle, quick liquor matured of the power in the earth and of the light in the sun. A cup from which he had not dared to drink. A cup that was now cracked and to be forever empty.

The deep dark of winter's night came swiftly and filled the room. Stars shone briefly unheeded but were soon obscured by cloud. For a long time the darkness stayed complete. The world was silent and inert, brought to a virtual standstill by the recent snowstorms. For a long time the silence stayed complete. Until Rowland fumbled for a candle and a match.

Squinting against the sudden light, he set the cheap, tallow fed flame upon the dresser betwixt mirror and photographic portrait. The silky light of the fragile flame was reflected by the glass of both objects. His cold fingers fumbled with the frame of the photograph and he turned it to look more closely at the picture in the dim light, driving more recent events from his mind as he thought of that earlier episode of his life; the happenings of '78 and '79, and the defeat at Maiwand in '80. Unconsciously he rubbed his aching leg.

The candle flickered in a sudden draught and, from the corner of his eye, he saw his reflection in the mirror. In that little, bright instant he was confronted by the truth and could no longer deny it with rational argument or with some false insight of his mortally educated intuitive being. He no longer had the strength of spirit or the strength of mind.

The two images were superimposed in his brain. He reached out with both hands and picked up the photograph and the mirror, turning his back to the light to see them more clearly. In the dim and cold night-time of his being, he looked back and forth from face to face. One was still, captured those five endless years ago, and the other was alive. Alive with a cold fear, pallid and wide-eyed, staring back from the shaking glass. Save for the expressions each face carried, there was no difference between the two. Yet the difference was there, despite each being the same. However, it was not the difference between his past and present self. It was the difference between himself and other men.

Carefully, he replaced both picture and mirror on the dresser laying them face down. There was no longer any escape from the consequences of what he had done. He could no longer pretend to himself. Bitter grief flooded through the darkness within him. Moving away from the dresser, he went and sat on his bed, lowering his head into his hands. Even that conspired against him. Against his palms he felt the smooth flesh of his face, recalled the jokes made at his expense because at the age of twenty-five he did not need to shave, as now at the age of thirty he still had not ever used a razor.

The photograph did not chain him to humanity as he had first thought it might when he had placed it on the dresser. It did nothing to make him more a part of the surface life of the valley. It served only to help remind him of the abyss between himself and the others. It was a hopeless chasm he might no longer cross. He had been given the chance. Yet the full truth had never been clear to him. In the past, everything that had been revealed to him had been revealed in the belief that he knew more than he did. But he had known nothing. And now he had nothing.

In the darkness he recalled her face, his lady of the dance. Why had she not told him that he might now rightfully be sleeping beneath the earth? Not cold, as the bones of the swan; not cold, as the flesh of John Elam in its slow dissolution; but warm, resting only before the dance of renewal. Why had she not said?

He wiped the cold tears from his eyes and then leaned forward to pinch out the candle flame. In the darkness he cast off his boots and socks before lying back on his bed. The sheets were cold and damp to the flesh of his hands and feet, musty, smelling of frosty soil. The astringent smoke of the smouldering candle wick filled the still air of the room and caught in his nostrils.

For what seemed hours he lay shivering in the open grave of his fears, turning this way and that, seeing in his mind's eye the warm hearth, the rich tapestries, the comfort, imagining the sleeping form, delicate and at peace, of his lady of the dance. Or did she sleep with a sadness in her heart, did she, perhaps, dream of this rough room?

Only at that moment when his sanity was in the balance did he finally admit to himself that he loved her. It was a complete acquiescence of a totally hopeless situation. In it he found a kind of peace. In it he found certainty. He knew that he wanted only to be with her. To dance. To learn to sing. To walk the paths, sit with the swans, touch the sea, watch the clouds, see roses in some distant high summer.

In his dreams he had these things. He shared them with her in an intimate paradise that lifted his soul to heights of ecstasy that he had never before experienced or believed possible. And then he lost them. A swelling darkness billowed out from some malevolent and noisy machine that gleamed in slick and foul oils and rumbled remorselessly towards him. He fought with the darkness, was left suddenly alone on a path above a strange and eerily quiet village.

She came to him then once again with words of comfort he could not quite hear above the sound of many people. She touched him and he had the feeling that she had promised it would not be long until they were together. And then she moved away from him, away down a slope through the noisy throng. She moved from person to person, greeting them as she went and then she was brightly alone in a smoky darkness - just one star awake - like a swan in the evening that moves on the lake. He took great joy in her promise and her appearance but knew at the same time that she was lost to him forever. The darkness returned and he no longer had the will to fight. In despair he gave up, the fading words of the song in his head.

Cold, pale light suffused the room to mark the time elapsed. Sweat from the dreaming frenzy, slick upon Rowland's skin, turned cold; deathly fingers caressed his body. The fear, the loss, the love, the cold, embroiled in his deep and fevered tiredness to concoct a madness. He rose swiftly from his bed in some earlier time with the song now strong in his memory. Barefoot, part dressed, a smile of peace on his face, he descended to his kitchen and thence into the yard. Everything now was all right.

Gleaming beneath the pale moon, a fresh and heavy frost lay across the deep frozen snow that covered the valley. An idle but slicing wind from the north cut through the meagre covering of his clothes. He did not feel it because he was elsewhere, his eyes fixed with his mind on the ghosts of the trees that once stood on Cobb Spur. Somewhere in the ghostly depths of that spectral wood a warm light danced - moonlight reflected in bright glittering sparks from the frost that covered the dead branches of the fallen trees. Rowland saw and began to run.

Crisp thumping muffled footfall along the road and over the bridge; across the river into some other place where he was finally lost. Into the meadow where his feet kicked up a mist of powdered snow as he went. By the time he reached the slope covered with the tangled mess of fallen trees, his flesh was blue and turning numb, his breath was burning in his lungs and clouds of exhaled steam sparkled as they crystallized about his face.

Rowland's eyes saw a different world - a land in high summer. Wildly, he danced up onto the lower slope, crawling then across the corpses of the trees, scraping his flesh, jerking in the spasmodic rhythms of his imagined dance. Upward under a darkening night sky until he finally stood between the summits above the hidden figure of the Newelm Man.

Half out of his madness, free for a moment of the memory fed illusions, he stood still and peaceful on the top of the world as more snow began to fall - cold points of softness on a cheek wet with tears. Light flurries dropped in their own twisting convoluted dances from the broken cloud and drifted by. Within, somewhere, his rational self knew exactly where he was and accepted what that must mean, accepted the inevitable end.

It was his final act of acceptance, a final consent. After one last brief glimpse of the world, his rational self yielded completely to the new world of the dream. Yet before his light finally flickered into darkness, he was sane enough to know that the rational world was fast becoming the realm of insanity, that his dream, however short-lived it may be, was far more worth living.

Across the valley, Wealden Hill stood clearly illuminated in the last of the moonlight. He looked at the gap between its slopes and those on which he stood, snow meadows crossed by a frozen river. It was not such a great divide, not the abyss he had thought. It would not, he smiled to himself, take long to cross. It did not matter to him that it was the wrong divide. He did not know.

Falling as he tried to move knocked some feeling back into his legs. He picked himself up to stumble again, half roll, half run and slide down the snow covered slope before him. Powdery snow flew into the air at his passing. The clouds grew thicker and the moonlight faded. In the growing darkness, the abyss deepened, but he had started now and would not ever stop. Larger, heavier flakes of snow began to appear in the light flurries, growing more numerous, driven now into his face by the increasing wind.

At the bottom of the slope, thick drifts of snow cushioned his headlong fall. He picked himself up, momentarily shaken, but still set on his course. Blundering on, he crossed the meadow, clambered up the bank of Cobb Reach, and went straight down onto the ice. Stone hard, it bore his weight at the edge, but was too fragile in the centre. It gave beneath him with a dry, creaking whine and he dropped into the water, breast high. Had his body temperature not already been so low, the shock would have killed him there. As it was, close to fainting, he struggled to the ice on the far bank.

When he reached it, there was an eruption of confused, feathery, white shapes appearing in a sudden evolution of form from rearing mounds of shaken off snow. A hissing filled the air and the shapes evolved further as they spread their grand and powerful wings to become swans. Induced to near panic by the sudden rising of the host he scrambled up onto the breaking ice into their midst and clawed his way onto the snow. Pushing his way through the swans, reeling from several stunning blows, he tumbled into the meadow beyond and staggered on into the night. The water of the Reach began to freeze in his clothes and hair.

Almost immediately he was climbing the rough, new slope of the railway embankment. At the top he caught his foot against the nearest rail and fell. Instinctively, his arms went out before him. The cracking of his collar bone he heard more than he felt, and that not very much, as he landed across the second rail. The flesh of his palms stuck to the frozen metal as he tried to push himself up, burning him badly. He collapsed to his knees. For a moment he felt trapped, exhausted beyond all recovery, but a sudden subconscious understanding of where he was tapped unsuspected reserves of energy. He was filled with a powerful rage at the machine that had caused all this and his rage pushed him on.

In the darkness and heavy snowfall he clambered down the other side of the embankment and began to climb, at last, the southern slope of Wealden Hill. He tired quickly as those final reserves of energy were used and as the pain and the cold reached deeply into the heart and soul of his being. The ice that had formed on his river soaked clothes stuck to his flesh, beaten against him by the driven snow, forming a broken crust.

Close to the top of the hill, he slipped on his lifeless feet and fell to his knees, the rhythm of his movement knocked from him. For a moment he lay completely still as if it were suddenly over and done with. Then, with broken bone grating within him and burned flesh screaming, he continued to scramble up through the snow until he reached the relatively sheltered hollow where the great doors into everlasting summer had once stood open.

Only the pain, burning as a fire, kept him going now as he began to dig at the snow. He flailed wildly with little control over his limbs. Scraping with ruined hands he finally cleared the snow and ice away to reveal nothing but withered grass and earth. He beat at it in a wild frenzy and then began to dig at the hard soil with his fingers. With some last reserve of strength driven by his passion, he forced his fingers into the frozen earth. And with that the spark, for so long sustained against all odds, finally died and he collapsed. His body was jerked spasmically by sobs that grew weaker until he lay still and cold, covered by the falling snow.

(Sunday 17 December - Sunday 24 December)
Ruth Beckett stood alone with her thoughts looking down at the small headstone. A chill wind had cleared it of its covering of snow, drifting it in a deep bank against the inside of the south wall of the churchyard. For the last five days she had come every day to the grave to pay her respects and though she was wrapped well against the weather she felt, as always, a different and deeper cold within.

Her grandfather had, during those days, told her all he knew of Rowland's life. It had been a gesture of atonement on his part. A lifetime of secrecy, even if from no one in particular, leaves an unpleasant shadow on the soul. He felt that she should know all there was to know, especially as he now felt his own end to be near. It had helped her to understand. Now she had the longer task of coming to terms with that understanding.

Many chances, she realized, had passed by, and much had gone forever. Not everything was a loss, however. She did not weep at the grave-side. That, she had come to know, would change nothing that had already been. Only now and in the future could changes be made. She shuddered from the cold within her. It was a frightening experience for she had laid to rest much of herself here along with the bodies that reposed in the earth beneath her feet.

Quietly, she turned away. There was much still to do and many emotions, as well as understanding, with which she had to learn to live. Once, she had played at being the modern woman, not really knowing what that meant. Once, she had played at being in love with Rowland Henty. Now she no longer played. The time for playing was over and done with. And the man she loved?

*

Rowland woke suddenly from an empty darkness into the mute light of a bright, snowy morning and gazed at the ceiling. An atmosphere of quiet calm pervaded the room and he lay, feeling relaxed and well rested. An empty calm filled his being and he knew little of what was beyond his immediate waking experience. He began to move and felt the pain. It brought a gasp to his lips.

"Fully with us at last? I should not move too much just yet."

The familiar but unidentifiable voice, tired but obviously relieved, came from somewhere beyond the foot of the bed. Rowland squinted along the length of his body and saw, beyond the tented covers, the rising bulk of Dr Joyce.

"A merry dance you have led one and many."

The mention of dance stirred something in Rowland's mind but he could not call it forth from his memory. The doctor, smoothing his hair back with stiff fingers, moved round to the side of the bed and Rowland now experienced a side of the man he had not before been aware of. There was none of the blustering bluntness of manner as he pulled back the covers and helped Rowland to sit up.

Gently, the doctor probed Rowland's right shoulder. Rowland was conscious of the existence of pain but it did not bother him. He felt detached from his physical self, slightly adrift and floating. It was not unpleasant but it was disconcerting.

"You will need a sling for a while yet," the doctor finally decided. "The bone will heal well enough. How are your hands?"

Rowland frowned and looked down. His hands were heavily bandaged. The doctor began to unwrap them, taking care not to disturb the shoulder. When the lengths of bandage had finally been removed Rowland was horrified by what was revealed. All his nails were gone and the flesh was blackened and swollen, the fingers torn, bad bruising and raw flesh on his palms.

"Such a mess as I have never seen." The doctor continued to speak as he carefully examined the damaged hands. "You will not lose any fingers, though I do not doubt that they will cause you problems as you get older. Being dug into the earth probably saved them." He shook his head at his own memories. "Never have I seen its like," he said softly. "Never."

"What…" began Rowland and then stopped. There was a blank. He simply did not know what to ask.

"It will doubtless come back to you. I am no expert at these things but my advice is do not worry at it. It will be painful enough remembering without you forcing it on yourself. Can you feel anything in those?" the doctor asked, nodding at the hands.

Rowland turned them gingerly. The wrists were extremely stiff. "There is a sort of… prickling."

"Good. Clench them into fists." Rowland tried hard but could only make the slightest movement with them. The doctor seemed satisfied. "Good. They will mend."

Doctor Joyce gathered up the bandages and went to the armchair by the fire place. Rowland looked about the room for the first time. From the view through the window, he knew he was in the vicarage. He did not how he had come there or why. He turned to watch the doctor who was putting on his collar and tie. When he was properly dressed, he came back to the side of the bed.

"I shall be off to my own bed. I have watched you for all you need of me for now." He sighed. "You were lucky with your hands, Mr Henty. But not so with your feet. Frostbite. You lost all of your toes. It will take some time learning to walk without them. You will always need your stick. I have no doubts, however, after everything else that you have come through that you will manage." He picked up his bag and moved to the door. "I will leave instructions with Miss Beckett and you, sir," he said more sternly, "will do exactly what she tells you to do."

With that admonition, the doctor left the room and Rowland sat staring into the fire that burned brightly in the hearth, trying with little success to come to some understanding about his injuries. Shortly, there came a tap at the door and Ruth Beckett came in carrying a tray. She looked at Rowland, sadness, anger, and a hint of fear playing with her features. And underlying these, the first signs of a calmer and deeper maturity than she had formerly possessed.

She placed the tray on a bedside table and drew up a chair. In silence she fed him. When she had finished, she re-bandaged his hands lightly with fresh linen strips and then sat back and looked at him.

"What happened, Miss Ruth?"

She looked surprised for an instant. "Do you not remember?"

He shook his head and then wished he hadn't. A sickening pain grated in his shoulder.

Ruth raised a hand to smooth the sudden furrows of pain from his brow but she stopped halfway and placed her hand in her lap. "Five days ago, in the morning, when he was delivering your milk, Robert Hall found the door of the schoolhouse wide open. There was a drift of snow in your kitchen. When grandfather went to see, he could find no trace of you. Parties were organized and sought for you. On the afternoon of the day following, you were found by Thomas Overbury, a shepherd."

"Where?" But suddenly he knew.

"On Wealden Hill. The shepherd was first attracted by a group of black swans on the hillside." Ruth was suddenly quiet and withdrawn, as if the strangeness of such a thing had only now occurred to her. "His dog found you. Or, rather, it found your stick protruding from the snow where the swans were gathered." She nodded to the corner of the room where stood a rosewood shaft shod with silver.

Rowland looked across at it with an almost dispassionate gaze that masked his disbelief and bewilderment. It was the shaft of rosewood that he had cut from the climbing rose that had been brought down by the storm. But he had done no more than cut the shaft. It would not even have had time to season properly. Yet there it was, its shape distinctive. He looked back at Ruth. "May I have it?"

Ruth looked at him curiously for a moment but decided to keep her own counsel. She rose and brought the stick to Rowland. He took it from her with difficulty and held it in his bandaged hands. Turning it clumsily, he gazed at the silver ferrule and at the delicate trace work of silver in the shape of a swan that was let into the handle. It was decorated exactly as he had thought he would like, yet he had told no one about it nor had he committed his ideas to paper. He looked at it for a long time. Finally he looked up at Ruth who was standing over him.

"The doctor said that you had some kind of fit." She faltered for a moment, looking down at her hands which were clasped tightly together. "You were nearly dead." She was now close to tears, tears for him and not for herself. "You are to stay here until you are well. Those are Dr Joyce's orders. And now, you must rest."

She picked up the tray and left the room. Rowland clutched the stick to him looking once more at the swan and seeing so much more. Nearly dead, he thought. He closed his eyes and slumped back into the pillows. So close to making an escape. And no second chance. Of that he was certain.

*

During the week that followed, Rowland began the painful task of learning to walk again. He made better progress than he had at first imagined he would. Faltering steps from bed to chair and back again were followed by slow and exhausting trips to the window. At first he needed a steadying hand to help him keep balance but his body soon learned the new and necessary disposition for him to manage on his own. Eventually he was able to venture short distances unaided, but the whole venture left him drained and depressed.

The shortest day came and went. The Christian festival gathered pace. Rowland let it pass him by. Late on Christmas Eve, he dressed and was helped down to the parlour of the vicarage and placed in a chair by the fire. There he sat alone, the lamp extinguished in case he wanted to sleep, while the Becketts went to church. In the silence, he watched the flames and thought of his lady of the dance, sleeping beneath the hill.

He had lost. It was all gone now, beyond his grasp forever. He had taken what he had thought to be the easy course, the selfish course of the coward, the blind course of the man who had not sought out the truth because he was convinced he already knew. And now he was trapped in this world of men and their machines. He had been dragged back into it and must now follow its ways to his death. Even his dream had deserted him.

Heavy of heart, he struggled up from the chair and, with the aid of his stick grasped painfully between his wrecked hands, hobbled to the window on feet that, though they could walk, would not and could not dance again. With difficulty, he turned and settled on the cushions of the window seat. Through the cold glass, he could see the villagers leaving the church, silhouetted in the arched doorway as they left the candle lit interior and moved out into the midnight snowscape. Mrs Reeve accompanied by her mill manager and his family. Farmer Hall with Mrs Hall, young Bobby and the others. The Keatons, Mr Wedland and his dog, the Tricketts. The downcast figures of the Elams whose Christmas would also be empty. Slowly they all went their ways, the pale flickering light of mortal lanterns moving into the darkness of the village and disappearing. There was a simple beauty in the scene but Rowland was blind to it.

Then the candles in the church were extinguished one by one until its dark bulk underwent the transformation from a living structure to a cold and lifeless moonlit shape. From that cold stone pile one last lantern emerged as the Reverend Beckett and Ruth made their way across the churchyard. The light flickered as they walked and then moved from his field of vision.

He suddenly felt desperately tired. His muscles ached with it and it plumbed the depths of his body through to his bones. Too tired now for anything. Too tired even to bother trying to end it all. Tears came into his burning eyes and he wiped them away with his bandaged hands. Such tiredness. He must sleep. Such tiredness. Yet he had woken from the dream and sleep, the sleep he so desperately wanted, was now denied him.

Turning his eyes with great effort, Rowland looked beyond the church towards the head of the snow covered valley. Brightly lit by the moon, it seemed, but only seemed, to be as bright as day. And looming there in the distance was the stark, smooth shape of Wealden Hill. Beyond, moving swiftly over the cold, harsh world of night was a swollen bank of cloud that dragged its curtain of snow. Over the hills it came, obscuring the moon from view until all was lost in the grey, flickering void.

Printed in the United Kingdom
by Lightning Source UK Ltd.
107347UKS00001B/164